THE OLD
CAPE BLOOD RUBY

BARBARA EPPICH STRUNA

B. E. Struna

Cover Designers: Timothy Struna, Timothy Graham
Edited by Nicola Burnell

*This is a work of fiction. Names, characters, places, brands, media, and
incidents are either the product of the author's imagination or are used
fictitiously. Any resemblance to similarly named places or to persons living
or deceased is unintentional.*

Print ISBN 978-0-9976-566-5-7
Ebook ISBN 978-0-9976-5662-6
Library of Congress Control No. 2021906119

"I enjoyed seeing such great historical and cultural detail in *The Old Cape Blood Ruby*. It's important to see Tlingit culture portrayed in a unique and compelling way."

-Peter Stanton, educator in Lingít Aaní
Tlingit Country, Southeast Alaska

"The story takes us from the eastern tip at Provincetown, Cape Cod to the western edge in Juneau, Alaska. Barbara Eppich Struna has spun an ambitious multi-generational saga that spans three hundred years. Struna has artfully woven historical events into the search for a valuable family heirloom. Filled with romance, tragedy, mystery, as well as loves lost and found, its gripping plot will keep you reading."

-Rick Cochran, Author, *Murder at Bound Brook,
Bound Brook Pond, Wellfleet Tales, Wellfleet Tales I*

To my children, Scott, Tim, Heather, Anna, and Michael…
They have always chosen the road not taken

1

Present Day
EASTHAM, CAPE COD

NEIL HALLETT CRUISED the Internet looking to purchase anything that was connected to his supposed ancestor, Maria Goody Hallett. His daily routine began with a search for 18th-century artifacts and usually ended with any news about the one person he hated the most, Nancy Caldwell, the woman who had sent him to prison. He reached for a bottle of painkillers for his shoulders and hands. His years in jail had taken a toll on his aging body. Now, approaching fifty, it was easy to blame Caldwell for his aches and pains instead of the unhealthy choices he'd made throughout his life.

After his release, twelve years ago, he'd returned to his Eastham house on Goody Hallett Drive. He had stayed quiet – and elusive thanks to a full beard he had grown in prison. The bushy cover served him well, even today. Occasional off-season odd jobs, working for an old friend who owned a small home security company, aided him in supplementing his income. He usually was assigned jobs in less populated areas of the Cape.

Hallett stayed close to home surrounded by his large collection of memorabilia relating to Cape Cod and his ancestor. His free rein across the internet enabled him to haggle and bid anonymously, something he enjoyed more than owning the items. His passion for anything related to his lineage and the infamous Goody Hallett was an obsession.

There was one item that hung above the fireplace mantle that he would never sell. It was a portrait of a beautiful middle-aged woman posing with a teacup and saucer; her hand was adorned with an exquisite ruby red ring. The painting, signed by an Abigail E., seemed to hold secrets that kept Hallett guessing about his past. The auctioneer who'd sold it to him had said it was a portrait of Goody Hallett, the lover of Sam Bellamy. It was painted around 1750 and had come from a home in Provincetown. The artwork had no authentication to that fact, but Hallett still loved to look at the portrait and dream, mostly about the ruby ring.

2

1780
CAPE COD

MARIA HALLETT ELLIS stepped across the dark wooden floorboards of her Barnstable home. It was her last day of freedom. Tomorrow, she would be subjected to the rules of another. The family house and belongings had been sold at auction and the proceeds given to her son for her care, as was the custom.

She walked a familiar path through the dining room and into the kitchen, where a single table and chair waited for her. Maria leaned her achy back against the worn wooden slats of the seat. A delicate, blue-flowered cup and saucer rested on the bare table. She longed to have one more cup of tea.

Maria squinted through the cloudy veil that had grown thicker over her eyes during recent years. Faded walls, once stenciled in bright colors, reflected her age and that of the house. The room, once filled with life, looked sad.

The old woman held a gathered square of colorful wool. She carefully unwrapped its folds across her lap to reveal a brown leather pouch. A grey tendril fell softly from a bun atop her head. Maria pushed the wispy evidence of aging and worry back into place. From within the sack, she withdrew a deep red ruby set into a gold ring.

The ruby reminded her of her first love, Sam Bellamy. A vision of him materialized in her mind. He was so handsome. She closed her eyes and recalled how the ring had hung from a gold chain near his heart. She slipped the love token onto her gnarled finger. It still fit.

The sound of a bell downstairs, followed by a door closing, interrupted her daydreaming. She quickly slid the golden band off, then hid it in her hand.

A woman's soft voice echoed up into the bare rooms. "Mother?" Dainty footsteps and the swish of skirts grew louder as Abigail Ellis Smith's bonneted head appeared at the top of the stairs. "We have a long ride ahead of us. The carriage is waiting."

"Yes, dear, I'm ready." Maria placed the ring alongside the teacup and saucer, nestled the treasures back into the pouch, then tied the woolen cloth's four ends into a knot for carrying.

Abigail adjusted her skirts and cape. "Mother, how long did Father own this building?"

"Over sixty years." Maria recalled the day her sweet husband, Matthew, had purchased the sturdy building after they escaped from Eastham. They'd been so hopeful. She smiled at the thought of their two beautiful children, who had blessed them with extra love and laughter. They had made a good life together. "I will miss my home."

"I know, Mother, but your health has not been good as of late."

"I am aware." The twelve steps down to the print shop and the return climb for a much-needed nap was becoming more difficult with each passing day.

"Please, Mother. It's beginning to storm."

The sound of thunder reminded Maria of the stormy night, so many years ago, when her pirate Sam Bellamy had returned to her, then days later, had slipped the ruby ring off the chain and onto her finger. He had knelt before her. "Maria, will you be my wife? I promise to take care of you and love you with all my heart."

Abigail interrupted once more. "Mother, are you ready?"

Maria looked around the house one last time, then whispered to the bare walls, "It's time to say goodbye, my old friends." To her left, a large black stain formed an odd-shaped circle on the floorboards. She laughed, "Oh Abigail, you were a handful…always drawing or painting your pictures. What a mess that ink made on the floor."

Abigail returned a smile and held her mother's hand. "Sorry, Mother. I so enjoyed my art, didn't I?"

"If I recall, your brother Matthew preferred toy ships."

They walked slowly toward the steep stairway, then descended carefully. At the bottom, both women paused and looked around the inside of the little print shop for the last time.

Abigail was anxious to go. "We must leave before it gets dark."

"Yes, dear, I know."

"Let me carry that for you." Her daughter reached for the tied pouch.

"No dear. I want to hold it." Maria clutched the gifts against her breast, cherished remnants from her long ago past that she refused to give up. They were hers and hers alone.

3

Spring 1780
PROVINCETOWN

A FEW WEEKS after leaving her Barnstable home, Maria became accustomed to her new surroundings in Provincetown. She never imagined she would ever return to the far end of Cape Cod to live out her final days in the Province-Lands. The two-story Colonial style house stood alone on the west end of the harbor, separate from most of the 100 families who had already settled there. It was adequate for her son's family and widowed daughter, Abigail. The additional room that her first-born son, Matthew, had built for his mother was connected to the rear of the new house. It was small, comfortable, and private. Maria had hoped the profits from her estate would have been greater and she wondered if all her money had been spent.

One afternoon, Maria was alone in the new house when she felt a chill. A steaming cup of tea would taste good. She picked up a treasured blue and white teacup from her bureau and passed through the parlor. A quick stop to admire her portrait above the mantle made her smile. She reminisced about her favorite red dress with its dainty lace circling the bodice. It was modest but so exciting. At the time of the sitting, her coal black hair had just started to exhibit hints of white and Abigail's artistic talent was at its peak.

She was proud of her daughter and, of course, felt blessed with the many years married to her Matthew and still missed him.

Maria continued on toward the kitchen, relieved that her children hadn't sold the painting. She was grateful that Abigail had sensed her desire to keep a few special items, including her tufted rocker and four-poster bed. Packed into a trunk for safekeeping and stored in the attic were her old journals, a decorative box for personal papers, mementos from when her children were young, and Abigail's sketchbook.

She heard someone approach from outside and hesitated to welcome anyone, considering she was alone, new to the area, and far away from other houses. The black iron circle announcing a visitor hit solid against the wooden door. As her hand reached for the doorknob, she heard her son Matthew, outside, greet the visitor with, "Mr. Paine, so happy to see you today. Won't you come in?"

Maria stepped back as the two men entered the foyer.

Matthew immediately signaled to Maria. "Mother Ellis, we would like to speak in private."

"Of course, I shall retire to my room." With empty cup in hand, she left, but made sure her door remained ajar. She was curious about Mr. Paine and wondered why the well-dressed gentleman was visiting the Ellis house today.

Matthew placed his hat on a side table in the small foyer. "Would you care to imbibe with me? I have procured a special beverage from my last voyage."

Mr. Paine took in the surroundings. "I certainly would." Maria's likeness above the fireplace caught his attention. He walked closer to the painting while Matthew busied himself at the liquor cabinet.

"It's beautiful, isn't it?" Matthew handed a small whisky to Paine. "My mother was a beauty. And my sister's a very talented artist."

Paine kept staring at the portrait. His eyes were not looking at Maria's lovely face but at the ring on her finger. He drank his refreshment, placed the glass on the mantle, then began to clean his spectacles, his focus returning to the ring.

Ignoring the inquisitive behavior of his guest, Matthew was eager to discuss the purchase of a new schooner on behalf of his sons, Benjamin and William. "Mr. Paine, I'm sure you're a busy man. I am also, but I would like to conclude my intentions to further our family's deep-sea whaling enterprise as soon as possible. Mr. Paine?"

The visitor spoke without turning around, his eyes steady on the ring gracing Maria's hand. It stood out against a black velvet shawl lying across Maria's lap. "Mr. Ellis, have you ever heard of a ruby called The Pigeon's Blood?"

The sounds of delicate china clinking together came from Maria's room and then the rustle of a skirt.

Paine explained. "The Pigeon's Blood is one of the most valuable stones in the world. It is said that a perfect ruby, possibly like this one in the painting, is the same color as the first two drops of blood from the nose of a killed pigeon. I would love to see it." Mr. Paine returned his gaze to the painting. "Mr. Ellis, do you believe your mother still has this ring?"

"I'm not aware of what she has in her possession at this time. But I will inquire about it."

Mr. Paine turned and moved closer to Ellis. "I would be very interested in purchasing the jewelry. Or might we be able to come to a mutual agreement involving the ring regarding your new schooner?"

Matthew Ellis looked eager to bargain.

Maria's door quietly closed with a hurried snap of the lock.

That evening, after dinner, Maria was resting in the parlor by the fire when Matthew entered. "Mother, I need a favor from you tomorrow."

"Of course, Matthew. What is it?"

"The mason, Mr. Nesbit, will be coming to finish the kitchen hearth. Will you be at home to see that all goes well? I must be away to Barnstable and everyone else will be busy." He poured himself a snifter of brandy.

"Yes, I will oblige you." Maria always tried to do as her son asked; he had a temper on occasion, and she knew when to be quiet and agree.

"Thank you, Mother." He sat on the tufted settee. "By the way, whatever happened to that lovely ring in your portrait? I've never actually seen it."

Maria hesitated. "If you recall, you couldn't be bothered with my stories. You always found other ways to amuse yourself."

Matthew swirled his liquor.

Maria sensed that, as usual, he really wasn't interested in her words. She loved her son, but he was nothing like his father, Matthew senior. "I must have the ring somewhere in my room. You know me, forgetful at times." She dabbed her dry nose with a lacey kerchief.

"I'd love to see it sometime. Maybe you could look for it tomorrow, while the mason is working in the kitchen?"

Maria knew her son was never one for admiring female attire. That was his way. She remembered the afternoon's conversation he'd had with Mr. Paine. "I'll try to locate it, Matthew, but I can't promise these old eyes will be able to find much of anything." She stood to retire. "Good night, son." As she walked past him, she thought, the ring was hers and it would be her decision to sell or keep it.

4

March 5, 1899
PROVINCETOWN, CAPE COD... 119 YEARS LATER

WALTER ELLIS, already old at thirty-five, awoke in the chilly upstairs room. Beside him lay his wife, Sarah, of fourteen years. He watched her sleeping for a few seconds, hoping to etch an image of her beauty into his memory. Maybe he shouldn't leave them, he thought.

He could see his breath. Shivers rippled through his warm body as his bare feet touched the cold floorboards. He quietly pulled on his suspendered pants and reached for his leather boots from the foot of the bed. His woolen socks were stuffed inside.

By the time he finished tying his laces, Sarah stirred under the tufted quilt behind him. "Oh Walter, I'm sorry I'm late in rising. It took me a while to fall asleep last night." She reached for her flannel robe. "I'll start breakfast. You gather your supplies."

He rose to sort the clothes and sundries needed for survival once he arrived at his destination in the remote and frigid Alaskan Territory. All lay ready on the top quilt of the bed, waiting to be stuffed into two large knapsacks. The most important items were his sealskin pants, three woolen shirts, beaver hat, four pairs of triple-thick woolen socks, and two sets of long underwear; one to wear and one extra while the dirtiest was washed. Walter began packing the bags. He grabbed the last item, a small pouch filled with an assortment of glass beads. He held it in the palm of his hand for only a second and then wedged the small bag deep into the middle of the knapsack. He hoped these trinkets would be attractive to the Indians for bartering. A portrait of the family was stored in his shirt pocket.

Walter listened to the gentle movements of his wife downstairs in the kitchen. He closed his eyes and tried to capture these precious sounds. He was ready. Because of the recent Portland Gale and the loss of his ship, it was the only way for him to provide for his family and protect his property. Amos Lindquist's letter lay on top of the bedside table. Its return address was Juneau, Alaska. Amos's encouraging words for the promise of gold soothed his guilt at leaving.

By the time his bags were hauled down the stairs, the kitchen was warm. Out of the corner of his eye, Walter noticed thirteen-year-old Grace Ellis was curled up in his stuffed chair by the fireplace in the parlor. When he came close, she childishly pulled a blanket over her head to hide.

Walter softly whispered in her ear, "Move over, my little Gracie." He eased his strong six-foot body next to hers and gently lifted her onto his lap. "You know I'll be home soon."

Grace dropped her cover, looked up at her father, then began to whimper.

Walter wiped away her tears and stroked her blonde hair. "While I'm gone, you must help your mother, and don't forget to play with Charles W. He's a handful."

Grace pointed to the framed picture that hung above the fireplace. "Tell me the story again, Father." She held her stare at the pretty lady in the red dress sitting next to a small table in the portrait. One hand was placed near a blue and white teacup and saucer. The other hand was adorned with a large red stone nestled in a gold band.

Walter could never resist his sentimental Grace, even now, as she grew into a young woman. "That lady is your beautiful great-great-great-great-great-grandmother Maria H. Ellis."

Grace sat still, ever fascinated with the portrait and her father's story. "Once upon a time, Maria was in love with a pirate. She knew their love was dangerous. He gave her jewels, gold, and delicate porcelain china to make her feel special whenever she partook of her daily teas. One night, there was a great fire and her pirate died, but

Maria escaped. She decided to live by herself in the woods because her neighbors didn't like her. They thought she was a witch. She kept her pirate's gold a secret for fear some people would steal it from her. It was very hard for lonely Maria. But she remained strong and eventually married your great-great-great-great-great-grandfather Matthew Ellis. The riches disappeared, but family stories tell of a ruby ring called the Pigeon's Blood, and a blue and white teacup and saucer that still remain."

"Is that the teacup and saucer?" She pointed to the china on the mantel next to the portrait.

"Yes, my angel. It is." Walter kissed his daughter on the head. One day, he thought, he'll find the ring, but for now, he must follow a different path to keep his family safe.

An ancient timepiece that hung next to the storage cabinet in the Ellis' kitchen ticked a steady beat. Its measured pulse filled the solemn room as Sarah sat reading the newspaper clipping that Amos had enclosed in his last letter to Walter. She placed her index finger on the headline from the Seattle Post-Intelligencer, July 17, 1897 – "Gold! Gold! Gold! Gold!" She read on, "Stacks of yellow metal – each miner reaped $100,000 and more!"

Walter held her shoulders from behind. "I'll be safe, and I know you'll be all right. Amos is a good man. He would never mislead me. I gave him a chance on my ship when he was in a desperate need. Now he seems to be steering me." He poured himself a cup of coffee.

Sarah rose from the table, looked in on Grace, now dozing in Walter's chair, then whispered to her husband, "You know she wants to go with you to the station, to say goodbye. I think I'll wake Charles W. so we can all go." She turned away as tears appeared in her eyes.

Walter sensed her anxiety and embraced her. "Back in 1780, when my great-great-great-great-grandfather came to Provincetown, the family was a brave lot, and so are we. After building this house, they had purchased the *Ellis* for whaling." He wiped a tear from his wife's eye. "They were successful. Even after my great-grandfather lost his brother at sea in 1840, he stayed strong and continued to take care of the family, just like I will."

They held each other, steadfast in their love, until four-year-old Charles W. stirred upstairs.

The schedule of the New York, New Haven, Hartford Railroad, or the NYNH&H, was oftentimes erratic. As the clock moved closer to 8:30 a.m., the Ellis' morning routine ratcheted to a frenzy. Walter wanted to be early; he could not miss his train to Boston.

5

Present Day - March - Nancy
CAPE COD TO ALASKA

THE PLYMOUTH BROCKTON bus to Boston would leave Hyannis on Cape Cod at 4:30 a.m. I secured and checked my baggage one more time, then slid my new identification tag with Nancy Caldwell, my address, and cell number into the small opening on the back side of the suitcase. My husband, Paul, had already started the car. He came into the foyer and grabbed my luggage.

"Is that everything?"

"I hope so. I have my ID, money, and meds. If I forgot anything, I can buy it."

I patted our old rescue beagle, Mac, goodbye. The sound of the rolling suitcase through the house, or on the wooden decking, always made him nervous. "I'll be back soon, buddy."

It was an easy drive. The roads were empty and dry this early in the morning.

Though always a little nervous whenever I flew, I was excited to travel to Alaska to see our son Brian and his wife Patty. This would be my fourth solo trip to visit them. Paul and I had visited several times before, but I would occasionally travel by myself. This time was special; they had recently moved from Anchorage to Juneau with their first child.

By the time my bus arrived at Logan airport, snow had begun to cover the ground. It was 30 degrees and just right for flakes to form.

Undeterred, I got through security and found my gate for departure. As I walked up the ramp to the Alaska Airlines gates, the runways turned white and snow blew in circles. Flights across the board began to delay, including mine, all due to visibility issues. I called Paul and got another cup of coffee. Within the second hour of waiting, my flight was delayed again. My connection was now in Portland, instead of Seattle, and I realized that I was going to miss that connecting flight. I waited again. Finally, our plane arrived. By the time it was cleaned and fueled, it ended up being the last out of Boston. All other flights were cancelled. I quickly texted Paul.

After landing in Portland, I found my connecting flight to Juneau had been rescheduled for the next morning. I tried to retrieve my luggage for a hotel stay but it was missing. By now it was close to midnight. I texted Paul again, to tell him I'd decided to stay overnight in the airport. Alaska Airlines gave me a small bag filled with toiletries and a blanket. I slept a little.

The next day, after I landed in Juneau, I hurried down to baggage claim. No luggage again. I called Brian and explained the situation; then asked for an extra jacket. The thought of having no clothes, toiletries, boots, or winter gear began to wear on my nerves.

Brian, dressed for winter and a rugged Alaskan environment, waited patiently for me to complete the papers stating the airlines had lost my luggage. I was grateful he'd brought the extra coat for me. The kind woman behind the counter said that if my luggage didn't show up tonight, I should call tomorrow with a short list of things I needed to buy, but only for a few days. She sounded confident that my luggage would be found.

It was sunny, with temperatures in the low 30s. Tired, but looking forward to a good night's sleep, I enjoyed the beautiful panorama of the snow-covered mountains that surrounded us at every turn on our journey to my son's new home. Even though Juneau is isolated, with access only by plane or boat, we still passed the familiar shopping centers, restaurants and grocery stores. Brian and Patty had chosen to live in a secluded area near Auke Bay and Tee Harbor, about 20 minutes from downtown Juneau. It was remote, sparsely populated and somewhat inconvenient, but the lovely views of the Pacific Ocean made it all worthwhile.

We pulled onto their driveway and drove down a slight incline to reach the single-story house. The home was long and narrow, with a wrap-around porch that faced the water with woods behind. It resembled a boat. Once inside, I breathed a sigh of relief.

Patty appeared with open arms; her blonde hair tied back in a ponytail. "Welcome, Grandma Nana! So happy you're here. The baby is sleeping. Why don't you take a nice warm shower and I'll have a cup of tea waiting for you?"

She took my borrowed coat and handed me a pair of Brian's warm fleece pajamas, woolen socks, and flannel robe. Patty was petite; I could never fit into her clothes. Fortunately, Brian's were nice and roomy. My airplane clothes went straight to the wash so I would have something clean to wear the next day. Even without my luggage, I felt welcomed and comfortable. Things will work out, I thought.

Once showered, I settled into a cushy chair by the blazing fireplace and waited patiently for my first grandchild to wake up so that I could hold her. I sipped my warm brew and surveyed the layout of the house. Three bedrooms were at one end and I had a separate suite on the other side. The kitchen and living area were in the middle of the house, with large windows for expansive views of eagles, seals, dolphins, and an occasional whale that came and went with the tides. Just as I finished my tea, I heard the soft stirring of little Sophia through the baby monitor. I quickly washed my hands so I would be ready to hold her.

The baby's room was dimly lit and cozy. I whispered, hoping not to startle the baby. "Oh, Patty, she's beautiful."

"She's such a good little girl. We're so lucky she's not colicky."

"I'm here to help you with whatever you need. Sophia comes first and foremost."

After Patty changed her, I scooped Sophia up and took a big whiff of that special baby smell. It had been a while since I'd held a little one. All of our five kids were grown, our last son, Danny, was headed for graduation from high school in a year. I felt comforted as memories of my own babies filtered through my thoughts.

6

THE ELLIS FAMILY walked a hurried pace along Commercial Street toward the train depot. Walter carried the lightest bag on his shoulder and gingerly pulled a wooden wagon stuffed with his heaviest bag. Little Charles W. perched his young body on top of the lumpy mass of brown canvas. Sarah held onto Grace's hand.

All stared straight ahead. On either side of the street, the destruction from the Portland Gale that had ripped through Provincetown five months earlier, left a grim reminder of everything that was lost and how everyone's lives had changed. The remnants of buildings along the harbor were strewn across the land and shoreline. Hundreds of people had died in that terrible storm. More than thirty Provincetown schooners were damaged or lost, including Walter's, and major wharves destroyed. The little family remained unwavering on their path to the depot.

Walter held Sarah once more. His touch was tender as he stroked her rosy cheek. "Don't be fearful, nor forget you have enough money hidden for survival while I'm gone." In the morning sun, Sarah looked like an angel to him; curly tendrils framed her lovely face. He pulled her closer for another embrace.

After a heartbreaking goodbye, Walter took his seat on the NYNH&H. He watched his little family wave to him from a side window through watery eyes. Once they disappeared from sight, his brow furrowed into a no-nonsense gaze. His choices had been made.

The small family, minus one member, turned and headed for the safety of their home. Breakfast had been quick, with only some crackers and milk, so their father wouldn't miss his train. Now everyone was extra hungry. Charles W. whined for biscuits and jam while Sarah scrambled to satisfy her children's empty stomachs. Every once in a while, she'd stop and stare into space, close her eyes, then breathe a deep sigh and wipe tears away.

Grace busied herself with folding a pile of clean clothes. Within the hour, the house was quiet as Grace finished her task and Charles W. played with his wooden trucks.

Sarah sat, and for the third time that morning, she read Amos' letter and newspaper clipping. Her thoughts went from excitement to dread, as she thought about the coming days without the presence of her husband.

Walter arrived in Boston by noon with time to make his connecting train to New York. After a bite to eat, he carried both duffel bags across his shoulders toward the New York terminal. He stopped to send a telegram to Sarah:

*I AM SAFE. LEAVING ON THE EARLY MORNING
RUN TO NEW YORK THEN RIDING THE
TRANSCONTINENTAL EXPRESS TO SAN
FRANCISCO.*

That night, after his first day of travel, Walter stretched out on a wooden bench, laid his head on one of the canvas bags and closed his eyes. His lips moved in silent prayer.

The next morning, Tuesday, March 6, a South Station constable shook Walter's shoulder. "Better get up, sir! You might miss your train. It's already 5:00 a.m." The policeman waited a few seconds to make sure the man lying across the hard bench was indeed awake.

Walter's back ached, his neck was stiff. As he massaged the back of his head, he saw the terminal had begun to fill with travelers. He grabbed his bags, thanked the man for waking him, then looked for a cup of coffee, some bread, and several hard-boiled eggs. His train to New York was scheduled to leave in less than an hour.

PROVINCETOWN

The day after Walter left, Charles W. woke Sarah around 6:00 a.m. He had soiled himself. She found him sitting upright and crying in his bed. "Accidents happen, my dear. You'll get better. Maybe you drank too much milk before bedtime."

He stopped crying when Sarah removed his wet nightshirt and started to strip his bed.

"I'm sorry, Mother."

"Not to worry. Now get some dry clothes on. Go downstairs and bring in coal from the back porch. I'll be right there."

Sarah dropped the wet sheets on the floor and returned to her room to get dressed. The empty space next to where she'd slept last night was enough to start her crying again. She whispered, "Oh God, Walter. I miss you. How am I going to do your work and mine?"

Throughout the morning, every corner, behind each door, across the surfaces of tables or bureaus, something always signaled to Sarah that Walter was gone. After breakfast, she sat at the kitchen table and made lists of chores that needed to be done and when they were to be completed.

NEW YORK TO SAN FRANCISCO

It was a long day for Walter, and he was hungry again as they finally pulled into Grand Central Station. The lateness of the day made his search for something hot to eat difficult. The lack of expendable money was another element that contributed to his discomfort. He carried $900 for the necessary supplies for his journey and very little extra for travelling incidentals so he kept his purchases cautionary. Walter checked the posted schedule for the Transcontinental Express to San Francisco and the hours of the ticket office. His worried face reflected the coming affliction of sleeping on a hard bench for another night.

On Wednesday, March 7, Walter stood impatiently on the platform clutching his $65 third-class ticket. It was a savings of $45 over the second-class ticket of $110, money that could be better spent on heartier meals besides hard-boiled eggs and bread over the four-day journey across country.

Confused as to which car to board, Walter accidently entered the second-class car. His face softened as he admired the tufted material that was stretched over the seats.

The train attendant soon pointed out his mistake and redirected him to third-class. Walking through the car, Walter discovered that his fellow passengers were mostly emigrant families gleaned from across the United States. He chose his seat, and once again, another stone-like wooden bench would be his bed and home for a while.

The first hours of the journey were spent introducing himself to those across the aisle and behind him and discovering that many essentials for purchase were unavailable in third-class. As the miles flew by, over the next four days, crying children, smells of small livestock, and a wide array of unusual aromas, ranging from personal body odors to diverse ethnic cooking, filled the train car. Even though the reality of communal travel had taken its toll on the usually patient man, Walter's underlying demeanor remained positive. As San Francisco finally approached, his stomach rumbled with a longing for Sarah's food and the serenity of the open sea.

7

Saturday, March 10, 1899
SAN FRANCISCO

CITY NOISES RATCHETED up with every step Walter took away from the train station.

A policeman pointed west. "Head toward the Port. You can buy a ticket at the Palace Hotel over on Montgomery Street."

Buildings soared above his head. Crossing the street was a death-defying act as horses, wagons, autos, trolleys, and people zigzagged to their destinations. Walter could see the blue ocean on the horizon. After he found the hotel and the Pacific Steamship ticket office, he was relieved to see that the S.S *Newport* would leave tomorrow for Seattle.

The port of San Francisco swarmed in the mid-day air with men filled with anger and impatience, shouting commanding words at hundreds of rag tag sailors and workmen. Walter maneuvered his best to avoid copious amounts of spittle, piss, and tobacco on the sloping streets, on his quest to find food. A sign on a small café to his right beckoned him with praises of coffee, meat, and pastries. He hurried across the narrow road and walked inside.

Hearty odors accosted his nose in a comforting way. An empty counter stool signaled an opportunity for something quick. He tipped his hat to the stranger next to him. "Mind if I sit here?"

The grizzled old-timer nodded, then returned to his plate of beef stew.

Walter leaned his bags against the far wall. He glanced at his neighbor's food. "Any good?"

"Fair to middlin', if you don't mind a bit of gristle."

Walter grinned, caught the attention of the young girl behind the counter, and pointed to the stew. "I'll have some of that."

The old man began his second course of apple pie and coffee. His hand gripped the spoon, and after each slow shovelful of the sweet morsels, he uttered a sigh of contentment. "Where you goin'?"

"Alaska." Walter observed the delectable treat of apples.

The old man never stopped his rhythm of enjoying the pastry. "Where you from?"

"Cape Cod. Provincetown."

"Any family?"

Walter pulled out the picture of him and the family from his shirt pocket. "Wife and two children."

After a quick glance and a shrug, the man replied, "Well, I hope you make it." He used his thumb to scoop the last flaky crumb from the plate.

Walter gestured for a piece of pie. "I'm hopeful that the good Lord will watch over me and my family."

"Seems like you're a God-fearing man." He stood next to Walter and eyed him up and down. "Strong lookin' too." He shoved a wad of tobacco into his cheek. "Lemme give you a piece of advice. Steer clear of that New Yorker Hotel. They're a bunch of crimps." He turned to leave.

Walter stopped eating and asked, "What do you mean, crimps?"

"Why, they get ya' lickered up, steal your money, then sell you to a Captain in need of crew, who'll then take ya' far away to some God forsaken place." He headed for the door.

"I thank you kindly, sir." Walter turned around for another bite of pie, put away the small photo into a vest pocket next to his money, and lowered the other hand to make sure the rest of his cash was still tied safely around his calf.

He picked up a newspaper from the counter and sipped his coffee while he scrutinized the classifieds for a boarding house where he could get a good night's sleep.

The young lady behind the counter watched him searching the paper. "If you're looking for a safe place to spend the night, my aunt has rooms over on Geary Street. A couple of miles away, but it's worth it." She began to wipe the counter.

"How much?"

"Well, it's got a double bed with a hair mattress and running water. Only $1.00 a day."

"Much obliged." He folded the newspaper under his arm and grabbed his bags. "Which way?"

"Left, past Montgomery Street, about a mile after that. Stay straight."

Walter discovered the boarding house was clean and had a lock on the door. The bed was a little short and his feet hung over the edge, but it still felt good to stretch out. The next morning, he bought his steamer ticket, telegraphed Sarah, returned to the café for some breakfast, and then walked to the Central Pier. The S.S. *Newport* steamship would leave at 10:00 a.m.

8

March 1899
SAN FRANCISCO

THIRD CLASS WAS again Walter's choice. His early boarding onto the steamship afforded him the bottom bunk in the tiny stateroom. As he was seeing to his duffle bags, a man's voice came from behind.

"Good morning," the young traveler greeted him.

A thin but muscular frame on the man was good news to Walter. No chance of the top bed above him giving way. "Yes, it is a good day." He extended his hand in friendship. "Walter Ellis, headed for Alaska."

A large smile spread across the other gentlemen's face. "Well, I'll be darned. Me too." He gripped the hand of his new acquaintance. "Harry Cavanaugh."

After all was settled, the two travelers went up on deck.

Above their heads, the ladies and gentlemen of first class waved goodbye as wildly as Walter's shipmates did in third class.

By the time San Francisco was a blur on the horizon, Walter and Harry were well acquainted. Harry's parents had both tragically died in a horse and buggy accident, a few months after he graduated from secondary school, so he was taking some time to heal. An adventure with the possibility of riches was just the thing he craved.

As the ocean surrounded the *Newport* and the miles sped by, Walter's body relaxed. He enjoyed the salty smell, brisk breezes, and now a friend.

The ship's band stopped playing above their heads, signaling the end of the official send-off. By 11:30 a.m., the faint odors of something good cooking drifted past their noses.

"I wonder what's for lunch?" Harry cocked his head upwards to the higher deck.

"Whatever it is, it almost smells like home." Walter turned his gaze back to the sea.

Harry took out a harmonica and played a soft tune while they waited.

The upper deck grew quiet as the wealthy were served their lunch first. At 1:30 p.m., third class was ready to eat.

In the salon on their level, a large table was set up in the middle of the room laden with three soup tureens, biscuits, jam, fresh fruit, and coffee. No utensils were laid out or tables to sit at. The two men were well acquainted with what third class offered. They stood ready with their own bowl, spoon, and cup. The chairs on deck were their preference for dining. None of their fellow passengers below minded the inconvenience; they found the food was tasty for all meals.

The night showed a clear sky. Thousands of stars twinkled across the blackness, but with stomachs filled and spirits high, the ship grew quiet early on that first night. The travelers would follow this routine over the next five days of steaming along the Pacific Coast, then change ship in Seattle for Alaska.

Each morning came with coffee, biscuits, jam, and oatmeal. Walter and Harry busied themselves between meals up on deck, comparing the necessary supplies that they would buy in Seattle, and dreaming of gold. They both agreed that their shopping choices would follow the advice from government officials and include cans of beans, beef, potatoes, coffee, eggs, butter, along with flour and sweetener to last for at least a year.

Harry pulled out a newspaper flyer that recommended what inventory was important. "Three pounds of food a day for one year. That's almost half a ton," Harry rubbed his forehead in amazement.

"That's only half of what we got to carry up over the pass. We've got to buy another half-ton of equipment." Walter kept reading. "And the miners have to make twenty or more trips carrying fifty to sixty pounds on their backs."

Harry gave a low whistle in bewilderment. "Ain't someone going to steal your supplies when you're carrying over the trail?"

"I've heard the men hire Indians to help carry or guard the stuff." Walter stuffed his list into his breast pocket. "I hope you've brought extra money." He breathed in the salty air with relief, remembering his bag of trinkets.

As Harry and Walter talked of their future plans on deck, Max Reynolds, dressed in a herring bone suit and vest, listened to their words from a few feet away.

Max was also headed in search of gold, but he needed help, and these two strapping men might be just what he was looking for. Max stood up and leaned over the rail near Harry. "Excuse me."

Harry turned toward the stranger, impressed with how this man dressed but cautious that he might be a con man.

Walter stepped to Harry's side to see who was interrupting their conversation. He spoke first. "What can we do for you?"

"I couldn't help overhear you two men talking on deck. So, you're headed for Alaska?"

Harry smiled. "Yup."

Walter nodded.

Max began with, "I'm going on the same hunt for gold."

The word gold piqued the interest of these two fledgling treasure hunters.

Max continued, "A while back, before we sailed from San Francisco, my partner took sick and returned home to Idaho, leaving me to fend for myself. I'm in need of some help and was wondering if you'd give me a bit of your time so I can explain my plans; hopefully they will include you fellows."

Harry and Walter looked at each other, shrugged their shoulders and nodded their heads in agreement, eager to listen.

The three men moved to wooden folding chairs next to one of the lifeboats. Max explained that he and his ex-partner had access to machines and equipment that would make their finding gold easier than using the placer method. Both men knew of placer mining, a back-breaking test of a man's strength and stamina.

Walter leaned against his chair. "Well, I think the proven way of panning the placer deposit is all we really need.

Harry added, "We know what we're doing." He recited his knowledge to impress Max. "A placer deposit is an accumulation of valuable materials, like gold, after it's separated from rock." He smiled at knowing the facts. "We'll be buying tools and pans for sifting all the gold that we find when we reach Seattle, on our way to the gold fields.

Max hesitated before he spoke. "All well and good, but do you realize that most of the gold is below the permafrost, about six feet down?" He waited for his words to sink in then added, "I've got machines to help you melt the ice and frost. Then you tunnel down and make a shaft to where the real treasure is lying. I can't do it by myself. I need partners. Are you interested?"

Walter stood up. "Tomorrow we land in Seattle. Can we sleep on it?"

"Of course." Max offered his hand. "I've been listening to you two talk over the past few days and have come to realize that both of you are honest and hard-working. I'll await your decision." He straightened his jacket and turned to leave. "See you tomorrow at breakfast."

Walter and Harry talked through the evening and examined Max's papers that showed proof of his machine purchases and other business credentials. Eventually, they decided that it would be to their advantage to join up with Max and his promise of using machines to find gold. They felt that with his support and backing, their fortune would come sooner.

Eager to talk with Max the next morning, the men were among the first passengers to gather their hearty breakfast.

As Walter filled his mug with coffee, Max came up behind him and placed his hand on his would-be partner's shoulder. "Well, what's your decision, young man?"

After a smile and a quick handshake, Walter's partnership was sealed. Harry repeated the same gesture with Max.

Max Reynolds appeared relieved as he piled his plate with muffins and jam. Looking up, he caught the attention of a man on the other side of the large buffet table. "Sinclair. Come on over here. I want you to meet my new partners on this adventure of a lifetime."

Sinclair made his way to the three men.

"This is Walter Ellis and Harry Cavanaugh."

The men exchanged handshakes.

"Tell the boys about your business." Max was ready for some coffee. "I'll be right back."

Sinclair took a deep breath. "I'm going to Alaska, too, but not for gold."

Max's new partners looked curious.

"I'm selling boots. I've brought with me 1500 rubber boots to sell to the miners." He waited to continue. "I know it sounds crazy but I'm confident. My wife is even with me. We'll probably only have to stay a few years and then hope to return to San Francisco with a ton of money."

Walter and Harry smiled to each other. Walter spoke up, "That sounds like a great plan. In fact, when we get to Seattle, maybe I'll buy a pair for myself."

Max returned and asked his partners for one last favor. "Boys, we need to document our partnership with a photograph. Meet me up on deck in ten minutes."

Walter tipped his hat. "Will do."

After breakfast, passengers had two to three hours to prepare themselves for their landing at Seattle. The ship was a-bustle with people readying for the next leg of their great adventure to Alaska.

9

Present Day - March
BREWSTER

THE SCREECH OF TIRES followed by a crunch caught Ally Grant's attention. With coffee cup in hand, she peered out the front window of her legal office at the two crumpled cars now stuck in the middle of Brewster's Main Street. Her red painted nails might hint at a stylish reluctance to get involved, but once Ally sees someone needing help, she usually jumps right in. She put her coffee down and flew out the door. "Everyone okay?"

The drivers had already exited their cars. The elderly man and middle-aged woman stood a short distance from their open doors, each shaking heads and rubbing necks.

Ally pulled out her cell. "Tony? There's been another accident in front of my office." She noticed the elderly man was grimacing. "Feeling okay, sir?"

He nodded.

Her attention focused back on her phone. "Yeah, everyone seems to be all right. Okay, honey, see you tonight."

Officer Thompson pulled up to the scene with lights flashing. Next came the ambulance and then the fire truck, all typical procedure for any auto accident.

Ally greeted Thompson. "I'll be in my office, if you need me."

"Thanks." Officer Thompson began asking questions as he stood on top of the shattered glass and pieces of metal.

Back at her desk, Ally skimmed through the case files piled to one side. Poor Mr. Jenkins let his house insurance lapse by one month only to have a chimney fire. Underneath his information was Peter Jericho, a sticky domestic violence issue.

The door opened. "Hi Ally." Lucy Sear's face always had a smile when she delivered the mail. "What about that accident?" She splayed the stack of letters across the desk like a deck of cards. "Anything interesting?"

Ally ignored the question. "Thanks Lucy." The local mail lady had a tendency to gossip too much. Ally changed the subject with, "How's your kitty doing?"

"Oh fine." Lucy exited the office with the disappointment of nothing new etched across her face. Halfway out of Ally's office, Lucy's expression quickly changed to a happy greeting. This time it was for the owner of the adjacent bookstore. "Hello Mary, what's new with you today?"

Realizing everyone was safe out on the street and used to the repeated accidents that occur in front of her office, Ally dove into the pile of mail on her desk. After sorting the important items out of the advertisements, she picked up a file she was ignoring but now needed her attention. She had been hired to liquidate an estate in Provincetown. A task she normally doesn't do but an old friend from Boston had asked this favor from her since she's now living on the Cape. The dilapidated house dated back to 1780 and had a buyer, if the house could be cleaned out by the first day of June.

Ally thought of her best friend, Nancy Caldwell. She was visiting her son and daughter-in-law in Juneau but would be home the following week. This is just what her friend liked to do; rummage through an old 18th century house that's hasn't been lived in for twenty years or more, searching for treasures.

10

AS THE STEAMSHIP made its way into port, third class passengers, mostly women, began to crowd around the top of the gaping cargo hold of the ship. All watched the men elbowing each other twenty feet beneath them, looking for their supplies. To the passengers on deck, it looked like a free-for-all; men crawling over boxes and crates to get to their provisions. First class baggage was stored in another hold with stewards retrieving personal items.

Sinclair turned to his wife before he descended the steps to claim his boxes of boots. "Stay up here, my dear." He pointed to the spectacle below. "That's no place for a woman."

Mrs. Sinclair listened with no question, but curious as ever, stepped a little closer to the edge. She could see Walter, Harry, and Max Reynolds. They stood next to large crates with the name, R E Y N O L D S, stamped across the sides and top of each box. She tensed as her husband appeared off to the right and then watched him dive into the scuffle.

Max yelled above the din to his two partners, "Stay put. I'll arrange to have the crates lifted onto the wharf. Once it begins, one of you needs to get up to the dock and stand by the equipment."

Walter and Harry nodded their heads.

It took several hours before Max's supplies were placed on the wharf. The men tied large tarps around two piles of wooden crates.

Harry stepped back and whistled. "Whew! I guess this is only the beginning of the work ahead of us."

Walter took off his cap and scratched his head. "Agreed, and you know what? I'm ready."

Harry and Max stood to the side with arms locked in approval.

Before their adventure continued to Alaska, the plan was for someone to stay and guard the supplies on the wharf for one night. The other partners would find a place to sleep. Harry agreed to the watch. Walter and Max separated, each finding their own selective accommodations. Max had money and was accustomed to the finer things.

By early evening, Walter had settled into a small hotel near Wharf 60. He was hungry. Before he left for dinner, he made sure his money was secure both in his pants pocket and a smaller amount tied to his upper thigh inside a leather holder.

The air grew damp and gray as Walter started his return trip to the hotel after a satisfying dinner. In the dusky evening, he became confused as to which way to walk. Within a few minutes, he realized he was heading in the wrong direction. He cut down an alley to get to the correct street.

He noticed several men crouched on the dirt, smoking and drinking, near the base of the brick buildings. Walter picked up his pace; cursing that his choice of a short cut was a mistake. He saw the glow of a gas streetlamp ahead of him. It felt reassuring but not for long. A strong hand grabbed his shoulder from behind and spun him around. Walter's chin collided with his attacker's fist, which sent him flat to the ground. Within seconds, he felt rough hands searching his clothes. He was groggy but still able to grab the man's hand that now held his money.

The two men struggled. Walter felt another paw on his shoulder, which slammed him backwards against the building. With the wind knocked out of him, he still ran after his money. All three reached the main street but as Walter turned the corner, his foot missed the wooden walkway and down he went. He tried to get to his feet but couldn't stand up. He lay there in excruciating pain.

The following morning, March 17, a menacing fog spread across Wharf 60 as Harry and Max waited for Walter.

Harry paced the wooden pier, trying to find his partner's face in the distance. "Where is he?" He stood on his toes to see above the masses of people waiting to board or say goodbye to loved ones.

Max checked his pocket watch. "It's almost 9:00 a.m., we've got to get in line. We can't wait any longer."

Harry yelled over the noise, "I'm going to check the ticket office, maybe I can leave a message for him." He pushed himself through the multitude of faces in the direction of the port authorities.

The steamship left on time at 10:00 a.m. without Walter. Max and Harry stood near the railing up on deck, searching and hoping to find their partner.

SEATTLE GENERAL

Walter lifted his hand to feel the ache pounding in his forehead. He quickly covered his nose as the antiseptic smell of the indigent ward at Seattle General blended with other bodily odors.

A soft voice spoke. "Mister. Glad to see you're awake."

He opened his eyes. "Oh Sarah, is that you?" He reached for her hand.

The young nurse, startled by Walter's response, drew back but quickly regained her composure. She touched his forearm. "Sir. You've had a bad accident. My name is Nurse Barnes."

Agitated, Walter rubbed his eyes. His face contorted into a scowl. He saw people lying in beds across and next to him. "Where am I? How did I get here?" He struggled to sit up. "I need to get to the wharf."

Rebecca Barnes gently pushed his shoulders back against the bed. "You are safe at Seattle General. You're also a very lucky man. If it hadn't been for the kind police sergeant, you may have laid there on the street for who knows how long before anyone found you."

Walter tried to sit up again, but the room spun. It hurt to move his leg. "What happened to me?"

The nurse straightened his coverings. "It seems you hit your head and received an injury to your ankle, probably a sprain. You should be better in a day or so. The doctor told me you may have to use crutches for a while."

Walter closed his eyes. Within seconds he opened them. "My God, what day is it?"

"March 17."

"Where are my things, my money?"

"They're safe in our offices."

He turned his head to the side in despair. "I've missed my chance. I'm sure they're gone by now."

Rebecca placed a glass of water near his lips. "Are you up to drinking?"

Walter lifted his head and accepted a few sips. "Please excuse my behavior earlier. You resemble my wife, back home, and I…I thought you were her."

She smiled at her patient. "Don't worry about that. It must have been quite a shock to find yourself in a hospital."

Walter watched her fussing about his bedside table.

She pivoted toward him. "Why do you need to get to the wharf?"

"We – my partners and I – were headed for Alaska. I was supposed to be with them. They have no idea what happened to me." He clenched his fists.

Rebecca patted his forearm sympathetically. "Now that you're awake, I'll be right back, but first, I need to tend to that gentlemen across the room." She moved on to her next patient.

Walter yearned for any word from the doctor. His wait turned into two hours of uncertainty, which dragged him further into a stupor of confusion and doubt.

Rebecca finally reappeared. "Now, let's see if you can sit up."

He did so with no dizziness.

"Can you move your leg?"

A few sways and lifts of his injured leg up and down proved successful.

"Excellent. I'll tell the doctor."

Walter felt better but still couldn't flex his foot. He sat on the edge of his bed for a few more minutes, swiveled his injured foot around to rest it on the white sheets, then leaned back against his pillow.

While he waited again, Rebecca brought him something to eat. "Mr. Ellis, my brother Lue works down on the wharf in one of the ticket offices."

Walter looked at her with hope.

Rebecca removed a metal cover from a dinner plate to reveal a meat sandwich and a pickle. "I think you'll be staying overnight at the hospital and I'm on shift again tomorrow. Maybe I can help you to get where you're supposed to be. Why don't you tell me your itinerary and what ship you were taking, and I'll ask Lue if he can be of any help."

"Thank you very much. You're so kind. I was supposed to leave with Harry Cavanaugh and Max Reynolds." He gave her the rest of the details.

Later that evening, the doctor told Walter that he had sustained a severe sprain, enough that bed rest was needed for at least a week, and then crutches. He would also need to stay through the night for observation because of his head injury. Discharge would be late afternoon tomorrow. The nurse would advise him about his living options.

"Good luck, Mr. Ellis." The doctor disappeared behind a white curtain across the room.

That night, Walter slept with a determination that he could handle what must be done. He was no quitter.

11

March 1899
SEATTLE - THE BARNES HOUSE

THE NEXT MORNING, Walter spoke to Rebecca of his family on Cape Cod, and how much he missed them. He beamed with pride as he showed her their picture. She admired his faithfulness and passion to provide for them against all odds. Knowing he had nowhere to go and had little money, Rebecca invited Walter to stay at her family's house.

"Are you sure your mother will be acceptable to me staying with you?"

"Mother occasionally takes in a boarder."

"I am forever grateful for your kindness. I will pay."

The following day, Rebecca and Lue helped Walter off the back of the delivery wagon and up the three steps that led into the family's front parlor. The Barnes house was small but tidy.

"Welcome, Mr. Ellis." Mrs. Barnes' round face, upturned hair and colorful apron looked heartwarming. The smell of home-cooked foods only added to Walter's welcome.

"Thank you very much for allowing me to stay here until my foot is better."

Mrs. Barnes directed him to sit in a stuffed chair. A colorful embroidered footstool was pushed under his sprained ankle.

"Mrs. Barnes, I assure you that I will be able to pay you for your kindness. Those bastar— I mean, ruffians didn't get all of my money. Excuse my language."

Mrs. Barnes shook her finger. "I understand your anger this time, but there'll be no cursing under my roof. Understood?"

"Yes, ma'am."

The lady of the house retreated into the kitchen, saying as she left, "I'll let you know when supper is ready."

Rebecca followed her mother.

Lue sat in the other chair. "Don't worry, Mother is a softy. She won't throw you out."

Walter scratched his calf.

"So, Rebecca tells me you were headed for Alaska?"

"That's right. But half my money's gone now. I'm not sure if I'm going to get there. I was counting on my partners to share expenses. They left without me."

Lue leaned in closer. "I've got some connections with the other steamship offices. Tomorrow, I'll ask if any messages were left for you. We might get lucky."

Dinner was just as expected – tasty. Coffee was poured and peach pie cut for all.

Walter looked to Lue. "Thanks again for retrieving my gear from the hotel." He glanced at his duffle bags on the floor in a small room off the kitchen. "I promise I'll repay."

Rebecca brought Walter a pencil and paper. "Now write down your address and what you want me to say in the telegram to your family. I can send it off in the morning. I'm sure they're worried."

Walter placed two dollars on the table and wrote these words:

SARAH ELLIS---DELAYED IN SEATTLE---STAYING WITH BARNES FAMILY---AS EVER---YOUR HUSBAND WALTER ELLIS

The bed was low, hard, and easy to lie down on. Walter retired early, at 9:30 p.m. but woke at midnight. His foot ached. He reached for the medication Rebecca had left on the little table near his bed.

While he waited for the pain numbing to circle through his body, his head filled with thoughts of his immediate future.

He hobbled into the kitchen and out the back door. The air was warm and the moon glowed large and yellow in the night sky. He thought of his Sarah and wondered if she was thinking of him and possibly looking at the same beautiful moon.

A week passed. Walter stayed off his feet, iced his ankle, and helped Mrs. Barnes in the kitchen, peeling potatoes or apples, or snapping beans. From years at sea, he knew his way around cooking and was not embarrassed to do woman's work. Lue couldn't find anyone who knew of messages left for a Walter Ellis. He did discover one thing – there might be several opportunities for Walter to work his way to Juneau, Alaska.

Over the following weeks, Walter realized that sending a telegraph was too costly. Instead, he sent letters home to Sarah and the family with news about his health and future prospects.

Postings by captains looking for able-bodied men to steam to Alaska were occasionally listed in the newspaper and Lue, becoming a fast friend, was able to recommend the good and bad for Walter, based on his local contacts from the wharf.

In the meantime, and throughout the month of April, Walter worked hard on getting his body in shape for whatever tasks he would be assigned on his up-coming journey to Alaska as part of a crew. He lifted bags of flour and dry goods for Mrs. Barnes' baking business. She supplied delicious desserts to several local hotels and cafés. Once his ankle was strong enough, he ran in the early morning hours, no matter what the weather, ate well, and slept even better. He experienced very few headaches as his physical strength returned.

On a rainy morning in May, Walter finished his running routine. He burst into the back door to see Lue sipping coffee.

"Any word about a job?" Rain dripped off Walter's cap.

"I think I've got something for you. Got in late last night but you were sleeping."

Walter took his wet jacket off, changed his pants then grabbed a cup for himself. "I'm all ears."

"Word is, the millionaire Harriman, from back east, is going on an expedition across the waters and coastal territory of Alaska." Lue reached for a slice of his mother's homemade oatmeal bread. "This man is bringing scientists, artists, photographers, and writers with him. They're going 9,000 miles, first across America, then they'll steam up and down the Alaskan coast, expecting to make 50 stops along the way. One of those is in Juneau."

Walter's eyes opened wide. "You think I can get work on board?"

"Some guys at the bar last night were making fun of it, calling it a circus. They heard Harriman bought the *George W. Elder* and completely refitted the ship with a stateroom for all his invitees. They're even bringing a piano, organ, and one of those new-fangled graphophones."

"I'm interested."

"I'll find out at work today what crew they're looking for."

"My thanks." Walter sat longer at the table by himself. He remembered Harry and Max mentioning Juneau and then Skagway/Dyea.

Towards evening, and after he'd completed his work for Mrs. Barnes, Walter wrote a letter to Sarah explaining the possibility of getting work on the *Elder* with an end goal of reaching Juneau.

Lue, home from work, walked into the kitchen as Walter finished his letter. He sat at the table next to him. "Good news and bad news, my friend."

The stranded adventurer listened.

"They're almost done with retrofitting the *Elder* as a luxury ship. The captain is looking for a few strong men. That's the good news." Lue reached for a beer. "The bad news is that he only needs stokers."

"What do you mean?"

"You know, stokers! They're down in the bowels of the ship shoveling coal into the boilers. I've heard it's 120 to160 degrees down there. It's tough work and the gangs are pretty rough men."

Walter sat back in his chair. "Never worked that kind of ship."

"Do you think you could handle it? I know it pays well and I'm pretty sure you can leave when you reach Juneau."

"When does it leave Seattle?

"May 31."

"Let me sleep on it."

After breakfast, Walter asked Lue if the captain would definitely allow him to leave when they reached Juneau.
"I'll ask the engineer on board. See you tonight."

Anxiety filled Walter's day as he followed his exercise routine and completed his duties for Mrs. Barnes.
That evening, Lue arrived home. "You're all set. Chief Engineer Scandrett had planned to have extra crews on board for the duration of the exploration. The work is strenuous and a fresh gang would deliver the best for Harriman's dollar plus they'll be stopping in Juneau."
Walter grew a smile across his face when he heard the news. Immediately after supper, he penned a letter to Sarah.

My dearest Sarah,

I have acquired passage to Juneau via working as a stoker on the 'George W. Elder' to Juneau. I will be working on the ship for six days. I hear it's hard work but nothing I cannot do. The 'Elder' does not leave until May 31. I have several weeks to continue building my health and Mrs. Barnes has been paying me for my work from her baking. Enclosed is $50.00. In God's plan to do right, I hope to find my partners, Harry Cavanaugh and Max Reynolds.

Give my love to the children.

Walter

May 31, 1899 arrived with sun and spring temperatures. As Walter said his goodbyes near the open door, Mrs. Barnes appeared, waving a letter in her hand. "Walter! I almost forgot. A letter arrived yesterday from your daughter, I think." She hurried over to him.
He took the missive, read its return and smiled. "It's from my Gracie." He tapped it across his palm in thought and decided to stow

it deep in his bag, so he wouldn't lose it. "I'll have plenty of time to read this later." He quickly waved another goodbye.

With good luck on their breaths, the Barnes family wished their new friend well on the next leg of his journey to success.

"Once I get settled, I'll send you a letter, and one to my Sarah, too. I hope the mail is good there."

Not sure what to expect over the following days, Walter took a deep breath, heaved two heavy bags over his shoulders, then headed toward the wharf.

12

May 31, 1899
GEORGE W. ELDER

BY 9:00 A.M., Walter had officially signed the roster as a crewmember. He was directed to his quarters deep below, near the boilers. The smell of coal and sulfur permeated the stoker's housing. On each side, six bunks filled the stark room for a total of twelve beds. Cautious and sensing very little privacy, Walter picked the last bottom bunk in the back.

A loud voice came from the open door behind him. "Hey!"

Walter turned around to see a smudged and grimy man wearing only a thin undershirt and black baggy pants. His shoes resembled clogs. "Get a move on. You're needed below."

The new stoker followed the man down the spiral staircase, or the *fireman's passage*, and into the boiler room. A burst of hot air hit Walter in the face. He couldn't breathe. He flung his jacket off. The doors of four double-ended boilers glowed red-hot. He stripped his shirt off, leaving only a thin undershirt.

"Put those on." The man pointed to a pair of black clogs with heavy wooden soles. "Keeps your feet from burning up."

Walter placed his leather shoes under the stairway.

"Grab that ash shovel." The man pointed to a nine-foot pole with a flat shovel on its end. "You'll be cleaning out the ash and smoothing out the coal."

Walter grabbed the tubular pole.

By 6 p.m., the *Elder* was underway.

Eight stokers were needed to maintain a rapid steam supply for the four boilers. Four extra men were slated to relieve the men every four hours, for at least 30 minutes. Walter cleaned the ash bed, smoothed new coal and filled in when necessary. No one talked; it was too hot below. The *black gang*, as they were called, kept to themselves.

It was nearing midnight before Walter was able to take a break. He and another stoker stood by an open porthole near the top of the spiral steps. The air was chilly, and the faces of the sweaty men were stoic and distant. Occasional breezes blew against Walter as he stood back behind his fellow stokers. "Pardon, could I stand a bit closer?"

One man spoke slow and threatening, "I'll move when I want to. The black gang takes nothing from nobody."

Undeterred, Walter stepped a little closer to breathe the fresh air.

Jimmy, as he was called, turned around and shoved a blackened finger in his face. "Listen. The last time someone pushed or bothered one of the black gang... that someone disappeared without a trace."

Walter stepped back.

On the fourth day of travel, food poisoning took over some of the black gang. Three of them stood vomiting out the portholes through the night. Walter and Gus Ercher, two of the four extra men hired for relief, were called down to the boiler room. Gus was short of stature but strong enough to break a two-by-four in half with his bare hands. With only two more days of travel before docking in Juneau, Walter consoled himself that he could make it through the intense heat and exhaustion that comes with stoking.

Unfamiliar with the routine of shoveling for the designated three minutes into the burning cavity and then stepping back and to the side for the draft of air to stimulate the flames, Walter hesitated in front of the gaping hole less than thirty seconds. It was an unfortunate mistake. A burst of heat and flame blew out and across the right side of his body.

Hoses were turned on and sprayed over Walter's writhing body until he eventually passed out from his pain. Gus carried him up the spiral stairway while Jimmy called for the ship's doctor, Edward Trudeau, Jr.

Upon examining his patient's burned flesh and state of being, Dr. Trudeau spoke with authority, "Before I can treat him, I need to calm him."

Walter moaned and thrashed about.

A note was handed to Gus:

Bring chloral hydrate, body bandages and ointment of grease.

"Find my nurse and give this to her. Tell her I need help with the bandaging."

The least sick man of the three poisoned was pulled from his bed and forced to replace the injured stoker.

The doctor tended to Walter and after a few more *knock-out drops*, he left with the confidence that his patient would sleep through the night.

Later, Archie Parks was on a break and the only one in the stoker quarters besides Walter. Most of the black gang distrusted him and a few even despised him. Archie knew no one was going to return until after 10:00 p.m. He crept closer to where Walter's bandaged head, face, and right arm rested. He could see the injured man's chest rise and fall in sleep. Slowly and methodically, he rifled through Walter's belongings, looking for anything of value. He heard footsteps on the steel staircase. In a panic, he only had time to grab the pouch of money, leaving the wallet intact. Walter lay asleep while Archie slipped past Gus in the doorway.

Dr. Trudeau came down in the early morning to check on his patient.

He pulled a stool close to the bedside and sat down. "What's your name, son?"

No response.

The doctor sat there, not wanting to touch the bandages for fear his patient would start to thrash about in pain. With calm and forthright words, he explained, "Son, you've had an accident and have acquired severe burns on the right side of your body."

Walter's one exposed eye flitted back and forth, as if trying to comprehend how bad his injuries were. He attempted to lift his left arm; his eye opened wide in pain.

Dr. Trudeau gently touched the raised hand. "Try to stay calm. We're arranging for you to disembark in Juneau. There's a hospital there, St. Ann's. They'll be able to treat your burns better than on the ship."

Walter tried to say his name, but nothing came out. Within seconds, he felt a liquid on his tongue and then everything went black.

Dr. Trudeau twisted the black medicine dropper closed on the chloral hydrate.

The chief engineer entered and stood near the doctor. "What's the verdict?"

"He needs to leave for St. Ann's as soon as we dock in Juneau. Do you have any papers on him?"

"All I know is, his name is Walter Ellis and headed to Juneau."

"Just as well, at least he's ending up where he wanted to go. It's a shame, if he's searching for gold; he's in for a big surprise. Chances of survival in *the inside* of Alaska and the likelihood that he'll find riches as a cripple and with one working eye are nearer to zero than one."

13

Present Day - March - Nancy
JUNEAU, ALASKA

ON THE THIRD DAY of my Alaskan visit, my luggage remained missing. Brian and I went into Juneau to purchase two more outfits, some toiletries, underwear, and a pair of hiking boots. When we returned, Sophia was still napping so we decided to go for a walk to explore the Point. I pulled on my new hikers, added ice cleats, then borrowed a walking pole from a small selection by the door. Brian grabbed his binoculars.

The house stood on the banks of an inlet from the ocean. We walked down the road behind the house to where the water met the Pacific. From the vantage of the Point, or *the edge of land*, Brian said we could see cruise ships and whales passing in the distance. We sat on the bench at the overlook.

"There's a neat trail called the Breadline." He pointed to our right. "It follows the coast along the bluff. I tried to walk it once but ran out of time. It's treacherous. In some parts, you're right on the edge, overlooking the water."

I was pleased to know my son made careful decisions. His stint in the Peace Corps had taught him a lot.

Brian hooked his binoculars around his neck. "Want to go down to the water's edge?"

"Sure. How do we get down?"

"Come on. Follow me."

Brian began to hike down the steep path on our left. The mossy rocks were slippery from Southeast Alaska's coastal temperate rainforests. I followed at a slower pace. We passed clumps of white snow lying next to beautiful moss and vivid green vegetation. It was interesting to see the verdant mix of whites and greens as we reached the huge cobbles and stones that covered the beach. Across the water, on the other side of the inlet, I noticed a series of poles and wires strung between them. "Are those telephone poles?"

"That's right. There were several canneries here in the 1900s. It was a big industry for Juneau back then." He pointed to a piece of a red brick among the rounded stones. "Once in a while, you'll see remnants of the old buildings." He picked up the smooth broken red brick to show me.

I looked behind me, toward the wooded land, at huge black rock outcrops, like platforms edged in moss, on one side of the path. I turned back to the water view and once again marveled at the majestic mountains that encircled us.

Brian checked his watch. "We'd better get back. Little Sophia is probably waking up."

I was starting to feel the wind increase and a chill went through my body. "Right behind you."

Brian led the way, turning around occasionally to see if I needed any help back up the steep path.

That night, 40-mph winds and torrential rains made the house creak and groan. Knowing it was fairly new construction, I felt safe enough to sleep better than usual.

Morning came early with the baby waking us all up around 6:30 a.m. I made the coffee while Patty tended to Sophia. Brian checked around the outside of the house for storm damage.

"Can I feed my little sweetheart?"

"Of course, Grandma Nana." Patty handed me a prepared bottle. "Want to sit by the windows? It's a beautiful view."

I moved the rocker in front of the window but remained standing, as I fed the baby, to observe the expansive low tide. I watched Brian walk toward the exposed ocean floor. His long strides quickly took him away from the house, his six-foot-tall body growing smaller and smaller the further he ventured out. "Where's he going?" I guessed he hadn't walked more than 500 feet, but knew that if the tide was in, he'd be under water.

Patty joined me and we both watched as he headed toward a large white object. The only sound was the baby drinking and cooing. When Brian picked up the mysterious white item, we saw that it was only a five-gallon plastic bucket. Then he placed it upright on the ground, took out his phone, bent over a bit, and looked as if he was taking pictures of something else he'd found. From inside, I looked at Patty for answers. She kept her stare on Brian. By the time we got the binoculars out, Brian had begun his return home.

As Brian's figure came closer to the house, Patty and I stood our ground until he disappeared beyond our sightline and into the garage attached to the house.

"What were you doing out there?" Patty's face looked anxious.

Brian crossed the room to his computer. After a few moments of silence, he said, "Take a look at what I found."

Sophia made a loud burp in my arms as I went to look at the computer screen.

All three of us stared at what seemed to be the skeleton of a complete leg, including the pelvis.

"Is that human or animal?" I craned my neck for a closer view.

Brian and Patty, both well versed in health sciences, were knowledgeable but stymied.

I was curious. "Should we call the police?"

"Not yet." Brian grabbed a cup of coffee to warm his hands. "I don't think it's human but let me do some searching on the internet before we call anyone. We have several hours before the tide comes back in and covers everything up."

I decided to change to indoor clothes. By the time I returned to the kitchen, Brian had found his answer.

"The pelvis is definitely too small for a human leg. Most likely it's from a deer or moose."

"Well, that's reassuring." I went to Sophia's bedroom to change her diapers.

After about three minutes, I returned to look at the pictures again. "I wonder how many people have disappeared out there, either falling overboard, or been conveniently done away with? It's such a remote area."

"Not to worry. We're fine out here." Patty looked over to Brian. "Our neighbors are all very nice and we look out for each other."

I started to load the dishwasher. "Do you think you'll ever move back to the lower forty-eight?"

"Nancy, we live in the last great frontier." Patty hugged Brian. "Every day is an adventure."

I nodded. "I have to agree with you on that point."

We all stood by the sliding glass door and reminisced about my escapades over the last twelve years. I was no stranger to danger or intrigue. Who was I to question the why or where these two decide to live? Living a life of love and being together is all that matters. Besides, all my kids are adventurous, and Patty was fitting nicely into the Caldwell family. As the tide slowly returned, I kept thinking that anything, human or otherwise, would easily be swept away and probably never be found again.

The following day, Sophia was scheduled for her three-month check-up in town; I stayed home to prepare dinner. The sun was shining, and the air was a brisk 35 degrees. I thought a good walk to the Point would energize me. Before I left, I Googled the Breadline Trail. Its first sentence read: "Not for whiners." Originally, the trail had been used by the men from Tee Harbor Cannery as a way to get to Amalga Harbor for nighttime entertainment. It followed the Favorite Channel high on the bluff, filled with mud, rocks, and precipitous climbs. I found an image of an old sign with warnings: Hazards include wild beasts, insects, falling trees, missteps, and bad luck.

Chuckling to myself, I ventured off to the Point.

The black ravens were talkative, their caws echoing high into the branches as I passed through the woods of gnarled pine trees. Dark green moss covered the forest floor like soft tufted patches of quilts.

When I reached the overlook bench, I sat to spot whales. On my left, I heard someone singing. I headed for the path down to the ocean and discovered a small girl squatting on one of the flat black outcrops. I smiled and said hello. Undeterred by my presence she kept playing.

I stopped directly opposite her on the path. She couldn't have been more than six or seven years old.

I walked closer. "What're you doing?"

"Just playing. My brother is down by the water." She had little dishes with moss and sticks displayed on them, as if preparing food. A dark, rusted metal box lay open to the side of the feast.

"Can I play?"

"Sure." She moved over to make room for me.

"I'm visiting up the road. I'm Grandma Nana."

She smiled. "Where the new baby lives?"

"Why, yes. That's right." I picked up a few pebbles for one of the plastic plates and offered them to her. "What's your name?"

"Elizabeth. But I like Lizzy." She reached for my contribution to her feast.

"What's in the box? Any treasures in there?" I leaned closer and noticed several beads inside. "Such beautiful blue stones." I pointed to some yellowed paper. "What's that?"

"An old letter, I think."

"Where did you find it?"

"It was in the box that I found inside there." She pointed to a deep opening in the rock.

"Wow. You're so lucky."

Lizzy lifted the folded stained paper and handed it to me. It was an envelope with no postage mark stamped on the outside. I squinted, trying to decipher the faded script. It read, C.C. MASS on the address. I turned toward better light. "I see the letter 'P'. I wonder if it was going to Provincetown?"

"Where's Provincetown?" Lizzy asked.

"It's on Cape Cod. There's no other town on the Cape that begins with the letter 'P'."

She handed me a moldy piece of leather. "This was in the box, too. The letter was inside."

It was an old wallet with the initials W. E. burned and stamped onto one of its corners.

"You can have them both, if you want them." She pointed to the wallet and letter in my hands.

I was thrilled with her gift to me. "Thank you so much. Are you sure you don't want them?"

"Nope." She nonchalantly returned to arranging her pretend feast across the flat black stone.

"I tell you what. If I find anything interesting about this old letter, I'll tell my son and his wife, and they can let you know what I found."

"Okay."

"I'll be leaving in a few days, but I'll be back in the fall. Maybe I'll bake you some cookies when I return. What's your favorite?"

Her eyes lit up. "Chocolate chip."

"Bye, now."

With the thought of chocolate chip cookies, I started to feel hungry as I climbed back up the rocky path to the lookout bench. I clutched the letter and wallet like a little kid on Christmas morning. As my curiosity piqued for more adventure, I headed for the Breadline Trail. Exposed roots and lumpy mounds of green moss, coupled with ankle-twisting rocks, slowed me down but only a little. After I hiked around 300 feet, I stopped to look around. I couldn't see the overlook bench. I'd been so careful not to twist an ankle or lose my footing along the edge of the cliff, that I hadn't noticed any markers to help me get back to the path and then out to the road. My heart quickened at the thought of being lost in a wild and unfamiliar woods. I reminded myself not to panic.

I tried to find my bearings in the dense foliage and tall cedars. I had started my walk with the water on my left, so it would have to be on my right for my return journey to the bench. Then I remembered that it was spring, and Brian had mentioned that bears were beginning to wake up from hibernation, "...take pepper spray whenever you go for a walk." I stuffed the letter and wallet into one pocket, felt for the pepper can in the other, turned around, then carefully walked ahead, listening to the water splashing below me on my right side.

Thankfully, I eventually spotted the bench, then the path heading out of the woods. Once my foot stepped onto the road the house came into sight. I breathed a sigh of relief when I saw Brian's car approach in the distance. As he drove down the driveway, I followed behind the car and was surprised to see my red suitcase by the back door of the house.

Once the car stopped, I reached to open the car door and pointed to the red beat-up bag. "They found my suitcase! And how was Sophia's checkup?"

"Everything's fine. She's doing well."

I grabbed the diaper bag from the car. No need to discuss the Breadline Trail; I was embarrassed enough that I almost got lost. I should have known better. As I wheeled my belongings into the house, eager to tell Brian and Patty about the mysterious wallet and letter, I couldn't help but wonder why the letter had never been mailed.

14

June 1899
JUNEAU

FROM A PORTHOLE of the *Elder*, Archie Parks watched Gus help carry Walter's bandaged body up from below on a stretcher, then down the gangplank and into a waiting wagon headed for St. Ann's Hospital. He grinned, thinking about the stolen money that now belonged to him.

As Gus was about to return to the ship, he noticed a sepia photo peeking out from under Walter's pillow. He tugged at it and saw a family. He slid the photo back into Walter's left shirt pocket, next to an ID tag tied through a buttonhole. Walter Ellis was a good man, Gus thought, and he hoped he would make it to wherever he was going.

Walter began to stir as the hospital wagon headed for Fifth and Harris Street. It was a short drive from the wharf. Unfortunately, the rutted roads did not favor an injured man. The hospital aide, waiting inside the wagon for the patient, could see the man was in a terrible state.

Walter stared at the watchful young woman with tears of pain in his eye.

Bessie Wright, barely eighteen years old, tucked her left leg under her skirt, habitually hiding her scarred foot. The burn accident that Bessie experienced as a child made her familiar with burns and the accompanying pain.

After checking Walter's ID tag, she noticed the family portrait. She missed her own family. Sad to leave them, several years ago, Bessie never questioned her father when he'd agreed to let his daughter leave the family house of Yaxhte Hít (Big Dipper House) in Aak'w Khwaán (Auke Bay) for St. Ann's Hospital. It was twenty miles away from her home and she was to learn the white man's ways in healing. The Order of the Sisters of St. Ann saw the girl, over the last three years, as a promising charge in their care and a quick learner, despite her limp.

Walter's eye closed at the gentle touch of Bessie's hand.

With sunrise the next day, Bessie began her daily rounds of toileting and cleaning in Ward 3, the indigent part of the hospital. Wards 1 and 2 were for Americans and the wealthy. She noticed the man she had accompanied from the harbor, the day before, lay still. As she moved from bed to bed, she watched him for any movement. It was going to be her task to change his bandages.

By 10:00 a.m. she was finished with her duties. The only patient left was Walter. Bessie readied the carron oil, a mixture of limewater liniment and linseed oil, to be applied to the burned skin with strips of cotton wool. Where the blisters had burst, solid nitrate of silver was used to reduce infection.

The doctor administered a drop of chloral hydrate to Walter. "Wait a few minutes before you begin the bandage change."

"I will." Bessie glanced at the family photograph she had placed on a small table next to Walter. The severity of Walter's injuries shocked Bessie when she gently removed his dressings. She hoped the man would survive the ordeal. She was also aware that the severe pain, during the daily bandage change, became the defining element in whether a burn victim lived or died.

Walter quietly endured the nightmarish ritual and by the fourth day, he was able to concentrate on the lovely face of Bessie, instead of his unbearable suffering. He focused on her unfamiliar appearance, which reflected the simple beauty of an Alaskan native; dark, mysterious oval eyes, bronze skin, and raven black hair. During the following weeks, her presence signaled torture but also the relief that he had survived another day.

PROVINCETOWN

July 1899 arrived with a fury to Provincetown. The air was steamy, and the streets were filled with artists and writers. Some came to learn from Charles Webster Hawthorne, at his newly opened Cape Cod School of Art, while others wanted to be inspired. Tourists arrived to experience a relaxing change from city life and watch the artists paint. It was a welcome blessing to the townsfolk after half the fishing fleet was destroyed due to the previous year's Portland Gale. Visitors could rent lodgings for the whole year or a season in the homes of people looking for extra income. Restaurants and cafés were busy, which also contributed to the local economy.

Sarah, hoping for word from Walter, left for the post office. "Grace, make sure Charles W. finishes his oatmeal. I'll return shortly." It had been over a month with no letter and Sarah was anxious.

She wormed her way through the crowds who were watching Hawthorne as he painted on the pier. Thoughts of when her Walter would return and her possible future of making do with scarce money drifted in and out of her head. How could she take advantage of the influx of people in her little town?

Grace had recently celebrated her fourteenth birthday and even though her blonde braided hair exhibited a child's hairstyle; she was growing into a beautiful young woman. She became her mother's strongest ally when days were lonely. It was difficult for Grace, always helping with chores during school days, but now that summer was here, it would be easier. She missed her father's presence as much as her mother did. Within the hour, dishes were cleaned, and a pile of Charles W.'s dirty linens was stacked in a corner of the kitchen. Grace grabbed the Borax and washboard as she went through the back door. "Charles W., go outside in the back and don't get into trouble. I have to start the laundry." He ran into the backyard with his wooden wagon and shovel. The sun was coming close to high noon and Grace wished the laundry were finished. Her little brother played quietly on the sand.

After each bucket of water was poured into the galvanized tubs, Grace wiped her brow. By the time the sheets were flapping in the wind, her mother appeared at the back door. Within seconds, the young girl knew from her mother's tearstained face that there was no letter from her father.

Sarah looked grim. "I'll be up in my room."

"Yes, Mother." Grace leaned back against the wooden wash table and covered her face to hide her tears.

Upstairs, Sarah threw herself across the bed and pounded the mattress with her fists. "Where are you, Walter?" she screamed. "Are you hurt somewhere in that godforsaken place?" As she rolled over, she cried, "Will I ever see you again?" Tears wet her face. She lay with arms outstretched and closed her puffy eyes. She thought of the last months without her husband. It wasn't a terribly long time, but she was desperate and missing a loved one, and it seemed like an eternity. After a few minutes, she had an idea.

First, she went into Grace's bedroom and then Charles W.'s. After glancing once more into her own bedroom, Sarah ran down the steps, wondering if the attached suite in the back of the house, now used as her sewing room plus storage, could accommodate a boarder. She smiled and decided it would work, with some reorganizing. The additional income would be helpful in maintaining her household budget. There was still money set aside from what Walter had left behind, but not enough. The rental would only add to the finances.

Sarah met Grace in the kitchen. "I need you to help me move all my sewing supplies from the back room upstairs to my bedroom. Then we'll clean out the old bureaus in the back area and move whatever boxes or trinkets are stored in there up to the attic."

Grace looked upset. "Mother, I just finished the laundry. Can't it wait until tomorrow? I'm supposed to meet Jenny Nickerson by Long Point in an hour." She stood next to the door, ready to stand her ground and refuse her mother's request of extra work.

Sarah rushed right past her daughter and grabbed a piece of paper and a pen from the desk in the living room. She stood by the table and scrawled in big letters:

ROOM TO RENT NEAR TOWN LANDING. PLEASE
SUPPLY REFERENCES. NO PETS. $50 PER/SEASON.
BREAKFAST/DINNER. INQUIRE AT POST OFFICE
REGARDING W. ELLIS HOUSE.

Sarah hurried to the door with the ad for the suite in her pocket and hope in her heart that things would work out. Before heading out to post her ad at the art school and around town, she quickly turned to Grace. "No questions now, we have a lot of work to do. You can visit your friend tomorrow. I'll explain later. We're going to be fine."

It only took a few days for furniture to be rearranged in the suite and anything extra carried up the stairs and into the attic room at the top of the house. Charles W. even helped lug his toys up next to his bed. Walls were scrubbed. The two windows that had views of the ocean were hung with new curtains. Each day after, Sarah checked for news about Walter and whether she might have a boarder.

A week passed and Sarah questioned her judgment. Had she priced her rental too high?

The following Monday morning, the two Ellis ladies were in the backyard engulfed in the weekly ritual of laundry. A bell rang: someone was at the front door. Sarah dropped a soapy pillowcase into the washtub. "I'll go. You stay to finish rinsing and the hanging." She crossed her fingers, hoping it was a new boarder as she walked through the house to greet whoever was knocking.

A handsome middle-aged man dressed in a white shirt, white pants, bow tie, and straw hat greeted Sarah as she opened the door. "Mrs. Ellis?"

"Yes."

"I'm inquiring about your room. If it's still available, I have papers for you to peruse." He pulled a brown envelope out of his pants pocket.

"I see. Mr.?"

"Fletcher. Andrew Fletcher. I'm from New York, here to study at the new Cape Cod School of Art."

"Mr. Fletcher, if you don't mind, I must look over your references. Are you staying in town or will you return in a few days?"

"I just arrived and was hoping to find a place right away."

Sarah felt that he had a kind face. "If you'd like, you can sit outside there on those steps near the path. I'll let you know my decision within the hour." She closed the door then ran to the back, where Grace was hanging the first sheet on the line.

She waved the envelope in the air to get her daughter's attention. "Come, look at our first boarder's credentials."

They sat outside at a small table in the shade of the house.

Grace, after reading out loud what was written, announced, "I think he sounds fine, Mother, and he's willing to pay for rent ahead."

Sarah reread his long list of references. "Interesting. It says here Mr. Fletcher is a friend of Mr. Hawthorne." She looked up to the heavens in deep thought. "I think you're right. Let's give him a try."

After hearing the room was available, Andrew Fletcher looked relieved.

"Would you care to see where you'll be staying?"

"Certainly."

Sarah closed the door behind her. "You'll have your own private entrance. Please follow me." She led him to the rear of the house.

Grace stopped rinsing and looked up at the new boarder.

Sarah introduced her. "This is my daughter, Grace. She or I will be here to answer any of your questions. Here is your key, your bed is ready, and I might add, you have a lovely view of the water."

Andrew looked out to the ocean and back to the house. "Beautiful, just what I was looking for."

"Breakfast and supper will be simple fare but hearty."

After a quick tour of the downstairs, Andrew walked back into town to retrieve his luggage.

Sarah hoped Mr. Fletcher would be settled by nightfall and her pocket filled with extra money.

When supper was finished, Mr. Fletcher retired to his room at an early hour. Sarah was exhausted on her first day as an innkeeper. Grace noticed the sluggishness of her mother and offered to clean the kitchen and set the dough to raise overnight for the morning biscuits. Sarah gratefully accepted. She stopped on the stairs going up to her bedroom. "Grace, thank you again for your offer to finish the day for me. Tomorrow, you can have the whole day to yourself."

The old clock on the wall signaled 10:00 p.m. Mr. Fletcher came into the kitchen. "May I have a cup of tea before I sleep?"

"Of course." Grace filled the kettle and placed it on the coal stove. The new boarder quietly watched the young girl. A few minutes of silence passed before he spoke. "Might I ask where your father is?"

Grace, hesitant to say anything her mother would not want known, answered, "He's away on business. We hope to hear from him any day now."

"Oh, I was just wondering." He spooned honey into his tea to sweeten it. "How old are you, Grace?"

"Old enough to know what hard work is." She mumbled to herself, thinking of more laundry that would need to be done.

"What's that you say?"

Grace wiped crumbs from the table and changed her thoughts of extra work to the idea of a new dress for the annual Fall Festival. "Nothing important. We're happy you're here." She removed her apron. "Do you work, Mr. Fletcher?"

He smiled. "Yes. Doesn't everyone?"

"I was wondering how you could leave your work and come here for the summer to learn about painting? Are you wealthy?" Grace was accustomed to fishermen and laborers in her little village.

"Let's say that I'm able to do what I want, when I want to do it." He rose to say goodnight. "Sleep well, Grace."

15

August 1899
JUNEAU

WALTER WOKE AFTER a restless night with the quiet stirring of Bessie completing her daily rounds in Ward 3. The shock of losing his eye had slowly lessened over the past two months as he became accustomed to focusing with only one. He had not left his bed without help since he'd arrived; his pain too unbearable to move. Today he felt different; he could lift his right leg a few inches from the bed using his own powers.

Bessie noticed his improvement and moved over to his bedside. "Are you feeling better today, Walter?"

"Yes, I believe so. In fact, I was wondering if I could sit up?"

"Let's give it a go." She brought a chair next to the left side of the bed for him to hold onto, just in case he wasn't strong enough.

"Are you ready?" Bessie took a deep breath to steady herself. "On the count of three, I'm going to swivel you around so your feet will touch the floor."

"I'm ready."

Carefully lifting the covers away from his body, she slid her arms under his left side and said, "One, two, three." And with the final count, she rotated him around.

Walter winced and struggled to steady himself on the edge of his bed. Bessie stood back and immediately noticed a look of satisfaction on his face. Then the two of them laughed in the joy of accomplishing such a difficult task.

After several seconds, Walter's body started to tilt to the right. Bessie caught his left shoulder and quickly swiveled him back to a lying position. She looked at him with understanding. "It's a start, Walter."

Every day after that, Walter began to gain more strength in his body. The bandage changes became less and less painful as his skin regenerated new layers. By the beginning of September, he was walking on his own, determined to train himself to function with the missing eye and weakened right arm.

St. Ann's did not have the staff that could assist Walter in learning how to deal with his disabilities. Bessie decided she could help him. Her older brother, now gone, had lost an eye in a terrible accident, a few years before, and she remembered some of his coping skills.

The young nurse noticed Walter usually made a mess if he poured himself a glass of water.

She took hold of his arm. "Now hold onto the glass with your injured hand. It will help you find the glass when you pour the liquid into it with the good hand."

Walter tried it. It worked. "Thank you, Bessie."

With only one eye, his visual perceptions regarding distance were troublesome. It was a slow process, learning one method of functionality at a time. He trained his head to always rotate toward his good side to steer him when walking and to aid him in avoiding missteps, especially when someone approached from his bad side.

As Walter's body recovered, thoughts of the future trickled into his head at first, but as time passed, they surged and preyed upon his fragile inner well-being. His head became filled with doubt. What was to become of him? He had little money to secure passage home to *the outside* and no way to earn the wages needed. He assumed his partners had moved on without him. It was just as well; he would only be a burden, unable to contribute his fair share of work in their search for gold.

Walter wanted to write to Sarah, but the words didn't come. How could he explain away his disfigured body? His family were better off without a cripple to care for. He especially did not want to be remembered as Walter Ellis, a worthless, no-good father who couldn't support his family.

On occasion, throughout sleepless nights, he considered taking his life, but he was a God-fearing man of faith. When these negative thoughts surfaced, he managed to keep them buried beneath his will to live and a strengthening acceptance of his Lord's plan. There must be a reason he survived.

16

Present Day - Late March
EASTHAM

RICK SANDERSON CHECKED his work schedule for the spring. He had to find someone to monitor the houses of two customers from April to June but could not afford to hire another employee for his home watch company, While You're Away. He was going to Florida and his one employee was having a hip replaced. He needed a friend who would watch the houses free.

Neil Hallett's phone rang.
 "Neil? It's Rick."
 "What's up?" Neil Hallett turned in his chair to face the window.
 "I need a favor."
 "Yeah…?"
 "I've got two houses in P-town that need to be checked. No big deal. Just a quick walk around and through, might take you less than 20 minutes."
 "I don't know."
 "Listen. You owe me from when I sent you those books and magazines in prison. Remember?" Rick rocked his pen back and forth over the calendar.
 "You know you could get in trouble for hiring me, an ex-con?"
 "I know you can keep your mouth shut. Are you going to help me out or not?"

"I guess so. What're the addresses?"

Rick slowly recited the street numbers to his friend then flipped a few pages of his daily calendar, looking for a particular day. "Oh, and one more thing, on Thursday, April 9, you need to meet some people at the second address at 10:00 a.m. so they can start cleaning the house out. Just give them the key. When they're done, tell them they can put it back in the fake rock on the front porch."

"Is that all?"

"You still have the company's hooded sweatshirt I gave you last year?"

"Yeah."

"Don't forget to wear it when you go. I wouldn't want anyone to think you're a crook." Rick was laughing when he hung up.

17

Monday, Late September 1899
JUNEAU, ALASKA

THE DARK DAYS of winter were on the horizon for Juneau, when daylight would show itself for only five to six hours. It was a hurried time for Alaskans if daytime duties were to be finished before the onset of lonely hours indoors, waiting for the sun to rise again.

Walter knew the winter solstice was coming as he sat by the sunny window at the end of a large dormitory-styled room in St. Ann's Hospital.

Sister Marie came quietly toward him with clipboard in hand. "Good afternoon, Walter." She pulled a white wooden chair close to him.

He nodded. "Sister Marie."

Dressed in the long black habit of St. Ann's Order, the circle of starched white material that edged her face hid her full cheeks. "I see from your chart that you've been getting stronger." She flipped a few pages, studied them and then laid them flat. "As you know, St. Ann's never turns away those who need help, as in your case."

Walter stared out the window, sensing what she was going to tell him. He knew it was time.

"I'm afraid that you'll have to leave St. Ann's. We cannot house you anymore here at the hospital."

He remained quiet.

"Walter?" Sister Marie placed her hand over his. "You're a very smart man and we know you understand our predicament."

"I do understand." He quickly glanced at the woman and then fell back to his blank stare and to thoughts of what he was going to do and where he was going to live.

Sister Marie stood to deliver her final words. Her somber colored skirts covered her sturdy black shoes. "I've spoken to Bessie. She has connections with the Indians. Her father is in need of help and he has offered a small cabin on his land for you to live in. If you're willing to work in trade for your accommodations, he would be agreeable."

Walter's face softened as he looked up at the sister. "I'll accept his offer. Thank you."

"You should thank Bessie." Sister Marie took a few steps away from him and then stopped. "We would like you to leave by the end of the week."

Walter waited in the morning for Bessie to begin her routine at the hospital. Over the previous months, they had become friends. At times, their laughter and conversation grew so relaxed that others, new to the ward, assumed they had known each other all their lives.

"Good morning, Bessie." Walter showed a broad smile and a wink.

Bessie bantered in return. "Good morning, Walter." She reached for the small table by his bed to refill his empty glass.

Walter kept his eye on her. "Sister Marie came by late yesterday."

Bessie faced him. "And…?"

He grinned from ear to ear. "I guess we'll be neighbors."

"You've accepted?"

"Indeed. I am ever so grateful to you and your family."

"I'm delighted. I know you'll do well, and my father will welcome your help. It's been hard for him since my brother died." She turned away to retrieve a clean water glass.

He stopped her, held her hand in his, then kissed it.

She blushed.

"I'll never be able to thank you enough for all your persistence and kindness in my recovery. You are my angel."

Bessie gently pulled her hand back, then hurried away. Once out of sight in the hallway, she leaned against the wall and closed her eyes. Her body trembled and her heart fluttered. After a few breaths to calm herself she straightened her apron, stood tall, pushed open the swinging doors of the kitchen and bumped right into Sister Marie. "I'm so sorry, Sister! Please excuse me." Embarrassed by her foolishness, the young girl ran to the washroom with Walter's kiss lingering in her thoughts.

Bessie hid in the bathroom for several minutes, trying to rein in her emotions, bracing herself to complete her nursing duties. Was she strong enough to hide the feelings building inside of her heart from those around her? She resolved that Walter and she could only ever be friends.

Determined to control herself, she hurried to the kitchen to fetch Walter's breakfast before returning to Ward 3.

She found him at the end of the ward, where sunlight filled a small alcove. Bessie placed the tray on a wooden table next to the window. She wore a smile but uttered no words.

"Everything all right, Bessie?"

"Of course. I have so much work today, I can't stay and talk." She quickly left to tend to her patients on the other side of the ward.

Unaware that his innocent gesture had triggered a spark in Bessie's heart, Walter sipped his coffee, enjoying the warmth and comfort of the sun.

18

Present Day - Nancy
JUNEAU

JUNEAU INTERNATIONAL Airport was bustling at 6 a.m. when Brian and I hugged goodbye at the main door.

"You want me to wait until you're checked in, just in case your bag is over the weight limit? I can ship stuff home to Cape Cod."

"I'll be fine. You get going." I knew the ins and outs of traveling; I wasn't worried. As I turned to give my son one more hug, I whispered, "We're so proud of you and Patty. You'll both be good parents to our little Sophia. Don't forget to hug each other every day."

"Thanks, Mom. Let me know what you discover about that mysterious letter and wallet." Brian waved goodbye one more time as he ducked into his car.

My old suitcase felt heavy, but I was confident that it would be under, or close to 50 lbs., even with the extra clothes I had to buy.

Once settled on the flight, and after reaching cruising speed, I took out the letter and wallet to continue examining my prize. With my small travel magnifying glass, I peered closer. I decided the 'P' definitely stood for Provincetown and that the letter was addressed to someone whose last name began with an 'E'. There was nothing else to be deciphered; most everything had faded away. I replaced the found items back into the safety of my backpack, leaned back, then closed my eyes for some much-needed rest.

NEW ENGLAND

On the ground in Boston, I claimed my bag, then waited at Terminal B for the Plymouth/Brockton bus to Cape Cod. Taking the time to check my email, I deleted spam and advertisements as I scrolled through the list. I opened an email from my dear friend, Ally, asking if I would I like to explore a late 1700 house in Provincetown. I quickly replied: *Absolutely! I'll call you.*

As we crossed the Sagamore bridge, I texted Paul: *See you at Barnstable in 20 minutes.*

I saw our white car waiting in the parking lot. It was nice to be home. I looked forward to a hug from my sweet husband, Paul, of thirty some years.

He delivered a big squeeze and grabbed my luggage. "So glad you're home."

"Me too."

I settled in for the thirty-minute ride to Brewster. Always thoughtful, Paul had a banana and a bottle of water waiting for me.

"How are the kids?"

"Well, since we last spoke, before you boarded in Juneau, the good news just rolled in one after the other. Casey had another profitable day at her gallery in Chatham. Jim got a part in a recurring commercial. Molly passed her final history exam and Danny got accepted into the National Honor Society."

"Wow. We're so blessed." I leaned back against the seat and closed my eyes. After a few minutes, I sat up. "I almost forgot. I found the neatest thing at the end of Brian's road. By the lookout bench."

"And…?"

"I met a little girl who gave me an item she'd found hidden in the rocks. It was an old wallet and a faded letter that had never been mailed. Addressed to someone on Cape Cod. I'll show it to you when we get home. Or maybe tomorrow. I'm really tired."

Before I closed my eyes, I could see Paul smiling as he drove home. I knew what he was thinking. There she goes again. And that's why I love him so much.

Next morning, the trail of fresh coffee slowly signaled me to wake up as the down quilt encouraged my tired body to sleep longer. Familiar surroundings nourished my soul. The comfort of my own pillow and bed hid the allure of far-away places.

But not the allure of coffee and husband. I rolled out of bed. "Good morning, Paul." I reached for a cup in the kitchen.

He came over to give me a hug. "Nice to be home, isn't it?"

"Definitely."

Paul took a refill of coffee, then returned to his iPad for more news from the *Cape Cod Times*.

Mac's tail was wagging as he followed me on my leisurely stroll, my coffee in hand, through our old 1880 house toward my front office. A pile of snail mail waited to be opened. I sipped my soothing drink while I sorted the envelopes addressed to me. Our senior beagle sighed as he settled in under the desk. I reached forward to make a pile of junk mail. Somehow, the bottom of my sleeve caught my coffee cup and the hot liquid spilled across the desk. "Oh, for heaven's sakes!"

Our old pup was right behind me as I ran to the kitchen. Paul was already gone into his studio. I grabbed a dishtowel and paper towels. By the time I returned to the accident, coffee was dripping onto the floor, courtesy of our crooked floorboards in the old house.

I knelt down to crawl under the desktop to wipe away the hot liquid. As I retreated backwards, something white caught my attention toward the rear of the old rolltop. It peeked out underneath the bottom of the closed drawer. I whispered to Mac, "What is that, boy? An envelope?" I wanted to grab it but couldn't reach it, so I returned to my office chair.

Mac sniffed at the coffee spill.

Paul came in and sat by the bay window. "I heard a commotion. You look a little stressed."

"Just clumsy. I was wiping up my coffee when I noticed something was sticking out the back of my desk. I can't get it out."

"Want me to get it for you?" Paul knew full well that I was curious about it.

"Thanks." I stood up to help and opened the drawer just a little. "I think this might be a two-person job, but not you, Mac. Move back."

Without hesitation, Paul put his coffee on the floor near the window, knelt down, then reached under the desktop. After a couple of pulls and jiggles, he stood up holding my prize for the day.

"Oh, thank you." I turned it over in my hand. "I remember this letter. I got it a few years ago but then forgot all about it when the kids invited us to visit them in Alaska. By the time we returned from the trip I couldn't find it. I'd assumed it was accidently thrown out when I went through the pile of old mail."

Paul returned to his window seat. "Danny likes to work at your desk when you're gone. He spreads his stuff out. It probably got pushed down into the back of the desk."

I looked at the return address and read aloud. "A. Baranova from Rhode Island." I opened the envelope and withdrew a picture of a familiar blue pattern on a china teacup and saucer.

19

WALTER DONNED the trousers and stained cotton shirt that he'd arrived in when he first came to St. Ann's. They were clean but ill-fitting and carried grim reminders of his injuries. Gone were his muscular arms that would haul in the bulky nets needed for his past life as a fisherman. His waistband puckered as he moved around in the old pants, even after he had punched new holes in his leather suspenders to lift the trousers higher. He adjusted the black eye patch over the scarred socket, where a healthy eye once guided him, then tucked a spare patch into his duffle bag. A list of supplies to buy was nestled alongside the family photo in his breast shirt pocket. He sat on the chair next to the bed and examined the contents of his monogrammed wallet. St. Ann's had given him money drawn from a charitable fund for indigents upon their discharge from the hospital. His guide, Sam James was waiting for him outside. The old Indian was to deliver him to Madsen's Rooming House, on the slope of Franklin Street, for one night and then guide him on to Juneau.

Bessie rushed to Ward 3 to say goodbye. Not wanting to appear anxious, she purposely slowed her pace as she approached. With cheeks flushed, she called out, "Walter."

He turned his head to the left to see her standing behind him. "Bessie, I'm glad you came." Dropping his bags, he took a step closer to her.

Bessie stood her ground.

Walter moved no further.

The two friends faced each other in an odd silence. With a sheepish look on his face and his head turned downward, Walter asked, "Could I have a goodbye hug?"

Bessie waited a few seconds and then took a deep breath. "Of course, Walter."

They embraced.

Walter closed his eye as unexpected flickers of passion rippled through his body. He breathed in her essence. It had been so long since he'd felt a woman's sensuality. He did not want to let her go.

Bessie pulled away. "I have to return to my duties."

"Certainly." Walter bent over to retrieve his duffel bags. "Will I see you again?"

"I rarely visit my family."

"I understand."

"Walter." Bessie's words tumbled from her lips. "Sam James is a good man. He will watch over you and guide you to where my father lives. The cabin is not far from our Raven Family House. I want you to know that before my brother passed, he carved his totem. It stands in front of the small house. His story was short-lived but beautiful." She stared at the man she wanted to open her heart to. She needed to tell him so, but she couldn't. Bessie's last words were, "Look for the black patch on the Raven's eye," and then she turned away so Walter would not see her tears.

He watched her disappear into the corridors of St. Ann's.

Nicknamed "Harriman," Sam James waited for Walter on the wooden sidewalk. His instructions were to take Walter to the rooming house for a night and then on to buy his supplies at Decker's. The following morning, the two men would set off along the coastline for the twenty-mile journey, with Harriman steering his cedar bark canoe toward the Wright's empty cabin and the beginning of Walter's isolation.

Walter dragged his bags through the front entrance of St. Ann's and onto the sidewalk.

"Walter Ellis?" Harriman asked.

"That's me. Sam James?"

"Call me Harriman." He grabbed the largest of the bags. "Adawóotl."

Both men spoke little as Walter struggled with the lighter bag and tried to figure out what Harriman had just said.

Harriman stood with hands on hips and a broad smile, waiting for Walter to catch up. "Looks like you could use some meat on those bones."

When Walter reached the top of the street, he was angry with himself for being out of breath. He reached for his kerchief to wipe his brow.

"Adawóotl!" Harriman ordered again and then continued his strong pace.

Walter followed as best as he could, vowing to get stronger.

At dawn, Harriman waited for Walter outside of Madsen's with a two-wheeled cart. He repeated his command. "Adawóotl!"

By now, Walter had figured out that Harriman was telling him to hurry up. With the guide's advice, a rifle and food supplies for the winter were purchased from Decker's. Walter also bought pencils, tablet and envelopes, in case he had the courage to write to Sarah. By the time they reached the water, the crisp weather had turned Walter's left cheek crimson. His scarred right cheek was only a light shade of pink.

Walter sat in the rear of the canoe with boxes and bags of various sizes, all filled with his supplies. Harriman was the lead man as they glided along the water, following the rocky coastline. The further they paddled away from the heart of Juneau, the denser the hillsides became. Giant lodgepole pines, with their branches sprouting only at the top, stood like tall soldiers guarding the water of the Favorite Channel. Sitka spruce and cedar filled in any openings with their eight-foot diameter trunks. By noon, the men hauled the canoe up onto the rock-strewn shore to rest.

Harriman had brought two small wooden boxes filled with Hooligan's.

"What are these?" Walter dipped his finger into the greasy food.

"Hooligan's. You'll like them."

Harriman pulled a tiny fish from the oil by its tail then swallowed it whole. He handed a sourdough biscuit to his passenger from a leather pouch.

Walter was hungry so he popped a fish into his mouth.

"What do you think? Good?" Harriman waited in anticipation.

Walter smiled and nodded. "Not bad. They taste like smoked herring from back home." He was curious about Sam James's nickname. "Why do they call you Harriman?"

"I guided the big man, Harriman, when he came with many men to study our territory."

"You mean the scientists and writers from the *Elder*?"

Harriman grinned. "He paid me well."

Within the hour, they resumed their journey. As the canoe skimmed across the sparkling water, Walter grew more curious about his new home. His full belly and a gentle sun quelled his anxiety and he began to whistle.

Harriman heard Walter's engaging sounds and smiled. As the cedar canoe slipped around a bend, near Auke Bay, the stark black raven's caw echoed up into the trees and across the water.

20

Present Day – Thursday, April 9 - Nancy
CAPE COD

BY THE END OF THE week, I was eager for my day to begin with Ally in Provincetown. I waited in the foyer dressed in jeans, sneakers, and an old navy-blue sweater. Ally was never late. Her car pulled in exactly at 9:00 a.m. Mac barked to let everybody know someone was outside. Paul looked through the window as he enjoyed his morning coffee in the kitchen.

I grabbed my purse. "Bye, honey. Talk later."

He gave me a big smile as he called out, "Have fun."

I fully intended to enjoy myself. Exploring an old house always satisfied my obsession for the unknown.

Sliding onto the front passenger seat, I greeted my best friend. "What a great day. A little cloudy but comfortable."

"Did you bring your flashlight?"

"Yes. Right here." I held up my trusty pen/flashlight combo. "I just love this gadget. The kids bought it for me when I started Geocaching last year."

Ally shook her head in wonderment. "You're too funny, Nancy. I don't know anyone else who enjoys digging around in the woods as much as you do."

"You can't say I'm not prepared. Give me a few clues and I'm off and running."

"Coffee at the Sparrow?"

"Great idea."

The Hot Chocolate Sparrow served delicious coffee and was a favorite with locals and tourists.

As the car rounded the rotary in Orleans, our fresh coffee in hand, we headed for Provincetown. The grey clouds grew darker as a fog rolled in from the water. I settled back in my seat. "You wouldn't believe what I found yesterday, stuck in the back of my desk."

"What?" The Eastham Windmill flew by the car's window.

"A few years ago, before Paul and I visited the kids in Alaska, I got a letter from someone in Rhode Island. I put it on my desk until we returned home, then forgot all about it. Paul said that Danny occasionally uses my desk when I'm travelling. The letter somehow got pushed into a drawer and then must have gotten stuck in the back."

"You only found it yesterday?"

"Yes. I spilled my coffee, and while I was wiping up the drips under the desktop, I saw the envelope. Paul helped me pull it out."

"What was inside?"

"A picture of a teacup and saucer with the same pattern as the old teapot I have on my bookshelf. Remember my Antigua escapades?"

Ally laughed. "You mean when you tore your rotator cuff in the woods because you fell into that old foundation looking for treasure? If I recall, you almost got yourself killed."

"I guess so, but I was careful." My sheepish smirk slowly turned into a mischievous grin.

"I know that look, Nancy, and believe me, today will be mild compared to your usual adventures. I hope you're not going to be bored and won't mind some dust and cobwebs?" Ally pulled to a stop at the Marconi Beach intersection on Route 6.

"Me? Bored? Never."

"So, what was the letter about?"

"Evidently, this woman named Abigail Baranova, was interested in finding more about her ancestry."

"Why would she write to you?"

"I guess the teacup and saucer has been in her family for years, but not much was known about it. She took it to an antique dealer who told her it was of the Kangzi Period. She googled Kangzi and up popped my face among the images, holding the old teapot." Trees and marshes whizzed by my window as I continued. "After a couple of clicks of my name, all my adventures appeared in her search. So, she wrote me a letter to see if I could help her."

We made a left onto Shore Road. As we passed the ocean blue of Provincetown Bay, fond memories of the times before Paul and I relocated our family to Cape Cod flickered in and out of my thoughts. Small cottages with flower names flew by our sightline and images of old quaint Cape Cod appeared every fifty feet. After a quick glance at Marilyn Monroe's face painted on two garage doors, we found ourselves driving through the East End of Provincetown.

"Oh, and one more thing... On my recent visit to Juneau, another mysterious letter landed in my hands."

Ally zigzagged the car down the narrow Commercial Street, past MacMillan Wharf, and into the West End.

"At the end of Brian's road is a lookout point. One morning, I met a little girl who was playing on the rocks. She had found an old metal box filled with beads and trinkets, plus an old wallet with a letter inside."

After a quick left where Tremont met Franklin Street, Ally continued driving toward the water and looked to her left. "There it is."

"Looks interesting." My phone was slid into a side pocket on my purse.

"Sorry, Nancy. I want to hear more about this letter, but first, I want to get in there."

"No problem."

She found an empty space on the street and turned the car off. "Let me check it out first," she said, climbing out of the car. "Wait here."

"Okay." I craned my neck to see what was happening and noticed Ally was talking to a man beside the house. He was wearing a sweatshirt with a While You're Away logo on the back. I couldn't see his face because it was covered with a big bushy beard and the hood on his sweatshirt was pulled down over his head.

After a minute, Ally waved me to come out.

I quickly exited the car and started across the grass. The man glanced over to me then did a double take, as if he knew me. He pulled his hood lower, pointed to the fake rock, handed over the key to Ally then took off toward his car. He kept his head down as he passed me.

I met Ally on the porch. "Strange guy. Do you know him? Seems to be in a hurry to leave."

"I don't recognize him," Ally said as she opened the grand but weathered front door of the 1780 house.

21

Fall 1899
PROVINCETOWN

OVER THE SUMMER, Andrew Fletcher had asked Grace to pose for him on the beach for some of his plein-air paintings. Other artists at the Hawthorne School did the same. It was extra income for the townsfolk.

Grace loved the fashionable dresses from her portrait sittings and the money came in handy on the day she bought supplies and clothes for the new school year. She made sure her wardrobe had no puffy sleeves: so old fashioned.

Before Andrew left, he told Sarah Ellis that he would return next summer and offered to pay double the rent for his room to ensure it would not be rented to someone else. Sarah accepted half in advance and promised not to procure any new summer boarders. Andrew also wondered if Sarah could join Grace as one of his models for the new 1900 season. The future looked rosy for the Ellis family.

Grace was disappointed when Andrew left for New York. He had been so nice to her and her mother; even Charles W. liked him. She would miss the extra groceries he contributed and his little gifts for everyone. The whole Ellis family was grateful for such kindnesses.

As October approached, and with no letters or news from her father, Grace noticed a slight decline in her mother's well-being. When

Andrew was staying with them, she smiled more, or at least on the surface she looked less melancholy.

One weekend, during the final days of fall, winter reared its ugly head on Cape Cod. A Nor'easter plowed its way across the tiny peninsula, bringing snow, wind, and cold temperatures. By Sunday, it was over, and Grace was anxious to get outside in the sunshine.

"Mother, can I walk over to Jenny's house?"

"Did you finish your studies?" Sarah wiped her hands on a dishtowel and took off her apron.

"Yes, Mother." Grace stood in anticipated approval from her mother.

"Run along. Be back before dinner."

Grace grabbed her cape, donned her galoshes and ran out the door.

The snow glistened under the sunshine like diamonds and ice crystals twinkled as Grace walked the path to her best friend's house. Before Jenny Nickerson was born, her family had lived on Long Point, a small village just off the coast of Provincetown. It was surrounded by water and cut off from everything and everyone. In 1860, the isolated community slowly disbanded. Coupled with the remoteness and the collapse of the salt industry, houses were moved and relocated to the mainland. These thirty plus houses were floated across the harbor to Provincetown. Jenny felt special because her house was a *floater*.

"Good morning, Mrs. Nickerson. Can Jenny go for a walk with me?" Grace stamped the snow from her boots.

"Jenny! Grace is here."

The two friends looked like sisters; same shape and height, but Jenny had brown hair and Grace was a blonde. Jenny even giggled with the same giddiness that Grace did. They left through the back door and headed to the beach near the lighthouse.

As long as the sun was shining, the brisk air didn't bother the two girls as they sat on the rocks by the shore.

"That lighthouse is so romantic." Grace sifted the sand through her gloved fingers.

"What do you mean?"

"I've only been over there twice, but I think the lighthouse has secrets. Remember when the light keeper's wife, Mrs. Smith, climbed twenty-five feet up the ladder, outside the bell tower, to oil the fog bell? She must have really loved her husband. He was sick at the time, and she risked her life in all that wind so that his job would be saved." Grace looked across the water at the keeper's house. "Wonder why they never had any children."

Jenny laughed. "Well, you can't say they never had the opportunity, you know, to do the deed. They were always alone, just the two of them."

A few clouds covered the sun and the girls started to shiver. "I guess we better get back." Jenny stood and brushed the sand from her backside.

"Yes, I'm cold," Grace agreed. "See you tomorrow at school."

The girls headed home along the beach.

As Grace entered the kitchen, she found her mother counting money at the kitchen table.

"Will we have enough for winter?" Grace hung her cape up and removed her outer boots.

"Never enough, but I think we'll be covered this year." Sarah rose to replace the old coffee can on the top shelf, next to the kitchen clock. "I pray every day that we get word from your father. I know something has happened to him. I wish I could go and find him." She leaned over the sink and bowed her head. "I just want to feel his arms around me again."

Grace held her mother's shoulders from behind. "We'll be fine, Mother. Love will prevail."

With such wise words coming from her almost grown daughter, Sarah smiled, comforted by a simple hug and the reminder of the love that she and Walter had between them.

22

October 1899
JUNEAU

HARRIMAN BEACHED the canoe on the shore. Walter climbed out and studied the tree line, trying to locate a way into the woods. "Where do we go from here?" His hand shielded his eyes from the bright sunshine.

Harriman was quiet as he righted the small cart on the sand so it could be filled with the supplies.

Walter assisted in filling the wooden carrier to the brim, then he lifted his duffle bags up onto his shoulders.

Harriman called out. "Adawóotl!"

It took the strength of both men to pull the cart over the rocky sand to a small opening up a grassy embankment, whereupon they stopped, took a deep breath then stepped off uphill, embarking on the last leg of Walter's journey.

The slope was too steep to go straight up; a zig-zag path was needed, which made their struggle to reach the flat forest floor a little easier, albeit longer.

Once they reached the top, a worn path leading into the woods was evident. Harriman pulled the cart ahead while Walter carried his own bags.

"How much further?" Walter was breathing hard.

Harriman said nothing again, concentrating his focus on keeping the cart straight and upright.

After ascending another brief incline, Walter could see the top of a small cabin. As they came closer, the totem Bessie had mentioned appeared in front of them. It was elegantly carved and topped with a raven, its wings spread and painted in red with a black eye patch on one of its eyes. With relief, Walter stopped and rested on a nearby rock and adjusted his own eye patch. The totem was his first welcoming sight.

He spotted a small pole structure, for drying salmon, next to the backside of the cabin. It needed repair, but nothing he couldn't fix. Harriman pulled the cart as close to the door as possible. Walter understood and rose to his feet to assist in unloading the supplies.

The door was unlocked. Inside, the 10x10 feet room was dark, with only a small window for light. The cabin had been built using a log frame with hand-split cedar planks as walls. The cracks between the boards were filled with moss for insulation, its earthy ribbons cascading down the planks, as if waving at the new tenant with each door opening.

A lone bed made of poles placed side by side was against one wall and formed a flat place on which Walter could lay a folded blanket for his mattress. In the middle of the room sat the sheet iron stove, which would be used for cooking and heat. There were a few shelves nailed to the wall, high to the ceiling, out of reach of animals. The floor was made of flat boards laid on the dirt, with wide gaps between, perfect for swallowing small items. Foodstuffs remained in the sealed boxes and stacked against the wall opposite the bed. Walter sat on the one chair next to a tiny wobbly table.

After Harriman brought in the last box, Walter stacked it in the corner. Harriman took his turn at the chair. Walter sat on the bed.

The old guide spoke one word. "Supper?"

Walter had a glazed look on his face.

"I'll stay tonight. Tomorrow I leave." Harriman went outside to gather wood for the stove.

Walter observed his guide prepare their food. No stranger to cooking, he could only watch due to sheer exhaustion. This newly arrived ex-treasure hunter was unaccustomed to living in the frigid wilderness and perplexed as to what he should do next.

It soon grew dark and the smell of sourdough biscuits fried in seal oil filled the tiny house. Walter's stomach grumbled. By the time they were able to eat, Walter had made his bed and was eager for food. As night set in, the frosty fall weather blanketed the forest around them with a deep cold. Inside the little cabin, the two men's eyes slowly closed, comforted by the soft warmth from the stove and full bellies. Walter motioned for Harriman to sleep on the plank bed; he would sleep on the floor. It was the least he could do for his new friend.

Unfamiliar night sounds gave Walter a restless night. He worried about the seclusion and bears, even questioning his ability to survive the coming harsh climate filled with snow, ice, wind, and possibly meager food. How would he earn enough money to go home to Cape Cod, if he had the courage to do so?

By sunrise, Harriman was ready to leave. He looked around the inside of the rustic cabin, put his hand on Walter's shoulder and said, "You will do okay. See you in spring."

Walter breathed in. As he let his breath out, his lips formed a small smile. Harriman was right. He would do just fine.

The two men retraced their steps down to the shoreline. With the tide out, Walter noticed a few spits of water shooting into the air. It was a good sign that meant food. As Harriman pushed his canoe out to the water, he turned toward the shore once more. A grin grew across his face when he saw Walter was digging for the juicy clams that lay buried in the sand.

Upon Walter's return to the cabin, he began to unpack his duffle bags. The sealskin coat and trousers were hung on one of two pegs to the rear, while his two flannel shirts and long underwear were hooked onto the second peg. He rolled his woolen socks and stuffed them into the coat pockets for safekeeping. The beaver hat with flaps topped his coat. He glanced around the cabin and found an adze; natives used it to carve large chunks of wood. It was like an axe, except that its blade was perpendicular to the handle. Maybe he'd be able to carve a canoe out of cedar for himself.

As he sorted through his belongings, his fingers touched paper. That's strange, he thought. It was Grace's letter. When he'd left Seattle, to sail on the *Elder*, Mrs. Barnes had given it to him. He quickly lit another candle and sat at the wooden table. His hand shook with excitement as he slowly opened the missive, dated May 25, 1899, sent almost five months ago.

My Dearest Father, he read out loud and smiled at his daughter's sweet greeting.

> *How are you? We are all fine. I am happy to hear you were*
> *able to find work on a steamer to Juneau. Please be careful*
> *and let us know what you are doing and where you are going.*
> *Mother misses you but does not cry as much as she did*
> *before. Charles W. caught a frog yesterday and wanted to*
> *keep him. Mother said no. Looking forward to summer. NO*
> *school!*

> *Please write back,*

> *Your loving daughter, almost grown up,*

> *Grace*

Walter reread his daughter's words over and over, each time looking for extra meaning in them. What did she mean, he wondered, Mother doesn't cry as much? Was she falling out of love with him? Did she meet someone else? Are they running out of money and does she think she needs to marry again? After a while, Walter calmed his thoughts and realized Grace's words were exactly what he'd read the first time - a simple letter from a young daughter telling her father about her day. His stomach began to rumble as he took out his tablet from a leather pouch that hung on a wooden peg by the door. Walter wrote down the time of low tide, so he could keep track of its flow. He had to be aware of when to gather shellfish. Before he left for the shore, he carefully put away the tablet, pushing it next to the beads and trinkets he'd brought for trading.

Earlier on the beach, before Harriman left, Walter had spotted an inlet a short distance from where he was digging for clams. Harriman had told Walter how to catch salmon at low tide by building small rock walls on the ocean floor. When the small barriers were submerged at high tide, salmon swam over them. Once they were trapped inside these channels at low tide, he could spear the silver salmon stuck between the rocks.

Walter planned his next day. In the morning, before the tide retreats, he'd have time to repair the poles for drying the salmon and then later, he would begin constructing the walls on the exposed ocean floor.

True to his plan, by the end of his second day, he had caught several salmon. His catch was quickly prepared and splayed across the drying poles behind the cabin. When finished, he strung a few empty cans across the fleshy salmon pieces, to warn him if a bear tried to steal his food.

After a week of discovering the land and its opportunities around his cabin and developing his survival methods using only one eye and a weakened arm, Walter wondered when Bessie's father would appear. He hoped they would get along and was eager to prove himself worthy of his hospitality.

23

March 1900
PROVINCETOWN

WITH THE ONSLAUGHT of consistent low temperatures in the New Year, the Ellis family budget was stretched as far as it could go to keep their house warm and comfortable. The wish for warmer weather was in Sarah's daily prayers, along with the hope of news about Walter. A year had passed since he'd left his family to search for gold in Alaska.

Grace came downstairs one damp, cold spring morning. "Mother, I was wondering if there was any spare money. I want to buy a little gift for Jenny's birthday. I saw a pretty fan at Nickerson's. I know Jenny would absolutely love it. It's so sophisticated."

"I'm afraid not." Sarah turned her back on Grace to stir the oatmeal.

"But, Mother…"

"No more talk about it." She plopped Grace's breakfast bowl on the kitchen table next to Charles W., who was playing with his sticky meal of oats.

In a huff, Grace sat down.

Everyone was silent as they finished their breakfast. Grace left for school and Charles W. ran up the stairs to his room. Sarah's eyes blurred as she grabbed the coffee can from the top shelf that held their monies. She sat with her morning coffee counting what was left of an expensive winter. How long could she hold out? Weary of living on a limited budget, her attitude was buoyed with thoughts of Andrew's arrival in a few months. His contributions would certainly help them, but how realistic was his return each summer? Maybe she could offer her services as a seamstress. Her sewing skills were good, and her threads and materials could be taken care of by asking customers to place deposits on their orders. "Charles W.! Get your coat on, we're going into town." While she waited for him to come downstairs, Sarah filled out several small squares of paper listing her seamstress advertisement and a new ad for an off-season boarder.

It might have been a springtime thaw, but the walking path to town and the planked sidewalks were still coated with ice. Sarah had grabbed a dime from the coffee can for a ride home. She rarely used the accommodations, the horse drawn carriages and more recently, the open-air busses that drove people and goods up and down Provincetown. Once near the middle of town, as Sarah and Charles W. walked past the First National Bank of Provincetown, she averted her eyes to the other side of the street for fear that Mr. Dyer, the Head Cashier, would start talking to her. She had been late on their payments only twice since Walter left, and was confident that with her new adventure in sewing repair and rental money all year round, she would get through the next winter.

As she exited Nickerson's, after posting her notices, she turned to see a woman writing down her information about sewing repairs. A look of satisfaction appeared across Sarah's face. With a skip in her step, she hailed her accommodation. On the way home, they passed the Masonic Hall. She cuddled Charles W. in the chilly air and remembered the warm summer night, in 1898, when Walter had reserved two tickets at 50 cents each for them to attend a performance by the Alabama Troubadours. The musical entertainment, brought to Provincetown by the Boston Opera House Co., was so romantic.

When they passed the wharf, remnants of destroyed ships still littered the beach, a grim reminder of the November Portland Gale of the same year that decimated the fishing fleet and their happy home. Her smile changed to a somber frown.

"I'm cold, Mother."

"We'll be home soon." Sarah covered her son with the long end of her scarf for the rest of their ride home.

Grace could hardly wait for the end of her first year at the high school and summer vacation to begin. Jenny and Grace were looking forward to the freedom of summertime, the arrival of Andrew, and the attention of the new boy at school, Donald Costa. He had arrived from Portugal with his family last October and Grace was certain he liked her and not Jenny.

On the last day of school, Grace found her mother reading a telegram at the kitchen table. She rushed over to see who had sent it. "Is it from Father?" She peered over her mother's shoulder. "Oh, please let it be from him." She crossed her fingers and closed her eyes in wishful prayer.

Sarah stood up and let Grace sit down to read it herself. "I'm afraid not, Grace." She stirred the stew cooking for dinner. "It's from Andrew, he'll be arriving next week."

"I think that's still good news. I mean, we now know Andrew's coming back for sure."

"Yes. I suppose you're right. And I have agreed to model for him, so we'll get paid double."

Grace ran upstairs to change her school dress. She was going to meet Jenny, Frank, and Donald for a walk on the beach within the hour.

Sarah called out as Grace flew through the back door. "Make sure you're home for dinner."

"I will, Mother."

Andrew arrived in June, on the day he said he would, and paid Sarah the extra $50 for his stay. He also had gifts for everyone, including the latest fashions for them to wear as his models. "I hope your winter wasn't too difficult. I worry about you and the children all alone." Andrew handed a narrow-wrapped bundle to each of the ladies.

"What is it?" Grace squealed in delight. She tore at the brown paper. "Oh, my gracious. It's beautiful." The lacey pink parasol was popped open in seconds.

Sarah laughed. "Grace, don't you know it's bad luck to open it inside?" She unwrapped her bundle and did the same thing. "It's so elegant, Andrew. It must have cost you a pretty penny."

The boarder, fast becoming a friend, casually said, "I'm calling it a business expense."

The two ladies twirled the parasols on their shoulders, laughing with each turn around the little kitchen. Charles W. sat on the floor with his toys, giggling and pointing at his mother and sister as they acted like two little girls. That evening, everyone kept laughing through dinner, filling the small kitchen with sounds of joy once again.

24

1900
PROVINCETOWN

ANDREW LAY IN BED near the end of August, listening to Sarah's quiet puttering in the kitchen. In New York, where Andrew was head of the family's business interests, he was an early riser. He enjoyed the peace of the morning before the harsh sights and sounds of everyday city life woke him. Today, he still enjoyed waking early. Sarah's daily tasks never bothered him, including the aroma of her special coffee, which eased him from his bed with a smile on his face. Her classic beauty was an added bonus. His affection for her and the children had grown stronger and he secretly wished he could be more than a friend.

This season, Andrew noticed a slight change in Sarah; she seemed preoccupied with her new business of sewing and mending. He missed the freedom of their conversation, laughter, and their time together. Andrew looked forward to his final scheduled sitting with Sarah as his model on the beach. He would have her all to himself.

Sarah stood waiting in the kitchen for Andrew, dressed in a frilly white dress, holding a pink parasol and a picnic basket filled with lunch for later. They did not have to walk far, only out the back door and 300 yards to the right, past several mid-size dunes.

The silvery grasses glistened in the morning sun as a lovely breeze swayed the green blades back and forth. As Sarah took her place on the sandy slope, Andrew stood and stared at the beautiful image before him.

She lowered the parasol. "Is everything all right Andrew?"

He stammered, "Yes, of course. Shall we begin?" He set his easel up, took hold of his brushes and began creating.

By noon, they sat on a blanket for lunch.

Sarah donned a straw hat to shade her head. "I know you like ham and cheese." She handed him a sandwich.

"You know me so well."

"Why shouldn't I? You live in my house for almost four months of the year."

He opened a bottle of malt. "Do you get lonely?"

His question stopped her, and she hesitated. "Of course, I do. But the uncertainty of the children's future far outweighs my personal wellbeing. I need to stay focused on surviving."

Andrew looked out to the water. "Do you miss the company of a man?"

"Mr. Fletcher, now you're asking too many private questions." She looked upset.

"I'm sorry." He finished his sandwich in silence and then held his stare at the blanket. Finally, he spoke. "Sarah, you must know I've grown attracted to you and the children. I care deeply about all of you."

She lowered her head. "I too, care about you, and have enjoyed your stays with us each summer."

"You know I will always return."

"I'm ever so grateful for that."

He took her hand. "I will keep returning. I pray that someday you will feel free enough to consider me more than a friend."

With these words, Sarah stood to leave. "I am a married woman."

"Please don't go." Andrew jumped to his feet and reached for her hand once more. "Forgive me for being so bold."

Sarah pulled away. "I'll see you back at the house. I feel a slight headache coming. Probably from too much sun." She gathered her things and retreated into the shade at the rear of the house and then went inside.

Guilt over Andrew's words pushed her up the stairs and a return to the tragic state of her life. She changed into everyday clothes and hung her frilly dress in the back of the closet.

Sarah sat on the bed and slid her hand across the quilt where Walter once slept. She did miss being with a man and longed for Walter's touch, his kisses, and his embraces. She was indeed lonely. Confused about her future, she wondered how long should she wait for Walter? Forever? Would she be able to provide for the family by herself? She was at a complete loss for answers. Her life seemed to change every day. One thing was certain in Sarah's heart; she'd always love Walter and be forever grateful for everything they had together.

When Andrew left the following week, the family said their goodbyes as usual.

25

November 1899 - June 1902
JUNEAU

WALTER'S FIRST MEETING with Bessie's father went well. He watched the elderly patriarch slowly follow the grassy path to return to the clan house, Big Dipper. Soon, Thomas of Tee Inlet, proved to be patient and fair with his new employee. He shared with Walter the ways of the Tlingit and appreciated his help and kindness on days when he wasn't feeling well.

1900 -1901

Over the next year, Walter's confidence grew after coming to such an unsettled and remote territory. His health and stamina improved. During the cold winter months, he had spent his isolation lifting heavy items from storage, using them as weights and building up his strength. He eventually adapted to the weakness in his right arm and to the difficulties of navigating with one eye. He took pride in his ability to steam and bend red cedar into bentwood boxes for food storage and carve his own bowls and spoons.

Walter's respect for the ancient ways and his hard work pleased Bessie's father. The two men were becoming friends.

The mountains that encircled Walter's cabin seemed to protect him with less snow and average temperatures. He had been lucky in catching salmon and preserving it for his food, along with hunting skills that brought meat from moose, seal, and bear. He was surviving on his own. But there was no shelter from his inner thoughts and regrets of not sending word home to his family on Cape Cod. He knew there would be no work in Provincetown for him because of his injuries; he would be the last person a sea captain would hire.

1902

In mid-January of 1902, Walter attempted to write to Sarah. Over two years had passed since his arrival at Tee Harbor.

My Dearest Sarah,

Endless guilt of not sending word to you has kept me from writing this letter. When I boarded the George W. Elder for Alaska on May 31, 1899, life dealt me a fate from which I fear I will never recover. There was an accident on board that left me crippled. Years have passed with horrific trials that took me further away from thoughts of returning to you and the children. As of this day, I remain in Alaska with no means to return home. I want to set you free and hope that you will seek someone else to love and support you. God knows you deserve this. Look no further for my arrival. Tell our children that their father loves them.

Walter Ellis

He folded the missive, sealed it into a small envelope addressed it to the Ellis Family of Provincetown, C.C. MASS, then placed it in his wallet. He would mail it when the first opportunity presented itself, if he had the courage to send it.

As the snow swirled around his cabin, nights of isolation pushed Walter further into deeper depression. Each time he thought of sending the letter, he succumbed to the embarrassment of his weakness and physical defects. Secluded and with no encouragement from anyone, his mind continually played tricks with his emotions. He blamed himself for his burn accident and remained convinced that his family was better off without him. His letter would only bring grief and sadness. Too much time had passed with no word. Walter couldn't bear to hurt them any more than he had already and hoped Sarah had remarried to keep the family safe.

By March, the King salmon were plentiful. The rush of catching the silver beauties was exhilarating after a winter's loneliness and inactivity.

On one crisp afternoon, Walter carefully finished gutting and filleting his catch for the day. He began to splay the slabs of fish across the drying poles when he heard a rustling behind him in the dense woods. Thinking bear, he slowly reached for his rifle that was leaning against the cabin to his left. He knew the bears were awakening from their hibernation and would be hungry. Cautiously taking hold of his weapon, he turned to face the intruder, pointed the barrel in the direction of the noises, then waited.

A soft voice called his name. "Walter?"

His eye looked away from the riflescope and strained to see into the brush.

"Walter? It's me. Bessie."

He lowered his weapon but stood his ground.

Bessie appeared at the edge of the woods then walked toward her friend. She carried two cloth sacks. "Wáa sá iyatee?"

There was no hello or goodbye in Tlingit, just a simple "How are you?" Walter repeated the greeting. "Wáa sá iyatee?

Bessie smiled as she came closer and offered the two filled sacks to him.

He ignored her gesture and resumed his task of attaching the salmon fillets to the poles.

She placed her gifts at his feet, knowing he would be upset with her because she had not visited him since he left St. Ann's in the fall of 1899.

Walter remained silent. With no response from him, Bessie twisted to leave.

He stared at the salmon and refused to focus on Bessie. Without looking at her, he finally asked in measured words, "Why didn't you come?"

She stopped, turned around and whispered, "I was afraid." She took a step closer. "Afraid I would fall deeper in love with you."

Walter stopped tying the sinew that attached the salmon to the pole but still couldn't look at her. She placed her hand on his arm in one final plea for his forgiveness. "I'm sorry, Walter. It was wrong of me not to come. I should have been strong enough to just be your friend."

He slowly faced her. She was beautiful. His loneliness and longing to hold her overpowered his will to ignore and his emotions exploded within. Even as his desires rose higher, his stubbornness still held him back from accepting her presence.

Bessie bent over to open one of the bundles. "Please let me show you the gifts I brought you."

In an instant, Walter succumbed to his heart by gently pulling her up and wrapping his arms around her. "I don't need those things. You are my gift." And with those words, they embraced.

Bessie never regretted her choices that day with Walter. She loved him and he loved her. Over the following weeks, she happily shared her time away from St. Ann's tending to her father and, of course, Walter.

On her return trip back to Juneau, by the end of April, she was eager to complete her studies at the hospital. The joy of helping people always gave her satisfaction. It was her passion. Every day, her pride swelled knowing that in a few months, she would be receiving her accreditation as a nurse and could return to visit Walter.

By mid-May, something felt different. Her energy level decreased and most food made her nauseous. She persevered in her studies but oftentimes found herself lagging in her hospital rounds. Her performance prior to this unhealthy demeanor had been excellent.

Bessie attributed the lateness of her period cycle to normal stress about her final exams, but as June approached, she knew she was pregnant. Thankfully, her uniform was loose-fitting and hid any swelling in her stomach. No one was aware of her condition. Two days before the ceremony to honor the nurses, she received a letter from Walter. Her hand trembled as she opened it. To her surprise and distress, it was not a love letter. It was about her father. He had taken ill and was asking for her to come home to Tee Harbor. He needed his daughter.

The following day, Bessie summoned Harriman to escort her home. The old guide waited for her outside of St. Ann's. Three suitcases were loaded into the waiting wooden cart.

"Adawóotl!" he called out.

Bessie followed the old guide down to the water in silence, worried about the coming canoe ride in the rough waters. She had vomited once this morning already. She spoke few words to Harriman, only smiling when he asked how she was. She stared straight ahead, trying to focus on the horizon, ignoring the beauty of the mountains and the power of the tall native trees.

They pulled ashore halfway into their journey to eat.

"Not hungry?" Harriman took a bite of smoked salmon.

Bessie took a sourdough roll from her pouch.

Harriman continued to eat his fish.

She finished the bread, then nibbled on salted crackers.

After Harriman relieved himself in the distant brush, he announced, "Adawóotl!"

Bessie followed him back into the canoe with a half-hearted smile. Staring ahead again, she wondered what Walter would do when he discovered she carried their child. Would she be able to keep this from her father? His eyesight had been declining over the last year. Would Walter marry her? She trailed her fingertips in the water and sprinkled the coolness against her face and neck. As they rounded the bend to Tee Harbor, her heart fluttered in anticipation of seeing Walter. Deep within, she knew he loved her; he had told her so when she came to him, months ago. Would he do the right thing? What about his family back home?

Suddenly, Harriman stopped paddling. Bessie felt the stillness of the canoe and asked, "What's wrong?"

Harriman stayed quiet and pointed out to sea.

A magnificent Orca whale breached into the air. Bessie gasped in its beauty. In seconds, it was gone.

The old guide turned to Bessie. "The Orca's presence is good luck for you." He smiled a toothless grin then continued pushing the canoe through the waves.

Bessie knew the legend of the Orca and its sign for goodness. Her body calmed and her heart beat in a steady rhythm. Walter will accept her, and they will become a family. This was their destiny.

26

WALTER HAD MIXED feelings in his heart upon hearing of Bessie's condition. Was a man able to love two women at the same time? With still no money to leave for the outside, his future seemed to be in Juneau. Almost three years had passed since he'd left his home. He could not expect Sarah to wait for him any longer. His choice became clearer every time Bessie came near him. She was radiant. He did love her, and she was carrying his child.

When Bessie told her father the news of the potential union between her and Walter, he welcomed his friend into their family as his future son-in-law, but not until Tlingit traditions were honored. Their marriage would not go forward until Walter became a member of another moiety, or a group of different descent, because one could not marry within the same moiety. Walter was eventually adopted as an Eagle so Bessie, a Raven, could marry him. She hoped that her father would live to see his first grandchild.

Darkness was constant across Tee Harbor. Walter moved into the Big House with his new bride and waited for the birth of his son. Walter stayed by Bessie's side. Now in her ninth month, she remained healthy and strong, dutifully tending to her father's every request, as he grew weaker by the day.

The clan house, Big Dipper, was large enough for all to live together, as was the custom. Bessie's Uncle William, her mother's brother, and his family shared one end of the long house, while Walter and Bessie, along with her father, who was the Chief, lived on the other side.

On the morning of December 10, as Walter awoke beneath warm blankets, he reached to touch his wife. She was gone. Her covers cool. He sat up. "Bessie?"

In the dimly lit house, he heard quiet sounds of women whispering. He rose to go nearer. Three women surrounded Bessie as she lay near the center sheet iron stove. Her labor had begun.

Walter felt helpless in the birth and decided to complete Bessie's duties in caring for her father; distraction was key to his composure. As the women's voices grew higher and faster, he concentrated on preparing food for the older man and keeping the stove hot.

By nightfall, the sounds of a new life echoed through the long house. It was music to Walter's ears. When Grace and Charles W. were born, he'd felt the same pride as he did now. He could see Bessie's face. How beautiful she was, even after her ordeal of giving birth.

He sat near his wife and she handed the male child to him. "His name shall be Matthew." They had discussed the choice of names prior to the birth and Walter was aware that the Tlingit society had a matrilineal clan system. One's identity was established through the mother's clan, so Bessie would name the child. It had been a long time since Walter had held a small infant. Little Matthew felt good in his arms and all was well.

In the months that followed, Bessie healed and the child flourished.

Walter's skillfulness in hunting began to spark attention in the village. People noticed his prowess. Bessie's father was again pleased. Bed-ridden and unable to care for himself, he was grateful for the help of his daughter and son-in-law. His new male grandchild was an added blessing.

On a cold day in late March 1903, Bessie summoned Walter to her father's bedside.

The old man lifted his head to speak. "Walter, I am filled with pride. You have shown to be of a strong character and standing in our family." His hands fumbled to pull a folded weaving from under him. "Let me help you?" Walter stood to assist. "No." With determination, Bessie's father pulled out a beautiful, beaded robe. He displayed it across his lap. The Chilkat weaving, with the crest of the Raven clan sewn into the middle, became a symbol of the father's trust in Walter. "I want you to take care of this for me." He handed it to Walter.

With utmost respect and knowledge that any sign of wealth, music, ideas, or stories can never be owned by a clan member, only protected and handed down to another Tlingit, Walter was honored. The exception to this tradition occurs when it's given to the most trustworthiest person for protection. He bowed his head in reverence for the old man and to thank him. "Gunalchéesh. I will guard it."

He took hold of Walter's hand. "You are now royalty." He closed his eyes.

As Walter walked past Uncle William carrying the cherished garment, he heard the uncle growl, "Beach Feeder."

He recognized the insult. No Tlingit would eat shellfish like he did when he first arrived at Juneau. It was contemptible and a sign of poverty. He knew the uncle's disrespect was also seeded in jealousy. Bessie's uncle was supposed to receive the father's Chilkat robe as the next in line of inheritance. From that day on, the two men grew more divided.

Within a few weeks, the traditional *Potlatch* which means, 'to give', marked the eventual death and passing of the clan chief, Thomas of Tee Inlet. Throughout the mourning preparations, Walter stayed near his wife and baby Matthew for support. He remained cautious and watchful whenever near the resentful uncle.

The deceased's clan, the Raven, remained in mourning, as was the custom. The opposite clan, the Eagle, provided the feasts, cremation, and all necessary planning. A celebration would commence over the following week, along with the destruction of the father's belongings. Walter found this custom confusing. Bessie assured him that the Eagle clan would restore the wealth of the Raven. These gifts to the Big Dipper house gave the Eagle clan prestige in the eyes of surrounding villages. It was a testimony to their wealth and generosity. In the final days of commemoration, speeches were given about the deceased and the last of the mourning would commence with a celebration of life.

27

February 1903
PROVINCETOWN

WITH NO WORD FROM Walter, Sarah changed her visits to the post office from daily to once a week. She hated the pitying looks from townsfolk about her missing husband as she did her errands. Her boarders in winter proved helpful for extra money and kept the gossipy tongues from wagging about any moral indiscretions that might be assumed between her and Andrew.

As spring neared, Sarah counted the money stored in the old coffee can every week. Sobering conclusions about her future spread deeper into her brain. It's been too long, she thought, he surely must be dead. Crying was not going to bring him home. She knew in her heart that Walter would probably not return. Sadness was not an option for her anymore. She also realized the health of Grace, Charles W., and yes, even herself was more important.

Sarah felt a chill as snow began to fall once more, and brewed a hot drink, then rubbed the top of her hand in a nervous habit. Her skin felt dry and aged. She looked in the hall mirror and stretched her cheeks back away from her cheekbones, examined the dark half circles under her eyes, and sadly found more wisps of grey hair. She recalled wise words from her mother, "Be careful, vanity can overcome common sense and wisdom." Sarah vowed to focus on finding ways to remain in the family house.

She finished her weekly dusting and moved the furniture further apart, hoping the room would not look so empty when Andrew arrived in a few months. She paid no mind to the front parlor's sparseness; another expensive winter had forced her to sell some of the family's treasured pieces to pay bills. Determined to survive, Sarah needed normalcy in her life, and if a few treasures went missing, then so be it.

Great-great-great-great-grandmother Ellis's beautiful settee had been the first to go. It was heartbreaking to Sarah but more difficult for Grace. The young girl was angry, and without her mother's knowledge, she began gathering decorative boxes, old letters, perfume bottles, household journals, even old scarves and shawls from her grandmother and hid them in the attic. When another small table was sold, Grace purposely locked the attic door and hid the key in her closet high on the inside of the door trim. Feigning ignorance of its whereabouts when asked about the key, her reply was always, "Sorry, Mother, I haven't seen it. Maybe Charles W. took it."

In April, a Nor'easter blew across Provincetown and delivered rain for several days and nights with hurricane force winds. Houses that had withstood storms in the past had their roofs torn away. The Ellis house did not go unscathed. A new roof was needed, and quickly, before another spring storm would arrive. Sarah was at a loss for solutions. There was not enough money saved for a repair and she certainly could not do it by herself.

One early morning, when the children were at school and Sarah was alone, the black iron circle on the front door sounded throughout the quiet house.

Hesitant to answer the door, she wondered if it might be a representative from the bank. She had heard officials were checking on the mortgaged houses for damage from the past storm. Rumors continued to circulate, stating the bank would force repairs to secure their investments. She had only been late once this past year and felt confident that the house would look worry free. Before she opened the door, pails were immediately picked up where the leaks had dripped and protective tarps were gathered from pieces of furniture. Sarah took a quick glance around; everything seemed to be in order. She greeted her visitor. "Good morning, Mr. Cook."

The banker stood in the foyer, waiting to be allowed further into the house.

"Won't you come in?"

Mr. Cook was not fond of his job of snooping on neighbors. To calm his guilt, he reasoned he was merely fulfilling his duties and protecting his own job. He stood in the foyer. "The First National Bank of Provincetown would like to make sure you fared well in the last storm."

"Certainly." Sarah crossed her fingers behind her back.

"May I?" Mr. Cook waved his hand toward the parlor.

"Of course. Please, sit down."

"Thank you."

Sarah watched the man's eyes skirt the walls, ceiling, and floors, looking for damage. She quickly added, "As you can see, we are fine."

After several minutes of awkward silence, the banker's gaze stopped at stains on the wallpaper in a dark corner. He rose to get a closer look. Upon touching the damp wall covering, he said, "So there was some damage?"

"Oh, very little. Nothing I can't take care of." Sarah began to wring her hands together.

"I'm afraid I'll have to order someone to access the damage."

"Might I be able to borrow against the house, if there are extensive repairs?"

"With your past delinquencies, that is out of the question. Have you considered selling?"

"No, I will never sell." Sarah stood by the mantle, next to Grandmother Ellis's painting.

"Mrs. Ellis, the bank is aware of your troubles, what with your husband unaccounted for, but we must protect our interests." He averted his stare from Sarah to the painting. "That's a lovely portrait. Maybe that treasure could be sold for a tidy sum from someone who collects fine art?" He stepped closer for a better look. "It is beautiful. You might be able to keep your house if you sold it."

"I don't know." She continued to wring her hands together.

Mr. Cook headed for the front door. "Let me ask around town to see if anyone is interested."

As the door closed behind the banker, Sarah peeked out from behind the small curtains in the parlor. She noticed him pull his collar higher in the cool spring air and glance back at the house from the path. He had a grave look on his face as he shook his head and headed for town.

She continued to watch him walk away. Her situation was severe, and with no husband and little money, she must make more hard decisions. By mid-morning, Sarah had wrapped the painting in a blanket, tied string around it for carrying, and summoned an accommodation.

As she watched the storefronts pass her view on her way to town, she wondered if some background about the painting and its family history might help secure a greater sum. Besides, it wasn't her ancestor. Stretching the truth and mentioning pirates, treasure, and the name Goody Hallett might help. Within the hour, Sarah stepped over the threshold of Provincetown Estates and Jewelry, on Commercial Street, hoping for a miracle.

That afternoon, Grace bounded into the kitchen with good news. "Mother, guess what?" Sarah was preparing dinner at the sink. "Mr. Silva said he would style my hair for graduation."

"We can't afford such a frivolous expense."

"Mr. Silva said he liked the way I cleaned the shop after school so much, he would keep me on and trade!"

"Are you sure?" Sarah wiped her hands and started up the stairs to her sewing room.

Grace grabbed a piece of bread and jam from the pantry. "It's all settled. I start working on trade tomorrow for a new hair style."

"I'm happy for you Grace, I'll be upstairs. Don't make a mess with that jam."

"Yes, Mother." Grace cleaned her hands and left for the parlor to look through the Provincetown Advocate for the latest fashion sales. Graduation would be so exciting.

Within minutes, Sarah heard Grace scream, "Where's Grandmother's painting?"

Sarah knew her daughter would be upset. She hurried downstairs.

"Where is it?" The young girl frantically searched the parlor, kitchen, and the guest room. "Please don't tell me you sold it?"

Sarah stood in silence, listening to her daughter scream and hunt for the cherished painting.

Not finding any trace of the beloved image of her grandmother, Grace collapsed on the small couch in tears. The ghostly outline of where the beloved painting once hung stared back at her.

28

Present Day - Thursday April 9 - Nancy
PROVINCETOWN

IT WASN'T OFTEN that I had the opportunity to explore an old house that had been closed up for almost twenty plus years. I was in a search-and-hunt mode.

"This is so exciting, Ally." I held my pen/flashlight combo in my hand, ready to uncover secrets. Musty smells never bothered me; it was a sure sign of things undisturbed. I looked for a light switch. "Is the electricity turned on in here?"

Ally ran her hand against the wall near the door jam in the dimly lit house. "I found it." A lone bulb in the center of the ceiling produced a yellow glow in the parlor. "That's better." She made her way around the fireplace wall and into the small kitchen.

I followed. "Typical house built with a center fireplace." I inspected the open hearth. "Nice masonry work. They built these homes to last." I peeked into one of the rooms off the kitchen. "This must be the borning room." But it looked different to me. "It's awful big for the small borning rooms of old. I wonder if this was just an extra room, maybe for an aged family member?" Next to the attached area was the bathroom, almost as big as its neighbor. "I'm going to check upstairs."

"Okay. Let me know if you find anything interesting." Ally proceeded to turn on a small lamp in the kitchen.

Upstairs, the three bedrooms were unexciting. Each had a bed and an empty dresser. A fourth door opened to eight steep steps leading up to another floor and a closed door. Now we're getting somewhere, I thought. After I climbed the narrow stairway and reached the sixth step, I found the door was locked. I steadied myself by holding onto a thin handrail so I could jiggle the doorknob. No luck. I returned to the parlor. "Well, not much upstairs. Just three rooms with beds and empty bureaus. There were some steps that led to an attic, I think, but the door was locked. Is there another key somewhere?"

"I don't have one; just the key in the fake rock."

"Too bad. I wonder what's up there?"

"I'll call the security company and ask about a second key. We've got a few weeks to explore before our deadline." Ally took off her jacket and began to browse through several filled bookcases. "Look for any first editions or things hidden within the pages."

"Will do," I said and joined her in the search.

By noon, I was getting hungry. "Want me to walk into town to find us a sandwich and coffee?"

"Great idea. Get me a cheese sandwich and see if the Portuguese bakery is open. If they are, pick up two of those fabulous fried malassadas."

"Okay." I could see Ally with her head buried in a box of books and called out as I closed the door. "Maybe we should skip the healthy sandwich and go right for the fried dough? Be right back."

The sun tried to show its warmth through dark clouds that covered the sky as I walked in search of something good to eat. As luck would have it, I found sandwiches, coffee, and the gift of sugary sweet fried dough.

On my return, I spotted a familiar image from my past visits. Up in the second-floor window of an old house at the intersection of Commercial, Tremont, and Franklin Streets, was a white bust depicting someone that I assumed was famous, although not sure who it was. I promised myself that one day, I'm going to knock on the door and ask who watches down on everyone as they walk by.

In about five minutes, I met Ally outside in the back yard, admiring the water view and on her phone. There was a picnic table with two chairs near a small porch attached to the house. I set out our lunch.

Ally joined me. "The dumpster won't arrive for a few days. Too bad, I was hoping for all this to go faster."

"I'm not complaining. This is fun. When you're done eating, don't forget to put in a call to the security company and ask about the attic key."

"Of course."

I grabbed the greasy bag of fried dough. "God, this is so tasty." I licked the sugar from my fingers.

Ally wiped hers on a paper napkin. "I wonder if someone who once lived in this house sat right here and ate these same sweet treats?"

I crumbled up the bag. "I'm sure it happened. I know the bakery up on Commercial Street opened over a century ago." I stared out into the ocean with my fingers splayed in a sticky mess. "I once read that before indoor plumbing was brought in for a bathroom, bathing took place on the back porch, near the kitchen, where they could get hot water from the stove." I glanced behind where we were sitting and pointed to the screened enclosure. "That porch looks small. I bet the bathroom was originally part of it. What's the history of this house?"

Ally wiped her hands again to look at her email. "From the legal documents and proof of title, the house was built in the 1780s by the Matthew Ellis family. Around 1801, smallpox invaded the town and wiped out some of the people, including those who lived in this house: Matthew, his wife Mary, and a widowed sister called Abigail. They all succumbed to the disease and were buried in a cemetery outside of town limits. Because the family had two sons who were away on a maiden voyage, the officials simply closed up the house. The sons stayed away from their home for almost ten years. Upon their return, in 1812, they claimed the house and all its contents."

Ally scrolled her phone. "More Ellises are listed after that. The two most recent owners were in 1885, with a Walter and Sarah Ellis, and in 1906 a Grace Costa bought the house for one dollar. That tells me it was probably a family transaction. Wonder what her maiden name was? Probably Ellis?"

Ally stood up, tried to brush her hands clean but they were still sticky. "In 1970, a trust was formed for the family and it was an investment rental up until the early 1990s, since then it's been empty. Let's get back to work. Maybe we could leave around three o'clock?"

"Sounds good to me."

With only a few hours left to explore, I stayed in the parlor with Ally sifting through the rest of the books. My eyes wandered to the painting above the mantle. "That's very nice." I stood to get a better look. "I always loved the Impressionistic plein-air paintings of the early 1900s. The art embodied everything of that era: women in flowing dresses billowed by soft sea breezes; faces hidden beneath large sun bonnets; quintessential images of time by the sea." I stepped closer. "I wonder if it's a print?"

With the aid of my little flashlight, I scanned the painting for a signature. "I see an A. Fletcher. Never heard of him." I turned around. "Do you think I could take it home? You know, our Casey is a bit of an art historian."

Ally blew her nose from all the dust. "That's a great idea. My job was to sift through everything, your job was to help me find anything of value and then get rid of the rest." She checked the time. "We'd better get going." She placed a thick black book in a box labeled, *books to be saved*. "I think that's a bible. When we come back next Wednesday, take a look and see what you can find."

"Okay." I removed the painting from the wall to place it in the car. As I turned around one more time, I noticed the faint outline of another smaller frame that must have been there before the Impressionist piece was hung.

29

1903
PROVINCETOWN

BY THE FIRST of June 1903, Andrew's telegram appeared as usual. He would be arriving in a few weeks, on June 20, for the summer. He wrote he was sorry that he would miss Grace's graduation but when he came, they'd have another celebration.

Grace remained sullen and aloof to her mother about the missing artwork. Sarah stayed patient. She had to be strong. Selling the painting was her only option for the roof repair; she was grateful that the Provincetown Estates proprietor had advanced her money against the painting's eventual sale.

Once school ended and graduation was over, Grace continued working for Mr. Silva at the hairdresser's shop on a fulltime basis. Disappointed there was no money for higher education in her future, she blamed her mother for whatever sadness she felt.

Even Charles W., now nine years old, noticed his sister's behavior. "Mother, what's wrong with Grace? I miss her. Why doesn't she laugh with me anymore?"

"Your sister is a grown woman. She has a job now."

Grace entered through the back door on her lunch hour, exhibiting her usual glowering demeanor.

Sarah stood by the stove. "How was your morning? Learn any new hair styles?"

"No." Grace grabbed a drink of water and made a sandwich. "I won't be home for dinner. I'm meeting Donald after work."

Sarah wanted to hug Grace, but she was gone in a flash.

Stay calm, she reminded herself. Grace will eventually grow up and realize life isn't always happy. She hoped Donald Costa's charm would soften her daughter's endless sullen mood.

At the close of day inside Silva's Hairdressing, Grace swept the last of the hair droppings into the waste bin.

Mr. Silva brushed past her. "Turn the lights off and make sure the door is locked, Grace."

"Of course, Mr. Silva." Grace wasn't mad at everyone in her life, only her mother. She called after him, "Give a kiss to your new little one for me."

"Will do. See you tomorrow."

As she flipped the closed sign over on the door, Donald appeared in her sight, his dark complexion, curly black hair, and rugged handsome appearance giving him a mysterious and romantic look. She was in love.

"Hello, Grace." He delivered a quick peck on her cheek and slipped into the shop. "Anything I can help you with?"

"No, thank you, Donald. I'll be ready to leave in a few minutes."

He waited outside for the love of his life. A little nervous today, he kept his hands in his pockets to steady himself.

As Grace locked the front door, she took Donald's hand. "Everything all right?" She noticed he was unusually quiet this evening. "Any news about your apprenticeship?"

"Not yet. But I'm hopeful. If Mr. Martin agrees to take me on as a mason after they finally build the memorial, I'll have a well-paying job for sure."

That was good news for Grace.

They headed hand-in-hand for Miss Dyer's dining room, down Commercial Street and past some of the new electric streetlamps.

After dinner, Donald suggested a stroll to Long Point. Later, they sat on the rocks in the moonlight. Donald cuddled Grace in his arms, waiting for the right moment. But first, he had to take care of one thing.

"Grace?"

"Yes, Donald."

"I think it's time for you to talk to your mother."

Confused, she asked, "About what?" She thought he was going to ask for her hand in marriage.

"About the two of us and our future together." He presented a small box with a ring inside.

Her heart skipped a beat. This was what she wanted to hear. She slipped the engagement token on her finger. It sparkled in the moonlight. "I love you, Donald."

They embraced.

Donald pulled away. "I know you're mad at your mother. I was hoping you could forgive her?" He held her hand in his. "I think she approves of me. It would make it so much easier for her to bless our marriage if you could put aside your anger over her selling that painting."

Grace gazed out to the water and twirled the ring around her finger.

He turned her face to his and gently kissed her lips. "What do you think? Will you forgive your mother?"

"I suppose I should." She leaned her head against his shoulder. "When I'm angry, I really don't like myself."

"That's why I love you so much, Grace. You wouldn't hurt a fly on the wall." He put his arm around her and they hugged even closer.

Grace melted into his arms. "Oh, Donald, I love you too."

As they held each other, the horizon slowly turned a darker blue. Grace whispered, "Thinking back to my mother, I probably would have made the same choice to save my family."

He faced her. "Then you'll talk to her?"

"Yes, it's time for me to forgive and let go...for us."

When they reached the front door of the Ellis house, Donald kissed Grace goodbye.

As Grace watched him walk away from the front parlor window, she felt relieved. The last thing she wanted to do was to lose contact with her mother. She had lost her father and that was enough.

She climbed the stairs and could see her mother's light was still on in her bedroom. She quietly rapped on the door. "May I come in?" The young woman honestly wanted to make amends with her mother and hoped she would find the right words. By nature, Grace was not mean-spirited.

Sarah gathered her robe to greet her daughter. "Come in. Did you have a nice time with Donald?"

Grace nodded.

"Was there something you wanted?" Sarah hoped for a pleasant talk between them. She missed the company of her daughter.

"Mother, I'm sorry for my angry behavior to you for selling the portrait." She stepped closer to the bed. "I can't blame you for what you did. I understand now. It's just that it was my favorite." She sat next to her mother and held her hand. "I want you to know that I don't think I would have been as strong as you have been over these last years...with father not being here."

Sarah hugged her daughter. After a few moments, she pulled away and asked, "Is Donald ever going to ask for your hand in marriage?"

Grace held her hand up and squealed. "I said yes!"

"I'm so happy for the both of you." They hugged again.

Grace stood and retreated for the door...all smiles. She caught sight of a telegram on the top of the bureau. "Is that from Andrew?" Grace had given up hope of ever hearing from her father.

Sarah's face lit up. "Yes, he's arriving at the end of the week."

In Grace's eyes, falling in love with Donald was the best thing to ever happen to her. Andrew returning to their home each season was second. "Andrew has been so good for you, Mother."

"I know. I look forward to his summer stays."

"Do you think you're falling in love with him?"

Sarah blushed. "Oh, Grace, don't be silly." But the idea of Andrew in her life was becoming more constant in her thoughts. He was kind and seemed to care so much for the children and her.

Grace yawned. "Mother, there's been a lot of excitement, I'm starting to feel very tired. Can we talk more tomorrow?"

"Absolutely." After another good night kiss, both Ellis women slept peacefully for the first time since the painting had left their house.

30

Summer 1903
PROVINCETOWN

ANDREW STEPPED OFF the train in Provincetown on June 20th. He immediately sensed happiness was ahead of him. Upon arriving at the Ellis house, family news buoyed his instincts even higher. He discovered Grace was in love with Donald and planning their marriage. Sarah was more joyful, secure that with a new roof, no big repairs were ahead of her.

Over the summer months, Andrew remained certain that Sarah would finally allow him to come closer to her heart.

Near the end of August, the advance of a storm cooled the night air. Sarah was alone in the parlor reading. Grace was spending the night at Jenny's, to plan the arrangements for her engagement party, and Charles W. was camping at the house of his best friend, Eddy Cook.

At 8:30 p.m., Andrew arrived home from his studio at Hawthorne's art school. Sarah heard him enter with his key and then wash his hands in the kitchen. She joined him. "Good evening, Andrew."

He glanced over at her. "Are you still up?" He dried his hands and leaned against the table. The soft glow of an oil lamp highlighted Sarah's classic beauty.

She lit the stove for a cup of tea. "Would you like some?"

He nodded.

She placed two teacups on the table.

He leaned closer to her then gently touched her fingertips. "Can we talk?"

Her heart skipped. "Of course, Andrew." As she reached for the steaming ironstone kettle, he moved between her and the stove.

"Sarah, you must know that I've been falling in love with you ever since I first met you, years ago." Andrew held her shoulders. He wanted her to look into his eyes, hoping she would see his devotion reflecting back at her. "I've waited for you. Please tell me you will consider me worthy of your love?"

Sarah wanted to tell him that she loved him too, but she stayed silent, held back by a deep guilt of being attracted to someone else besides Walter. But within seconds, her hidden emotions rose from within as Andrew's profession of love filled her with excitement, flushed her cheeks, and extinguished any feelings of unfaithfulness.

He pulled her closer in a loving embrace. Tears filled her eyes as he kissed her with such eagerness that she felt faint. Sarah returned the kiss with the same fervor.

Later that evening, among empty canvasses, exquisite paintings, and the glow of soft candles, Andrew and Sarah finally fulfilled their passions for each other.

Grace and Charles W. arrived home early the next morning. Sarah sat at the kitchen table sipping coffee.

"Did Andrew leave for the art school?" Grace grabbed a cup for herself.

Sarah laughed. "He was gone at the crack of dawn."

Grace noticed her mother's calm and glowing face.

Sarah tucked a curl behind her ear. "He told me he had a surprise for everyone when he returns, mid-morning."

"Oh, Mother, how exciting."

Charles grabbed the milk from the icebox. "Wonder what he's up to?" He began to drink out of the bottle.

For the first time in a long time, Sarah didn't correct him.

All three sat enjoying their morning drinks, each one lost in their own thoughts about what the surprise would be.

Andrew appeared on the back porch within the hour. "Glad you're all here. I have something to tell you."

Everyone sat straighter.

"With your mother's permission, I would like to bring the Ellis house into modern times." Andrew sat down ready to explain further. "How would you like to be able to take your weekly bath in private?"

Sarah and Grace looked wide-eyed. Charles W. shrugged his shoulders and took another drink.

"And...there'll be no more trips outside in the middle of the night or in the snow for...", he started to laugh, "...those private tasks."

The ladies of the house shrieked in eager unison, "A bathroom?"

Charles W. looked unimpressed as he put the milk back into the icebox. "I'll get started on the wood pile."

Questions erupted from the two Ellis women. "When?" "How?" "How much is this going to cost?" "Where will you put it?"

Andrew was calm as he explained, even though he too was thrilled. "I've arranged for Mr. Smith to begin enclosing half of the back porch for your new bathroom!" He looked at Sarah. "With your approval."

Sarah couldn't control her excitement. She hugged Andrew. Grace noticed a stronger connection other than friends between her mother and Andrew, but she kept quiet.

"Then it's final. I'm going to wire to New York for the supplies needed. My apartment in New York was recently improved with the new ultimate in flushing water closets, patented by Mr. Thomas Crapper, and I love it. You should be sitting pretty in a few months."

As laughter erupted in the kitchen, Andrew almost fell out of his chair at the idea of sitting pretty in the new bathroom.

A week passed and it was time for Andrew to say goodbye for the season. He and Sarah were alone again in the house. She was folding clothes in the kitchen. He put his suitcase by the front door and moved nearer to Sarah. "I can't stop loving you." He hugged her.

She closed her eyes and sank into his arms.

Andrew lifted her face to his. "I love you, Sarah."

She whispered, "I've been thinking about my future. I want you by my side."

He took her hand and led her into the parlor then moved a small fireside chair to face the mantle. "Sit here and close your eyes."

Sarah waited in anticipation.

"You can open them now."

In front of Sarah, one of Andrew's latest paintings hung above the mantle. It was one of her favorites, artfully rendered of her and Grace on the sandy bluffs. The art piece more than covered the emptiness where Grandmother Ellis's portrait once hung. It was beautiful.

"Do you like it?" He knelt before her. "Sarah, do you like it?"

She pulled him to her. "Oh, Andrew, of course, I do." She kissed him. "Thank you."

After they hugged goodbye for the last time, Sarah watched him walk toward the center of town. She felt no guilt, only a sense of relief. It was almost as if Walter had sent Andrew to them...to save his family.

31

Present Day – Thursday, April 9
CAPE COD

MEMORIES OF HIS encounter, years ago, with Nancy Caldwell agitated Neil Hallett more than usual as he drove home to Eastham from Provincetown. He gripped the steering wheel in a wild urge to settle the scores between them.

What was she doing at the house he was watching? What was so special about the old place? He tried to make connections between the house and Caldwell as he drove home to Eastham through the early afternoon light.

When he pulled onto the sandy road by his house, he remained tense and puzzled. After parking alongside the garage decorated with a quarter board that read *Goody Hallett*, he went inside, threw his keys on the desk, grabbed a beer, and checked his emails. He leaned back in his desk chair and stared at the painting above the dusty mantle. He rubbed his balding head and whispered, "Goody Hallett. Provincetown. 1780. Nancy Caldwell." He slowly repeated the words, immediately something clicked in his head. He grabbed his keys and drove to the offices of While You're Away, in Wellfleet.

The code numbers on the business's lock box were straightforward. Rick always told Neil that no one ever expects a simple code, and the lockbox hadn't changed for several years, so he dialed in 54321. It worked.

Once inside, Hallett headed for the metal file cabinet. The manila folders were alphabetical by town instead of client's names, and stored on paper, old-school style. He laughed, knowing Rick was never computer smart. The file on Provincetown held only two accounts. He read the information: Estate of Ellis Family; built in 1780; rental property since 1970; currently vacant. He searched through Rick's desk drawers for anything else that was related, but he found nothing.

Neil's phone signaled an incoming text. It was from the woman back at the house, Ally Grant. *There's a locked attic room, is there another key?*

Within seconds, he decided a locked room sounded intriguing, and if Nancy Caldwell was involved, he wanted to beat her for a first look. He texted back: *I'll look in the office. When will you return to P-town?*

His phone binged again: *Next week - Wednesday or Thursday.*

He checked the file once more and found no extra key: *No key. Don't break lock. I'll be in touch.*

When Neil left the office, he drove to one of his favorite places - Marconi Beach. He knew of a secret path that afforded panoramic views atop high cliffs and was a desolate spot for productive thoughts. He cut through the woods up to the top of the dunes, pulled out a cigar, lit up, then speculated about what might lie before him if he followed Caldwell's trail again. She was lucky in finding treasure. This time he'd be more careful.

By the time Neil got home, the sun was setting. He heated up a frozen pizza. While he waited, he collected his hammer, screwdriver, two small steel picks, and a revolver, then shoved them into his backpack for a return to the Provincetown house. He swiveled the desk chair to face his favorite painting. The auctioneer had told him it came from a home in Provincetown and might have been painted in the late 1700s. He repeated the name of the artist, "Abigail E." With a light-hearted step into the kitchen, he got a plate for his dinner, turned on the TV for Thursday Night Football, and hoped he was onto something that might lead him to good fortune.

That night, Neil Hallett dreamed of the red ruby ring from the painting and all the wealth that would go with its discovery. He woke with the decision of definitely exploring the house by himself. But first, he was to meet with Dominic DeSorta, one of his dealers, at The Watering Hole in Hyannis, about an old coin dating from 1715.

The Watering Hole was a bar Neil could enter, where no one would know him.

It was around noon when he ordered a beer and sat at the back booth near the bathrooms. His buddy was already there. "You brought it?" Neil flipped his hood off.

The unshaven middle-aged man reached in his pocket and laid a gold 1715 coin on the table. He slid it nearer his buyer.

Neil picked it up and pulled his magnifying glass out to examine it. "How much?"

"$90,000."

Neil remained calm on the outside but was overwhelmed on the inside at the price. He slid it back to the man. "Too rich for me. What else you got?"

The seller pocketed the coin and pulled out two uneven shaped gold coins. "How about these? They're Spanish. I can let you have them for $100 each."

"Deal." Neil passed two folded hundred-dollar bills to the man.

The man pushed the coins closer to Neil. He then ordered another round of beers.

After about twenty minutes, the grizzled-looking man seemed relaxed and began talking more to Neil. "You wouldn't believe what happened to me yesterday."

Neil was interested; he rather enjoyed a conversation with someone who liked the same things he did.

"I was looking at this oil painting over in Osterville and the guy wanted to sell it to me for $500." He finished his fifth beer.

This time Neil ordered a round.

"So I was examining it, you know, with my special glasses, but couldn't find any signature. I wasn't going to hand over $500, so I offered him $200. The man acted insulted."

"How old do you think the painting was? Was it an original or a print?'

"Oh, it was real. I could tell by the condition of the backside of the canvas. It looked familiar to me, like maybe it could have been a George Henry Durrie."

"Who?"

"Durrie! He's the guy famous for his paintings being made into prints for Currier and Ives. It looked real to me. A long-lost painting, maybe."

"So, what did you do?"

"The guy's phone rang, and he left for his back room. I moved out of his eyesight, upended the painting and shook it." The seller explained. "That's an old trick of mine. You'd be surprised what falls out."

Neil was now interested. "And…?"

"A small faded piece of paper fell out from between the canvas and the frame. I picked it up. With a quick glance, I saw the name Durrie printed on it. Before the guy came back in, I pocketed the little scrap."

Another round was drunk. "When he returned, I could tell he was in a hurry, so I offered him $300. He took it."

"Was it a Durrie?"

"Absolutely. I've got a buyer online as we speak. "$30,000!"

With that, Neil felt it was time to leave. He was out of his league. "Nice doing business with you. I gotta go."

Driving home on the mid-cape highway, Neil felt depressed about his monies but not totally devoid of hope. He decided to go home and give his favorite painting a good shake.

32

February 1904
PROVINCETOWN

LETTERS FROM ANDREW arrived weekly from New York throughout the winter. Today, the sun was shining and didn't feel like February, so Sarah decided to walk into town.

"Good morning, Sarah." The Provincetown postmaster handed yesterday's mail to her. "Another letter from that Mr. Fletcher."

"Yes. Thank you." Sarah headed toward the door, not wanting to talk any more than she needed to.

"Have you had any news from your dear husband?" The man knew everything about little Provincetown and enjoyed spreading the latest gossip.

"I'm afraid not." She stepped out onto the street, eager to open Andrew's letter in private. She pulled her scarf tighter as she passed the office of the town's new lawyer, Mr. Hopkins. She wanted to schedule an appointment with him. Legal matters were never her specialty. Walter had always handled that.

Thinking about Walter made her uneasy again. He'd been missing since May of 1899. Almost five full years had passed.

Sarah stopped at the wharf and leaned against a piling to feel the warmth of the sun and sea breeze. She didn't know what to think. She didn't even know if she was legally married or not; perhaps Mr. Hopkins would guide her. With the thought of returning for advice, she hurried to the safety of her home.

Andrew's letter rested unopened on the kitchen table throughout the morning. Every time she walked by it; recurring thoughts of Walter pushed her deeper into guilt. Andrew's news was always something to look forward to. Somehow today felt different.

It was a little after high noon; Sarah was tidying up the dishes from lunch. As she was about to open Andrew's letter, a knock interrupted. It was young Johnny Nickerson, the delivery boy from the post office.

"Hi, Mrs. Ellis, this came special delivery for you. The Postmaster thought you might want to read it right away." He pointed to the return address. "Look, it's from Alaska." He waited a few minutes for a tip, but Sarah closed the door.

Her hands trembled as she read aloud who it was addressed to, "Walter Ellis & Family." She felt the urge to open it as soon as possible but thought maybe Grace should be with her. She would need her daughter's support.

The rest of the day, she stayed upstairs in her sewing room and purposely avoided the sight of the two unopened letters on the kitchen table. Just as she couldn't wait any longer to open the envelopes, Grace came home.

Noticing her mother's agitation, she asked, "Is everything all right?"

Sarah pointed to the two letters. "I wanted to wait for you."

Grace studied both. "Which one should we open first?"

"The Alaska one." Sarah sat down and rubbed her hands together in her nervous habit.

"Shall I?" Grace was fearful but anxious to hear whatever the letter held.

"Yes, please."

She used a small knife to open it.

Sarah watched the blade slide across the top.

Dear Walter and family,

Walter, I hope this missive finds you safe at home with your family. When we parted in Seattle for the night, we never expected you not to appear the next morning of March 17, 1899. By the time the ship left the harbor, Max and I assumed you had decided to return to your family in Provincetown. But if that was not the case and you wanted to continue your journey to Alaska with us, I fear that something terrible has happened to you.

Sarah's heart pounded. She felt faint. Grace held her mother's hand and continued to read.

If you are alive, please contact me at my return address. I would like to repay you for your original investment based on the good faith that you were going to be a good partner in our enterprise of mining.

If your wife is reading this and crying, then I will respectfully request that she contact me. I have a sum of money that I would like to award to her. However, this story concludes, please contact me.

Sincerely,

Harry Cavanaugh

Grace held her head, thinking. "I remember Father explaining how he was robbed and had to stay in Seattle. But he wrote he was all right. These men, according to this, never knew why he didn't meet them."

She slid the letter closer to her mother. From the parlor desk, Grace retrieved her father's letters to check the dates. "The last contact we received from father was sent from the Barnes House, dated May 15, 1899, telling us he got work on the *Elder* for his passage to Juneau on May 31, 1899. He never did reply to my letter."

"What should we do?" Sarah began to pace the kitchen. "I don't think I can compose a letter to this Harry Cavanaugh."

"Shall I write it for you?"

"Thank you, Grace." Sarah returned to her chair. "We'll do it together."

Andrew's letter remained unopened.

33

Present Day - April Saturday and Sunday - Nancy
CAPE COD

AFTER A FEW DAYS of thinking about the locked attic door, I decided to call Ally to see if she wanted to return to Provincetown on Sunday. I couldn't stop wondering what was locked in the attic.

"Hi, Ally. Want to revisit Provincetown on Sunday instead of next Wednesday? It's going to be a nice day. I really want to get into that upstairs room. I've got some ideas of where the key might be. Over the years of discovering the curious habits of people from the past, I'm betting it's somewhere in the house."

"Let me look at my schedule."

I could hear some shuffling of papers in the background.

"Sure. Is 9 o'clock too early?"

"Absolutely not."

Sunday couldn't come soon enough. By the time we reached the old house, I was chomping at the investigative bit. While Ally retrieved the key in the fake rock, I lifted the old iron circle on the door and let it drop. Its ancient clang echoed back to days gone by. I did it again.

Ally laughed. "Take it easy, Nancy, we don't want to wake up any spirits."

"Maybe we should. We need some answers."

The house was just as we left it, with boxes of books in the middle of the parlor and an empty space above the mantle, exposing the ghostly images of where two paintings once hung.

I left Ally downstairs and climbed the stairs to the locked door. I jiggled the doorknob. For some reason, I had hoped it would open, thinking it was just stuck. It was still locked. I pulled on the knob, disregarding Ally's caution of 'no breaking the door'. It didn't budge.

I went downstairs into the kitchen to continue exploring and looking for any secret hiding places. The fireplace had no loose bricks; they were all solid. I walked around the edges of the room for any ill-fitting floorboards. I ran my fingers along the tops of the doorframes and looked behind everything hanging on the walls, even the old antique clock above the stove. I did the same in all the other downstairs rooms.

"Find anything?" Ally sealed up one box of books with duct tape and then shoved it closer to the entranceway.

"Not yet." I went back upstairs to look, using the same methods of searching. In the last bedroom, one more hiding place popped into my head. I remembered reading about a woman who hid her diary from a jealous husband up inside her closet. He eventually murdered her, then fifty years later, the new owners of the house found the book during a renovation.

I walked into the closet, turned around to face out and ran my fingertips along the top of the inside door trim. "Ouch" I yelped. A big sliver stuck out of my finger. I pulled at it then went downstairs to get something to stand on. I was determined to get a better look.

"Everything okay?" Ally finished marking another sealed box.

"Yes. I need something to stand on." I spotted a folding chair next to a cabinet and lugged it back up the stairs.

In the closet, the floors proved uneven. The chair rocked as I tried to stand on the seat. Finally, with feet flat, I slumped over to look closer. Out came my flashlight to reveal a secret. Before me was a narrow opening in the plaster, about six inches long, on top of the wooden board. I poked the other end of the flashlight in to clear away the dirt and dust then softly blew into the hole. With one more flash of the light, I saw it… the missing key.

34

May 1904
JUNEAU

WALTER AND BESSIE doted on two-year-old Matthew and never left him alone in the long house. Tlingit tradition demanded that when a child was born, the wife's nearest male relation would carry out all discipline of any children. Walter didn't trust Bessie's Uncle William and stayed cautious and protective of his son.

News had reached Bessie that her friend, Sister Marie of St. Ann's Hospital, had died. The young woman had a soft spot in her heart for her mentor and wanted to attend her memorial. The sister had always been strict but kind to Bessie when she first arrived for her training at the hospital.

"So, we will go as a family?" Bessie asked Walter one morning.

"Yes. I'll make arrangements. It might be fun to see the big city." Walter offered breakfast to his son and ruffled the boy's silken blonde hair.

By midweek, the family was ready for their trip to Juneau by canoe. The weather was sunny and warm. Bessie insisted that Matthew wear his cloth hat. The little boy fidgeted under the warm material. Bessie was adamant. She knew the face of a Tlingit and the hair of a white man would forever hinder the child, no matter what age he was or where he traveled. Matthew's hair color would always make him different from other Tlingits.

The journey to Juneau was beautiful and Matthew watched everything that swirled around him. After their lunch on a beach, the little boy fell asleep for the final hours.

It was dusk as they reached Madsen's rooming house, their home away from home for the next few days. Not very fancy, Walter remembered it from his stay, many years ago, after his release from the hospital. After settling in on the second floor, the family slept well for their first night.

The following morning, all were up early and dressed. Bessie grabbed her woolen jacket. "I can hardly wait for Matthew to meet my friend, Sister Elizabeth."

Walter fastened the little boy's hat. "I remember her. Very kind."

"Yes. Elizabeth said she would watch Matthew for us tomorrow, if we wanted to go for a nice meal somewhere."

Walter opened the door for his family to leave the small hotel room. "Great. And not to worry, I'll make sure Matthew is well behaved at the memorial."

As the family walked to St. Ann's, no one really paid attention to the couple. Mixed marriages were common in many of the remote areas of Alaska. But there were always a few that frowned upon those who chose to form such relationships.

The smells, sights, and sounds of St. Ann's fueled only good memories for Bessie. She enjoyed helping others and always took pride in her duties as a nurse. Walter remembered only pain, except for his interactions with Bessie. The chance meeting of his future wife at the hospital softened his agonizing memories and evoked his gratitude.

After several hours of listening, talking, and displaying their best social behavior, the family retired to their hotel room. Walter asked, "Are you hungry?"

"Not especially. The reception after the memorial filled me up." Bessie took out some sourdough rolls and cheese from her bag. "I took some food for us to nibble on later." She held Matthew on the edge of the bed as he ate the leftovers. "What about you?"

"If you don't mind, I might go for a walk."

"You go. We'll be fine. Take the key. I'm sure we'll be asleep early."

"I love you." Walter pocketed the key and left to explore the town of Juneau.

His first stop was the Imperial Billiards and Bar on Front Street. Walter wanted to remain invisible; he was not a talker. He remembered the bar was a place for beer or whiskey and not too many *percentage girls*. Those women would cozy up to the male customers, soliciting water-downed drinks for a kickback of 25% from the bartenders. He ordered a beer directly from the bartender for ten cents.

As he finished his drink, Walter heard a commotion behind him by the door. There was a scuffle which resulted in a native Alaskan or *Indian* being thrown out. The man had grown a beard and covered his head, trying to disguise his native identity for some alcohol. It didn't work. The law was strict in Alaska. No liquor could be served or sold to Indians. Court appearances would be held for those who did, and fines leveled. Walter assumed that the hooch or *Hoot-chinoo* that the Hutsnuwu Indians made was not strong enough for this man. When the struggle was over, he quietly left for the hotel.

By mid-morning, everyone was awake and ready to walk to St. Ann's to drop off Matthew. When the little boy was safe with Sister Elizabeth, the couple stood on the sidewalk in front of the hospital. Walter asked, "Where shall we go?"

Bessie thought a while then answered, "There's a restaurant next to the Lourve Theatre. Maybe after we eat, we could see if there's some entertainment we could attend."

"Sounds like a nice idea."

The two walked side by side until the restaurant came into view. Bessie stopped.

Walter looked to her. "What's wrong? Are you ill?"

She pointed to the sign above the eatery's door.

MEALS AT ALL HOURS – RESTAURANT

ALL WHITE HELP

Walter's face grew crimson. His anger for the prejudice that people held for the Alaskan natives burned him deep into his core. "I'll take care of this," he said and stepped toward the entrance.

Bessie held him back. "No Walter. It's not necessary. Let's find another restaurant."

"But Bessie, someone needs to tell them it's not right."

"Please. I want to leave." Bessie held her tears back so her frustration and anger wouldn't channel to Walter and encourage him to do something that may prove fatal. When she worked at St. Ann's, she had seen her share of injuries from men who fought over the smallest of disagreements.

As they continued through the town, more signs of racism appeared on other eateries and establishments. They left for Tee Harbor early the next morning. Walter vowed never to return to Juneau.

35

THE LOST SKELETON KEY clicked in the lock and the door opened. A rush of air stirred the sticky cobwebs that guarded the entrance to the attic room. I was never a fan of walking through wispy trails of white made from spiders, but I pushed through, even though the idea of long-legged crawlers getting caught in my hair or clothes made me uneasy.

After I brushed my clothes off, I stopped and stood, speechless. Before me were old tables, settees, bureaus, trunks, and file cabinets. Behind a tall clothes rack were stacks of canvasses, some painted and others half-finished. "Ally, you better get up here."

"Coming."

She stood by my side, taking in the same sight. "Boy, do we have a lot of work ahead of us."

"Yes, but what an adventure. If you don't mind, I'll stay up here; this is where the real treasures are stored. You want to finish the downstairs?"

"Okay. I'll let you go. This seems to be your territory."

Not sure where to begin, I looked around. The artwork piqued my interest first. I searched for signatures. I saw an Andrew Fletcher and an A. Fletcher. They matched the name on the painting I had taken home from above the fireplace. I took pictures of the different names for future reference.

Brown tinted documents were pulled from the top drawers of a file cabinet, mostly copies of payments from prior renters, seasonal to yearly leases, with dates from the early turn of century. The bottom drawer had aged papers listing sewing repairs and more contracts from summer boarders. Several names stood out: Sarah Ellis, Grace Costa – I knew they were owners of the house – and Andrew Fletcher, the artist. Well, at least a few mysteries were solved. I sat down on one of the covered chairs to sift through more of the papers. I didn't want to miss anything. Then I heard Ally come back up the stairs.

"So…did you find anything interesting?"

"Well, the artist from the painting I took home lived here as a boarder." I held up some of the contracts. "But why are his paintings stored up here? He was only a renter."

"Good question." She took a seat on the top step of the stairs. "It's only noon, we can stay longer if you want."

"I would like to stay." I focused on a large trunk against one wall.

"Okay." Ally stood up and began looking over the dated items on the clothes rack.

I walked toward the back of the attic room, then I flipped the brass circular lock down on the front of the black leather trunk. It made a clank as it bounced against the side. I was able, with some effort, to open the rounded top. I pulled my chair closer.

Folded in a cotton sheet were silk scarves, handkerchiefs, lace collars, and a beautiful black velvet shawl. Underneath, I could see a shoebox filled with perfume and ink bottles. To one side of the box lay ink penholders, tied together with string, and pen nibs in a brown envelope. Beneath the brittle storage container lay a black metal moneybox that held receipts for items dating back to 1885, including a mortgage document from the Provincetown National Bank with Walter and Sarah Ellis's names. I lifted another sheet with a red dress and several skirts wrapped inside. Near the bottom was an 11" x 14" leather bound drawing/sketch book.

My brain went into overdrive as I pored over all the artifacts that looked like they hadn't seen the light of day for over a century.

Ally woke me from my imaginings. "What's in the trunk?"

"You wouldn't believe it. Come take a look."

Ally picked up the black velvet shawl. "This is beautiful." Her cell phone rang. Ally headed for the stairway down. She stopped and called over her shoulder, "This time I'll get us lunch. Be back soon." The sketchbook intrigued me. I wiped off the front with a rag and uncovered, at the bottom right, the name Abigail Ellis embossed in gold. Another family connection to the house, but it wasn't Fletcher, as in the stored canvasses. I opened the portfolio across my lap.

36

1904
PROVINCETOWN

GRACE SEALED THEIR letter of response into the envelope addressed to Harry Cavanaugh and placed a stamp in the corner.

Sarah sat next to her daughter at the kitchen table, holding her head. "It's so final. Your father must truly be gone. He will never return to us."

"One day, Mother, I will find out what happened to him. One day. I promise." Grace left for the post office.

Sarah crumpled the practice papers that held all of their thoughts and broken sentences and threw them into a wastebasket. She was thankful Grace helped her craft their final words to the man from Alaska.

Andrew's weekly letter was still unopened. With mixed emotions and a little less guilt, she finally opened it. It was Andrew's third marriage proposal. Before she could finally commit to him, she needed to visit the new lawyer in town, Mr. Hopkins.

Amidst the preparations for Grace's wedding to Donald Costa, the last thing Sarah wanted to do was sit in a stuffy office and expose her struggles, both personally and financially, to a stranger. However, Andrew would be arriving in a month and she needed clarity in her life. Her appointment with the lawyer was on Wednesday at 10:00 am.

The weather was warm, so Sarah decided to walk into town. There was a light wind that felt good. As she passed the bank, she waved at the cashier with confidence, being up to date in her mortgage, thanks to Grandmother Ellis's painting sale and now Andrew, who was sending her extra money every other month.

Sarah reached the lawyer's office within minutes.

"Won't you come in, Mrs. Ellis?"

Sarah took her seat opposite Mr. Hopkins, who sat across from her behind a sturdy oak desk. On the walls were evidences of his education and to the side was a family portrait; his wife was stylishly dressed and holding their new baby.

"Lovely family." Sarah straightened her skirts.

"Thank you." Mr. Hopkins folded his hands. "Now, how can I help you?"

"As you know, my husband left in March of 1899 to find gold in Alaska."

"Yes. That is what I've heard."

"The last letter we received from him was dated May 15, 1899. What are my legal paths?"

"It depends on where your future lies."

"I'm not sure."

"Have you considered remarrying?"

"I have thought of it. Mind you, only for my children's sake."

"I understand. Whatever reasons you have are of no concern to me. Legally, I would advise you to wait a bit to marry again. Seven years total is a standard time to wait for persons 'in absentia' or to consider them legally dead."

The words 'legally dead' took Sarah's breath away.

Mr. Hopkins continued. "Five years have passed, so I think a few more years is a respectable choice."

She quickly regained her composure and replied, "Thank you, Mr. Hopkins. I will take into consideration all that you have told me today." She stood to leave. "May I call on you if I need your assistance again?"

"Of course, Mrs. Ellis."

"Good day, Mr. Hopkins."

Walking home, Sarah's head pounded. She had to accept the word *dead* when thinking of her husband. Walter was definitely gone. She passed the bank on her return and reminded herself to remember only the good things about Walter, and to remain thankful for the time they had together. By the time she reached the town wharf, the wind had grown stronger. It didn't seem to bother her; instead, she felt as if the burdens of uncertainty were slowly dropping away as rough edges were smoothed by the wind's force.

Sarah picked up her pace and a small smile grew across her face. When she arrived home, she was eager to write a letter to Andrew. A letter that would finally express her feelings for him. A letter that he would receive before he left New York and buoy him all the way to Provincetown. A letter that would invite him into her heart.

37

WALTER HEARD FROM several members of the Eagle Clan that someone was looking for the one- eyed white man who lived near Tee Harbor. Unsure why anyone would want or need him, other than his family, he kept himself on high alert.

Behind the long house, Bessie grabbed a fresh hide that Walter had just delivered to her. "Just because you have one eye, that doesn't mean they're looking for you." She began to prepare the tanning of the fur. "Are you worried?"

Walter started for the back door. "You need not be concerned. I can take care of myself. Rest assured, you and Matthew are safe."

Near the end of the day, the rumor proved itself true. A fist pounded on the door of the Big Dipper house as all sat for eating.

From outside, a loud voice boomed, "I'm looking for a one-eyed white man."

Walter rose from the table with his gun drawn, then stood behind the closed door and yelled, "Who wants to know?"

"Ivan Baranov. I bring no harm. I only seek the skill of one-eye."

Walter slowly opened the wooden door. Before him stood a six-foot mound of fur and muscle.

Ivan smiled as he saw the patch over Walter's eye. "You're a sight for sore eyes." He laughed and offered a hand in friendship.

"Walter Ellis. What do you want with me?"

"I would like to do business with you."

"What kind of business?" Walter stepped out and closed the door behind him.

The burly man asked, "May we sit and talk somewhere?"

Walter led the visitor to several tree stumps on the side of the house.

Ivan leaned his rifle against a tree then unbuttoned his seal jacket. "It's good to sit. I've been travelling for a week now." His belt held the largest Bowie knife Walter had ever seen.

"I'll ask again. Why are you looking for me?"

"You have quite a reputation for your hides. I'm interested in hiring you."

"For what?"

"I'm a trader from Sitka."

"Sea otters are finished here. I can't help you." Walter started to stand.

"I have connections with the Alaskan Commercial Company."

Walter listened. He knew about the ACC.

"I can still get good prices for your furs and hides."

Hesitant to get involved with big companies, preferring his life of seclusion with Bessie and his son, Walter shook his head and stood to leave but stopped as Matthew's blonde head appeared in the doorway.

Ivan saw the child and lowered his head. In one last attempt to get the one-eyed man to join him in trade, he said, "We have some things in common."

"What do you mean?'

"My father was part of the Russian American Company before Americans bought this beautiful land and delivered pain to all of us. Many left for St. Petersburg, my father and mother stayed. I am what you call Creole, or half-breed."

"Why are you telling me this?"

He looked up at the blonde-haired boy. "My mother was Tlingit. I understand."

Walter shooed Matthew away from the door opening and returned to his wooden seat to talk more. "I am worried about my son."

Ivan hung his head down in agreement. "As you should be."

"I want to protect him, but don't see how I will ever be able to shield him from the meanness of some people."

"If you join me, I can bring you money. Money enough for you to leave and take your family where no one will harm them. Maybe to the outside."

Walter was quiet, lost in his thoughts, but only for a short time. He was eager to talk to Baranov and, if possible, finalize a partnership. The Russian was invited to share his table.

Even though Bessie had grown to love Walter, other white men still made her nervous, and based on her last experience in Juneau, she remained cautious. But, as a devoted wife, she accepted Ivan Baranov into their home.

After a few days, everyone became more comfortable with the Russian visitor sharing the long house. His interesting stories entertained them through the evening hours.

The big man was kind and offered to bring in wood for the stove and anything else needed while Walter busied himself with other chores. The Russian had never seen such silkiness in beaver fur and praised Bessie's skill in preparing the hides. She appreciated his compliments.

One morning, when the spring temperatures had grown warm overnight, Ivan appeared, clean-shaven and smelled fresh. Bessie almost didn't recognize their guest. She was amazed to discover he was about the same age as Walter and even pleasant to look at.

A few days before Ivan was to leave, Walter had gone fishing and Matthew was misbehaving, as all children do. Ivan noticed Bessie's impatience and took the boy outside to play catch. Not having a family of his own, he enjoyed young Matthew. The little three-year-old threw a wild toss right through one of the two windows in the long house, on Uncle William's side. Within minutes, the uncle came storming outside holding his belt.

Ivan stood in front of Matthew. "Now hold on, old man, it was an accident."

"Out of the way." He kept trying to grab hold of Matthew. "It is my duty to discipline."

Walter appeared at the edge of the brush line carrying several fish. He saw the confrontation and yelled, "Déi áwé!"

Ivan knew, from when he was a boy, that Walter meant, 'STOP'.

"Déi áwé!" Walter rushed to the uncle and grabbed the leather belt from his grip.

Uncle William's face turned red with anger. "Tlingit demands that I discipline the boy."

"I don't care. You will not touch him."

Standing behind Walter, Ivan drew his Bowie knife in view of the enraged uncle.

Uncle William slowly stood down but kept his stare on Walter. "This will not be the last of my contempt for your disrespect." The older man turned and hurried into his side of the long house.

Ivan moved alongside Walter.

Walter scooped Matthew up into his arms and gave him a small white stone. "For you, my son, it's beautiful, isn't it?" He turned to Ivan. "Thank you. Your support is appreciated."

The young boy examined the marbled stone in his tiny hand, then ran to his mother to show her his prize.

The following day, Walter shook hands with Ivan and exchanged a trade in gold for the hides that Walter had on hand.

"I'll see you in the spring, my friend." Ivan held his knife in the air. "Here's to a successful winter of fur!"

Bessie called out from the open door. "Tsu yei ikhwasatéen."

Ivan repeated in English, "I'll see you again."

38

IT WAS LATE BY THE TIME Neil Hallett arrived home from his meeting at the bar. Anxious to take a closer look at his favorite painting, he didn't even take his jacket off. With a flip of the overhead light switch, the painting glared at him in the harsh brightness. Both hands reached out to remove it from the wall where it had hung, undisturbed, for over ten years.

He shook it side to side. Nothing. He moved it up and down then turned it upside down. This time, the edge of a small brown paper stuck out from between the frame and the canvas. He thought of taking the frame off, but the nails were rusted, and he didn't want to take a chance of ruining the canvas. Neil leaned the art piece on the floor against his desk, careful not to let anything poke at it from the backside. Using a flashlight and a pair of small tweezers, he pulled straight up. The top edge of the paper tore away from the bottom. "Shit." He tried to get the bottom half out, but it kept tearing and shredding.

He turned on the desk light for a closer look at whatever came out in one piece. The only words he could see were, *Provincetown Estates and…* The rest were gone.

"Provincetown Estates and… what?" he booted up the computer and Googled the words he was sure of. Nothing relating to the exact words of *Provincetown Estates* appeared, but several antique and jewelry shops did. He wrote their addresses down. He grabbed a little ziplock plastic bag, placed the brown paper scrap inside, taped it to the back of the frame for safekeeping then replaced the painting on the wall.

He'd get to that mystery soon enough.

After his trip over the bridge, to deliver a package for a guy in Boston on Monday, he would go back early on Tuesday to Provincetown, before the women returned. Right now, he planned to spend the weekend on eBay, searching, selling, and maybe buying.

39

Spring 1908
JUNEAU

THE SUN SHONE bright and made the temperatures warmer than normal for early spring. Walter checked his salmon catch in the inlet. He stopped when he heard a commotion to his right. Men were arguing. He stood upright to listen better then walked closer. Ivan was expected to return as he always had, over the last years, but none of the men resembled his Russian friend.

Two white men and two Tlingit men of the Eagle clan stood on the shoreline. All four spewed words and flailed their arms in the air. Walter hurried toward them and called out to the Tlingits, "Charlie!" "Tommy!"

He favored peaceful interactions between the Tlingit clans and whites, which was not always easy to maintain. The two Tlingits turned to Walter. At the same moment, and before Walter reached the men, the whites tried to escape back into their canoe.

Charlie, a Tlingit, attempted to grab a sack from the boat.

The bearded white man held on to the goods.

Charlie's friend, Tommy, reached for his knife.

Walter yelled again, "Déi áwé!"

In the following scuffle, Walter recognized the clean-shaven white man. "Amos? Amos Lindquist? Is that you?"

Amos cocked his head to take a closer look at who was trying to make nice. "Walter Ellis? What the heck happened to you?" He stared at Walter's eye patch, then held his partner's arm back to stop any more threatening moves toward the Tlingits.

Charlie and Tommy stepped away and turned to leave, thinking the argument with the white men wasn't worth it, and they trusted their adopted brother. They left disappointed in not reaping any extra goods for themselves. They did, however, look back over their shoulders every so often, making sure no trouble would follow them.

"Thanks, Walter. Wasn't sure if we'd leave with our lives." Amos gave his old friend a rough hug. "This here's my captain, from when I sailed out of Provincetown." His partner nodded hello.

Amos hoisted his pants up. "Got some time to catch up?"

Walter agreed. He had some questions also. First, he told Amos of the trials he encountered during his search for gold.

Amos whistled a somber regret. "Sorry, I steered you wrong."

"I can't blame you. Your letter was straight up, and I believed your words."

Amos took off his hat and smoothed his tussled hair. "You know, when I ran out of the gold, I went to the outside, back to Provincetown."

"When?"

"Spring '05. Of course, I found out, city life and fishing ain't for me. Why, I'm a free spirit here." He noticed his partner was anxious to leave and stood to join him.

Walter took hold of Amos' shoulder. "I need to ask. Did you come across my wife, Sarah? Is she all right?"

"Can't say I saw her; not sure I'd even recognize her. Lots of new people in town, what with all the artsy people staying there and all."

"Well, thank you kindly for what you've told me."

"Wait. Come to think of it. On my last night in town, I met an old friend. A roofer. We got to talking and he said he hadn't had much work since a big storm blew through town a few years back. It ripped all the roofs off. I asked him about your house, cuz' we sailed together. Just curious, you know. He said, 'Yep, the Ellis house, too.'"

"What about my family?"

"Don't know. He did mention that the woman of the house, reckon it was your wife?"

Walter nodded.

"Well, she was taking in boarders and rumors included that she was in cahoots with some rich artist from New York."

Walter frowned.

"Don't know much more. Sorry, mate."

With mixed feelings, Walter retrieved his salmon and started for home. He thought of the nine years since he had seen his Provincetown family. By the time he reached the long house, his anger softened into relief at knowing that Sarah was doing what she needed to do for herself and the children. At the sight of his Alaskan son, his heart leapt with joy. He, too, was getting a second chance at love and family.

Matthew came running up to his father with a hug. "Axh éesh." He held a small white marbled stone in his hand. "For you!"

Walter took it and put it in his pocket. "Gunalchéesh."

Thirty miles away, in Juneau, Ivan Baranov hoisted a drink at the Imperial Billiards & Bar on Front Street. In the morning, he'd journey to Tee Harbor and then on to see his friend *one-eye* Walter. A grizzled fellow drinker started a conversation and issued a friendly warning to Ivan.

"Be careful, my friend. I just saw my old partner over at St. Ann's. He's in bad shape but will survive. We were out over by Douglas Island. I went off by myself for part of the day. He stayed behind. From what he told us, a brown bear came up to our campsite. He scurried up a tree to wait until the bear was gone." He finished his drink and banged the glass on the counter. "That gall-danged beast went after him and knocked him out of the tree. Then he tore off part of his scalp, crushed his right wrist and bit through one lung. Left him for dead."

Ivan listened in agony, picturing himself in the grip of a furry beast. "Thank you, friend. I'll be watchful."

As he gathered his things to leave for the hotel, he thought he had a good partnership with Walter and a fine friend. It had been profitable for both and he looked forward to seeing the new furs that awaited him. Rest assured, he would be careful.

40

Present Day Sunday
PROVINCETOWN

THE SOUNDS OF THE ROARING ocean affected my psyche as I scanned the pages of the sketchbook in the dusty attic. With each turn of the page, my curiosity rose higher. The incoming tide below the third-floor window of the old house matched my tension as it came closer to its crest. Who was this Abigail Ellis? I knew she was part of the family, but what was her life like? Female artists were not held in high esteem at the turn of the century, or even in later years. Was she persecuted for her talent or just labeled as strange?

I saw sketches of birds, houses, hands, and several practice drawings. In the middle of the book, individual pictures repeated, each one growing better than the first attempts. Two hands folded on top of each other were strong and yet, I could tell they were a woman's. On the following page, a ring was drawn and after five attempts, watercolor was added. The large red ruby stone sat atop a golden band and then the beautiful ring appeared on the folded hands in another image. In the margin of this page the words *Pigeon's Blood* was written. I remembered hearing about this prized ruby when I was researching the jewels and necklaces from the treasure I had found on our Cape property.

Outlines of a woman's face came next. The woman's hair was long and wavy. A few wrinkles showed her age, but her natural beauty overpowered the ugliness of whatever trials she may have encountered.

An ink drawing of what looked like the final painting was on a page by itself. In the margins were linear measurements – 24x20 inches.

Ally called up the stairs, "Lunch!"

I closed the book, eager to tell Ally about what I'd found and also to fill my growling stomach.

The wind got stronger and rain started to fall as we sat at the small table in the kitchen. After each bite and a few chews, I explained what was in the book.

"So, do you think the painting from the sketchbook might still be in the house?"

"I don't know. It could be here." I drank soda to wash my food down. "I was successful in finding the key."

Ally smiled and began to clean the table. "Get back upstairs and keep looking."

As I rounded the banister railing and stepped on the second step, I glanced over to the mantle, where images of the two paintings once hung. I had an idea. First, I must find a measuring tape. I asked Ally if she had one.

"In my purse," she replied.

Having found the tape, I walked closer to the empty mantle. The smaller ghostly outline measured 28x24 inches. That would fit a 24x20-inch canvas with a two-inch frame. Perfect, I thought, just like the measurements in the sketch book.

Ally watched me from her stool in front of other boxes of books.

I turned to her with a big confident grin on my face. "Guess what? I'm sure the mystery painting once hung in this house. In fact, right here above the mantle, and then this larger one replaced it. I just know I'm right."

"You think so?"

"Well, the one I'm going to have Casey look at is too big and doesn't match the dimensions from the sketchbook."

Ally's cell rang.

Upstairs, I took the sketchbook and placed it by the steps to take home for more study. A few smaller trunks and boxes surrounded me along the edges of the walls. Will I ever be able to go through everything? I questioned my schedule. This was turning into a lot more than I expected. Now the rain outside was blowing sideways.

Ally appeared. "Do you mind waiting until the storm passes?"

I agreed and continued to look through a box to my right. By 4:00 p.m., I was getting bleary-eyed and ready to call it a day. Ally and I left by 4:30 p.m. with several boxes and trunks still unopened.

On the ride home, I called Casey to let her know that I wanted to stop by her gallery tomorrow to show her what I had uncovered.

Back in Brewster, I stood by the opened car door holding the sketchbook covered with a plastic bag. "Pick me up on Wednesday?"

"See you then." Ally pulled out of the driveway and headed west for her office.

As I reached the door, the rain started to pick up its speed. I found the door was locked. "Crap." Then I remembered that Paul now locks the front door if he's in the back studio. My last escapade had turned us all into slightly paranoid homeowners. I punched in the security code and the door opened. After hanging up my raincoat, I scurried out to the studio with the sketchbook in-hand.

"Look what I found." I carefully slid the book out of the wet plastic.

Paul gave a quiet whistle of appreciation for a fine example of the process an artist goes through in creating a work of art. Coming from someone with a career of over thirty years in painting, I knew he would enjoy looking through the book.

Paul carefully turned the pages. "This is interesting. Are you going to show it to Casey?"

"Of course. I'm going to the gallery tomorrow."

"I'll be anxious to hear what she has to say."

"Did Danny call?"

"He's over at Jimmy's working on their group project. He'll be home around 6:00."

"What're you hungry for?" I was hoping he'd say leftovers; cooking was not on my list for today.

"Had a late lunch, so I'm not starving. Whatever you've got in the fridge is fine with me."

"Great. I'll start heating up the stew from yesterday."

Sunday night football was approaching halftime. I snuggled next to Paul on the couch. Danny was home and upstairs, finishing his paper that was due on Monday.

Paul muted the half time show. "You know, I've been thinking about the letter and wallet you brought home from Juneau."

"What about them?"

"It might be possible they could be connected to the house you're liquidating."

"You think so?"

"Well, the initials of W. E. embossed on the wallet could very likely stand for the Walter Ellis that was listed as an owner, and the faded letter inside was headed for Provincetown. It is a possibility."

I sat there for a moment. "You might be right. If I've learned anything these past years, it's that life is filled with coincidences." I planted a big kiss on his lips. "It could happen." Then I thought, I need to think smarter. Concentrating on details and missing the big picture was always a setback in detecting.

When the game resumed, I retreated to my office, but not before telling Paul, "You know what? After all these years of you putting up with my adventures, some of my inquisitiveness has finally rubbed off on you."

41

MATTHEW'S SIXTH birthday arrived with a celebration. Bessie prepared his favorite dessert, a creamy blend of soapberries and seal oil. Traditionally, *Indian Ice Cream* was made without sweetener, but to mask the bitter taste, Bessie sweetened it for her young son. Uncle William scowled and took no part in her choice of an unconventional change in taste. To him, the red-tinted ice cream represented pure beauty and Tlingit tradition.

Walter presented Matthew with his first small knife and leather sheath.

At six years old, the young boy, carefully taught by his father, was already adept at carving, "Thank you, Father! It will be great when we take our first camping trip together this summer." He held the small blade in his hand. "I'll be able to cut wood stakes for my shelter all by myself."

"Yes, you will." Walter tousled his son's blonde hair then watched Matthew slide the knife into its casing and affix it to his belt.

Over the spring months, preparations continued for the big camping trip, delayed a few weeks due to Walter's severe chest cold. As he sipped liquid from boiled hemlock needles, he reassured his wife, "Not to worry. With your expert nursing, I'm feeling better already."

Bessie listened to his chest with her nurse's stethoscope, a gift from Sister Elizabeth. "Sounds clear." She refilled his cup. "Mind you, listen to my instructions. Your son is worried about you after Christopher John's father succumbed to pneumonia last month."

"I will."

As he recovered, Walter limited his outside work, looking for things to do inside instead. He built a small shelf for Bessie in the kitchen for her herbs and salves, and he repaired the handle on the stove. While sorting through his belongings, he perused his old journal from when he'd first arrived in Alaska. It had been stored in his knapsack, along with Grace's letter. Walter opened the pouch of trinkets and beads he'd brought for trade. They would make a nice gift to Matthew. The little boy could use some bargaining power for new possessions from his friends. At the bottom of his sack was a small metal box with a lid; perfect to put the beads in. He would give these gifts to his son on their trip together in early June.

June 1909

The plan was to walk to Tee Harbor, cross to the other side of the inlet by foot and camp near the point. Walter was familiar with the rocky, tidal terrain from past hunting days. If there was time, and Matthew was up to it, they might walk the Breadline Trail to Amalga Harbor.

Matthew's excitement prevented him from sleeping the night before their camping trip. But the next night, all the walking, building shelter, and preparing food made him fall asleep with little resistance. Even the obstacle of only a few hours of darkness, brought on by more than eighteen hours of daylight, couldn't interrupt a good night's sleep for the young boy in the wilderness. Walter had to wake him up to catch fish for breakfast. Finally, he gave his son the pouch of trinkets and the metal box. "For your trading."

The happy boy opened the pouch's contents into the box. Out poured delicate blue beads, pearls, and ivory buttons. "They're beautiful!"

"I thought you would like them."

"My friends will want some of these." He picked out the shiniest item then put the others back in the box. "Would you carry the box back home for me? It's so heavy."

Once more wanting to teach his son the meaning of work, Walter replied, "Son, you need to carry it home yourself, when we leave."

Matthew decided to leave the box at their campsite, hidden under some tree branches, as the two explored the rocky cliffs and then watched for whales.

After walking half of the Breadline Trail, the young boy began to slow down. When Walter suggested they turn around, Matthew nodded. Walter wanted to pick his son up and carry him, but he also needed to teach him to be strong, so they walked, rested, then walked again. At the end of the trail, the tree line stopped at a steep winding downhill path. Halfway down, Walter noticed an outcrop of black stone. They stopped to rest on the flat surface and ate chunks of dried berries brought from home. The berries tasted good as Walter and Matthew watched the water flow in and out against the large boulders below them. As Walter leaned back, his fingertips felt a large opening. Turning, he pushed his whole hand into the rock's crevice. "What a great place to hide things."

Matthew knelt down to observe what his father had found. "I'll be right back." He climbed down off the rock and ran back to their shelter, returning with the metal box in-hand. "Maybe I could keep this inside the hole?" He opened the box to reveal a few beads. The rest were in his pocket.

"If you'd like to." Disappointed, Walter thought perhaps Matthew didn't like the gift, but it belonged to the boy now; he could do what he wanted with it.

Matthew pushed the box deep inside the hole. "Father, this spot can hold our secret. No one but us will ever find this box. Next summer, we can come again and put more treasures in it. Agreed?"

Walter saw through the clever boy's idea. Matthew had made his father happy while also lightening his load home. Matthew's heart was where it should be. Maybe he didn't have to worry so much about his little half-breed after all.

42

GRACE ELLIS COSTA hung the last of the laundry outside their Provincetown house. As sheets billowed in the warm afternoon sun, sounds of the ocean waves against the shoreline and fresh sea air enticed her to take the rest of the afternoon to do what she wanted to do.

She quickly climbed the steps to her bedroom for some money. A sugary malasada from the Portuguese bakery in town would satisfy her sweet tooth, and a nice walk would be good exercise before she had to start dinner for Donald.

The old coffee can that once held the Ellis household money in the kitchen had been replaced with a stylish leather clutch that was now stored in the top drawer of her bureau. Three framed photos of family were prominently displayed atop her dresser. One was a family portrait taken right before her father left for Alaska, on the other end of the bureau was an image of her mother and Andrew at their wedding reception. Her own special day with Donald at her side was nestled between them. All three portraits represented happy times in Grace's young life.

How fortunate her family was after they received a generous check of $2,000.00 from Harry Cavanaugh. The family was able to open their first savings account at the local bank. Soon after the windfall, her mother had married dear Andrew and the happy couple moved to New York City with Charles W., leaving the house to Grace and Donald. Money was never an issue with her stepfather. He had eliminated all worry for his Sarah when he paid the balance owed on the mortgage. Grace recalled the day she and Donald moved into the family house: it was a day of changes, all good changes. The house had been legally bought from her mother for $1.00 and Grace had the paper to prove it. It was now her and Donald's home. Andrew had also set aside extra funds for Grace and her brother.

With a skip in her step, the sugary smells of the bakery on Commercial Street pulled Grace closer to her treat. The small bag that held the pastry on her return trip was marked with the delicious greasy taste of crispy fried dough. Not waiting to eat, she nibbled at it all the way home. In her back yard, on the small outside settee, Grace licked the last of the sugar from her fingertips with sweet delight.

The old clock in the kitchen moved closer to 5:00 p.m. Donald would be coming home soon from working on the new memorial monument on High Pole Hill. A quick ham sandwich with potato salad on the beach and a leisurely stroll into town for a chocolate egg shake would be a wonderful way to end this fine June day.

As Grace finished preparing the sandwiches, Donald appeared at the door.

He took his muddy shoes off on the back porch and then hung his cap behind the door.

Grace gave him a big hug and kiss. "How was your day?"

"Back-breaking but satisfying. What about yours?"

"Laundry and walking. How about a picnic?"

Always ready to please his wife, he agreed, "Give me a few minutes to wash up."

After the couple enjoyed their evening meal on a blanket near the shoreline, they talked more of their future.

"Come August, we'll be done with the tower," Donald reported. "The town is planning a big dedication on August 21st. Then there's more work inside, with the ramps and steps to build."

"So, you'll be at the monument longer?"

"Yes, then after it's finished, I'll begin working with the mason, Mr. Martin, as the number two man in his masonry company."

"That's wonderful, Donald. I'm proud of you and love you so much."

On Saturday, August 21, 1909, the final stone was put in place on the memorial's monument tower. A small group of townspeople, including Grace and Donald, had gathered to watch the installation of the one-ton stone. Mr. Clarke, the government inspector, Mr. Person, the derrick man who had directed all the raising of the stones, and two young ladies, Miss Isabel George, age eleven, and Miss Annie Cromar, age eleven, all assisted and oversaw the pulleys.

Immediately on Monday, following the setting of the stone, the inside work on ramps and steps began and continued through the winter of the following year. The heavy framework platforms needed to install the stones remained inside the tower and were reused as the ramps and steps were built from the top down. Final dedication was slated for a year later, on August 5, 1910.

By mid-July, before the celebration, Donald's work at the monument came to an end. Mr. Martin had a full schedule for the fall and was pleased that his new partner would soon join him for an early start. A two-story colonial style house was in need of a new chimney and the repair had been postponed until Donald was available.

"See you later, my love." Donald grabbed his tool belt and exited the back door.

"Love you." Grace carried the soiled clothes for Monday wash down the stairs.

On his walk to the job site, Donald thought about how wonderful his life was with Grace. He wished they could start a family. The doctor had said they were both healthy, and to go home and keep trying. His smile grew with thoughts of the coming evening with his beautiful Grace.

Mr. Martin had caught a summer cold but still felt well enough to be working on the roof, with Donald on the ground. Martin's new partner looked up at his boss, "I don't mind going up there. With your sneezing and dripping nose, you might be better off down below."

"Now, Donald, don't you worry. I've been climbing around roofs since long before you were born. My footing is sure."

Donald stood a short distance away as old bricks were carefully dropped below the edge of the roofline, using a pulley and bucket.

The sun rose higher; the time was twelve noon. Mr. Martin stretched tall as his feet straddled the edges of the gabled roofline near the pulley and bucket. "Let's break for lunch."

Down below, Donald decided it was safe enough to move the old bricks from the ground into a waiting wheelbarrow. As he bent over to pick up the red stones, above his head he heard Martin let out a powerful sneeze. The older man's body reacted with a violent bounce and dislodged his footing. Within seconds, his shoe had accidently knocked a large brick over the edge. The solid red missile crashed down, landing on top of Donald's head. He fell to the ground.

"Donald!" Martin yelled as he descended the roof as fast as he could. "Donald!"

Blood dripped down his partner's forehead and into his eyes as he lay quiet on the ground.

Martin shook him. "Donald, can you hear me?"

No response from the bloodied man.

"Oh, dear God, what have I done?" Martin's heart raced with guilt. He looked around for someone to help. "I need help!"

Donald slowly opened his eyes.

Martin stared at his friend. "Oh, thank God, you're alive." He helped him to a standing position, then walked him over to the rock wall that lined the property. "Sit here. Are you feeling all right?" Martin's lips moved in silent prayer as he handed Donald his handkerchief.

Donald wiped his bloodstained face. "I think I'm all right. Feeling a bit off, is all."

"Let's call it a day." Martin started to collect his tools. "Get in the wagon and I'll take you home."

Grace was having lunch when she heard Mr. Martin pull up out front. He never came to the house. Her stomach turned at the possibility that something was wrong. As she ran outside, she caught sight of Donald's bloody face as he leaned against the wooden slats. She ran faster and screamed, "Donald!"

Grace and Martin helped him limp into the house. "I'll get him upstairs." Grace ordered. "You fetch the doctor."

Once her husband was settled in his bed, and after the doctor left, Grace never left his side. Her instructions were to watch him through the night, to wake him every hour to check his eyes, and to ask how he was feeling.

It was one-in-the-morning when Donald finally spoke to his wife. "My head hurts."

Grace replaced the soiled cloth on his forehead with a clean one, then held his hand. "The doctor said I must watch you all night. I'll stay right by your side."

Donald smiled and closed his eyes for another hour. As the night progressed, whenever Grace woke him up, Donald's eyes seemed to be focusing the way they should be. By seven o'clock the following morning, husband and wife were sitting at the kitchen table drinking tea. Walter sported a large ice pack.

"How are you now?"

"I think all right, but I still feel a little foggy in my head." He reached for his coffee and knocked it to the floor. 'Oh Grace, I'm so sorry. Let me clean it up."

"Never you mind. I'll do it. Please just sit still. If you're thirsty I can help you." She put another cup to his lips and he took a sip.

"Thank you." He sat back in his chair. "Don't worry, I'll be up and back to work in no time."

"You're not going anywhere until the doctor says you're well enough to work."

Donald tried to stay awake for most of that day but by 6:00 p.m. he couldn't keep his eyes open and fell asleep in the fireside chair.

Grace sat opposite him in the parlor, watching him sleep. She worried he wouldn't make it up the stairs. "Wake up, Donald. Are you strong enough to get up to bed?"

"I think so." He struggled to stand. "Okay, I'm up." Standing straighter, he took hold of Grace's hand. She held his shoulder with the other hand as they climbed the steps together. When they reached the top, she asked again, "How are you feeling now?"

"Still a little off." He rubbed the back of his neck.

"Let's get you into bed."

Once he was under the covers, Grace watched her husband sleep until midnight, then she crawled into bed next to him. Exhausted, she fell into a deep sleep.

At ten o'clock the next morning, Donald was still asleep. When Grace couldn't wake him up, she summoned the doctor. By noon, Donald was gone.

43

UNCLE WILLIAM SAT by the sheet stove with his drink of choice, *hooch*. He mumbled under his alcohol-tainted breath, "I'm the one who should be the head of this house. It was my honor and that beach feeder stole it from me." Since Matthew's birth, the uncle had treated his nephew with scorn and tried to blame him for everything that went wrong. Today was no different.

Matthew moved closer to his uncle to deliver wood for the stove.

"Half-breed. Tell your mother to bring me more hooch." He threw the empty cup on the floor.

The boy was cautious and had the bruises to support his fear. Matthew reached for a long stick to push the cup away from his uncle, so he would not have to get closer to the old man. He grabbed the empty cup, ran toward his mother, then placed it on the table. "When will father return?"

She hugged her first-born. "Soon, my son. I'll take the drink to him. Go outside, the sun is shining." She took the filled cup and headed toward the stove.

Matthew accepted his mother's words and scooted out the door.

As Bessie approached her uncle, she noticed he had one shoe off and his knife was open. "Is everything all right, Uncle?"

He quickly hid the knife. "No. It is not. Your half-breed cut a hole into my shoe while I was dozing." He pointed to a small hole in the top of the leather shoe. "When he returns, I will whip him."

Bessie grew angry. "You leave him alone. I saw your knife shining in the light. My Matthew would not do that."

"Are you questioning my authority? Maybe I should whip you instead." He rose, as if to strike his niece. "Maybe your white husband will leave you and this house if you are scarred." He stood taller, with a piece of wood in his hand, held like a club.

Bessie knew better. She quickly retreated into a dark alcove of the cooking area. She hoped his angry mood would lessen if he drank more and then fell asleep in a drunken stupor. By that time, Walter would be home.

Over the deep winter, Matthew had become adept with the knife his father had given him. His carvings were rough but recognizable as he whittled symbols of fish, bear, or raven. As a spring snow softly fell, he went back inside with a small carving of his latest piece of art.

"*Shhh.*" Bessie warned her son to be quiet. "Uncle is sleeping, Matthew. Did you use your knife to damage his shoe?"

"No, Mother. I know better than to make him angry." He placed the piece of carved wood on the table. "I made this for you. It's a raven."

Bessie examined it. "You're getting very good with your knife. Promise me you'll never use it to hurt."

"Yes, Mother. I promise." He grabbed a cracker and snuck to his bed in the far corner.

Walter arrived home as the sun set in the afternoon. "The salmon are plentiful this year." He lay his catch on a sideboard.

Bessie inspected the fish.

"How goes your day?" Walter took his wet boots off by the back door and replaced them with softer shoes.

"Uncle has been up to his old tricks again."

"How so?"

"He led me to believe Matthew cut into one of his shoes with his knife. I did not believe him and told him so."

"Good."

"Walter, I feel as each day goes by, I become more fearful of that man. He hates you so much and sometimes it spills over onto us." Bessie served Walter a warm cup of soup.

"I've been thinking, too. Would you be against us leaving for the outside?"

44

Present Day, Monday - Nancy
CHATHAM

ON MY WAY TO CHATHAM, to show Casey the painting, my thoughts focused on the coincidences that kept popping up about the Provincetown house. Paul could be right. What if everything was related and fate was pointing the way?

The beauty of Pleasant Bay, as I drove along Route 28, distracted me in a nice way. Its history and local color reminded me of why we had moved to Cape Cod. Just a few fishing boats in the water, still too early in the season for sailboats and the perfect time to visit Casey, when there are fewer tourists. Her decision to open an art gallery that represented her father had been a smart move on her part. After receiving her degree in Art History and Business, the logical path was to become part of Cape Cod's art scene, aided by a well-known artist, her father. It was a perfect match.

I carefully carried the mystery painting into the gallery. "Casey?"

"Hi Mom." She came out of her office and gave me a big hug and then turned her attention to the painting. "Let's take a closer look."

"Okay. You get started. I'll be right back. I want to show you something else I found in Provincetown." I hurried to the car to retrieve the sketchbook. By the time I returned, Casey was searching the internet.

Without losing her concentration on the computer she told me, "I don't think it's a print faked to look like an oil."

I waited for more information.

"Mom, let me search some more. What was the artist's name?"

"Andrew Fletcher. Try Abigail Ellis, too."

"I don't see anything relevant to his name or even hers as painters or artists." Casey adjusted her glasses. "Wait. Here's an Isaac Fletcher, wealthy businessman and banker who lived in New York City. It says he collected art and then on his death in 1917, he donated the whole collection to the Metropolitan Museum of Fine Art, including Rembrandt, Rubens, Gainsborough, and others." She smiled as her fingers flew across the keyboard. "Let me try something else."

"You know," I mused, "this guy, Andrew, could be related to the man from New York."

Casey's screen filled up with rows of impressionistic images of women on the beach in flowing skirts with parasols and wispy tendrils of fluffy hair. She moved the computer closer to me. "Take a look. Maybe you'll notice something similar to the other paintings you found in the attic."

As I was scrolling through the images, Casey went to her office to get a few tools. "I'd like to check the physical canvas and frame again. You keep looking on the internet."

After several pages, I looked over to Casey, who already had the painting out of its frame and was examining it with her magnifying glass.

"No visible dot patterns, so it's definitely not a reproduction. It's been stretched on the canvas with small nails." She held the painting on its backside. "They didn't use staples until after 1940. I also see paint splotches on the canvas edges; a good sign for an original." She reached for her iPhone and snapped an image. "I've got one more idea."

I watched my talented daughter do her thing. Within seconds, the image appeared in her photo library. She then uploaded the image to Google's reverse image app then pressed the enter key.

"Let's see if Google can find any matches."

I made us some coffee.

"No luck. I don't see anything that comes close to this image. It's one of a kind. The women are beautiful." Casey sipped her brew. "Mom, do you think these women lived in that house with Andrew Fletcher?"

"My guess would be a yes. Andrew was also a boarder." I gave Casey a quick history sound bite. "I know that when Provincetown was hit by the Portland Gale, in 1898, the whole town was affected by it. Hawthorne started his art school the year after that and the townspeople took advantage of the newcomers. They rented out rooms or their entire houses, worked for the art school, sold supplies, and many posed for artists to earn extra money. It's possible the ladies were locals."

Casey began to replace the painting back in its frame. "Interesting. So, it was the beginning of the tourist industry for Provincetown?"

"I believe so." My visit wasn't over yet. I removed the painting and leaned it against the wall then slowly brought the black sketchbook into view. "I almost forgot about this."

Casey stood next to me. She ran her fingers across the leather, traced the gold letters at the bottom of the book and carefully opened it up to the first page. The sketchbook was intriguing as ever to both of us, especially the drawings of the Pigeon's Blood ring.

"Did you find any paintings in the attic that could be related to these sketches?" Casey carefully flipped through the pages of the leather book.

"Not any that I could see, just the coincidence that the dimensions of the painting in the sketchbook match the outline on the wall I found underneath the painting we're looking at today."

"When are you going back to the house?"

"Wednesday morning, with Ally."

I began to gather my things to leave. "I hope to find more interesting items."

"Good luck, Mom."

Tuesday

The next day arrived with warm temperatures and less wind. Paul and I drove to Nauset Beach for a walk along the popular shoreline. As it was still off-season, few people appeared within our view. We strolled hand-in-hand past bunches of sea hay, mounds of rocks, and twisted remnants of uprooted trees and branches. We stopped to listen to the rocks and pebbles rumbling and crackling in the sea as waves pushed them up onto the beach. It was eerily quiet, devoid of any human sounds and yet comfortable with only the sounds of nature.

"No treasures for me today."

Paul leaned in to give me a quick kiss. "Oh, I never worry about you being disappointed. You have a knack of always finding something that's intriguing."

Paul was right.

"Anxious to get back into that attic in Provincetown?"

"Absolutely." My cell rang. With scant reception on the beach, I said, "Ally's calling. Maybe we should get back to the parking lot."

We turned around and as we headed back, the wind picked up and blew into our faces. Too windy to talk, we kept our heads down as our shoes sank into the sand with every step. Winded and out of breath, I was happy to get inside the car. "Boy, that wind came up fast."

"Yep. Let's get home."

As we drove further away from Nauset, phone reception grew to three bars. I returned Ally's call. "Hi, what's up?"

"I just wanted to let you know that I went back to the old house today to clean out the boxes of books in the parlor."

"Oh?"

"A friend of mine in Provincetown said he had a client who specialized in old books. He'd like to see them so he can tell us which ones are more valuable than others."

"Are we still going back to the house tomorrow?"

"Of course. I wouldn't leave you out. You have the attic to rummage around in."

"Okay. See you tomorrow."

A little disappointed at not having the opportunity of searching through the old books, I accepted the task of exploring the attic with anticipation. And with that, my plans changed, just like the winds.

45

Late August 1910 – March 1911
PROVINCETOWN

JENNY HELD GRACE'S hand. No words were spoken between the two childhood friends as they sat in the parlor.

Grace's face, wet and swollen from tears, showed no expression.

Jenny grieved for dear Grace with a heart filled with sadness. At the same time, fear crowded her thoughts with the idea that something might happen to her own husband, Jonathan Mendes. They were newly married, as of three months ago. If a simple accident could take Donald away, then death could easily touch her own life, too.

Donald's burial invoice lay across Grace's black dress. Her damp handkerchief wet the papers. Jenny reached over and put the official documents into the parlor desk. "Would you like a cup of tea?"

Grace shook her head.

"Please Grace, you need to drink or eat something, even if it's a cracker and water."

Grace held her head and sniffled. "No more walks together. No holding hands. No more picnics on the beach. No nothing."

Jenny placed a cup of hot tea and a cookie on the round table next to the settee. "Your mother will return from town soon. She's very worried about you and so am I." She rejoined the distressed young widow. "I'm here for you."

Jenny was true to her word, over the following days, her best friend stayed with her for most of the daytime but went home at suppertime each night.

Grace had hoped her mother and Andrew could have stayed longer, but there was some trouble in the family business, so Andrew felt it necessary to return to New York. Grace understood.

One week had passed since Donald's funeral but it seemed like an eternity to the young widow. When alone, she'd walk around the house touching Donald's clothes, brushing her hair with his hairbrush, holding his favorite pen at the desk, and refusing to wash the bed linens from where he last lay. When did she kiss him last? She blamed herself for not being a better wife and kept thinking about the final day she was with him. Why didn't she kiss him goodbye that morning? Why was she so concerned about dirty linens and not a loving goodbye to her husband? Goddamn the laundry.

Her only comfort was that the Provincetown house always calmed her, whether she was alone or with family. It held so many cherished memories. She stood near the hearth and admired the masonry. Donald often commented on how well the bricks were laid and, how one day, he would be able to place his mark on the final brick of a stone project, just like the original bricklayer had in the Ellis house. She touched the small circle to the left of the open hearth depicting a miniature compass rose. Donald's dreams were gone now. What about her dreams? Would she have any now that Donald was not in her life anymore?

By the middle of the second week, Jenny had a doctor's appointment and couldn't come over. Grace began to feel hungry again and thought it must have been the exertion of finally washing Donald's linens, the day before. She found enough strength to prepare her own meal, a simple grilled cheese sandwich with a pickle, which tasted good. She grabbed a cookie left over from the mountains of food that neighbors had delivered, then she climbed the stairs to the attic, hoping to find a few extra memories of Donald.

Several trunks held the drawings, baby shoes, and other memorabilia of when she and Charles W. were little. The christening dress and bonnet that the Ellis family had used for all the children was wrapped in a white cotton cloth. Grace quickly closed the chest, thinking she would never have use for the ceremonial outfit now that Donald was gone.

The sun from the back window cast a beam of light on the wooden flooring. It led her eyes to another leather chest.

Upon opening it, she remembered when she willfully hid her great-great-great-great-great-grandmother's treasures so that her mother wouldn't sell them. It brought a smile to her face, thinking what a mischievous and stubborn child she was. She whispered, "Sorry, Mother."

Grace dug deeper and found her grandmother's journal. She recalled reading it as a young girl, secluded up on the top floor. The beautifully scripted words related the everyday life of her grandmother. Years ago, the young girl loved to immerse herself in the late 1700s, too naive to understand the secrets the journal held, including her grandmother's last entry before she died. No one ever questioned the strange words and their meaning, no one except her father, and he was a dreamer. Family attributed the written words, *Pigeon's Blood*, to nothing more than an older woman's fantasies.

Grace found a small case that held some of Donald's items dating back to when he was very small. There were only a few. When his family emigrated from Portugal, they took only what they could carry plus the money garnered from selling everything back home. Donald had saved his memories deep inside him, but now they were lost to her.

She heard the door open downstairs.

Jenny called through the house. "Hello? Grace? Where are you?"

"I'm upstairs in the attic. I'll be right down."

Jenny took off her hat and plopped into the stuffed chair by the fireplace hearth.

Grace sat opposite her. "How was your appointment?"

"Exciting. But I'm so exhausted." She stood up. "I'm hungry. Did you eat?"

Grace felt a tinge of normalcy. Their conversation had no sad news. "What's so exciting?"

"I need something to drink first." She poured a glassful of water. "That's better. It looks like my lazy days are over." She leaned back in the kitchen chair.

"Tell me more."

"Jonathan and I are going to have... a baby." She waited for a reaction.

Grace sat quiet.

"Please be happy for me." Jenny took her friend's hand. "I know you're sad but now I'm going to need you."

Grace listened and agreed but her heart still ached for Donald. "I'll do my best."

"That's all I need to hear."

The two women embraced.

A month passed and Grace was now visiting Jenny every day. She had no time to think about herself or her future; she was focused on preparations for the Mendes's coming child. Jenny and Jonathan had been living in close quarters with the Nickerson family but were hopeful of finding their own place to raise the baby. Jonathan was waiting on some new job prospects that paid more than he was getting from the railroad as a baggage handler.

At the Ellis house, weekly letters arrived from her mother. Grace skimmed over the usual repetitive questions about her future from a concerned mother and concentrated on whatever news there was from the big city of New York. She didn't want to think about what lay ahead of her, not just yet. The winter would be here soon enough, and with it, loneliness. She counted on that. Hopefully taking care of Jenny would mask her recurring sad thoughts and any impending decisions about her own life.

Christmas came and went with subdued celebration. By the time the New Year broke through the winter, Donald's official death certificate, delayed because of the government's new form, arrived in the mail. Grace filed it in the desk for safekeeping, among other envelopes and letters of condolences, without opening the legal document.

February quickly slipped away into the frigid New England cold. Grace left the house only to visit Jenny. She had her essential groceries delivered, not wanting to face or talk with townsfolk about her sad life without a husband.

By March, the temperatures mimicked spring and Grace was finally eager to take a walk by the sea. She had purposely deprived herself of the pleasure of sea breezes against her face since Donald's passing. Today, she stood on the shore behind the house with no hat, dressed only in her long coat and mittens. It was invigorating. She loved to feel the force of the wind and had missed it. Any notions of sadness were discarded as she remembered all the things that had made her fall in love with Donald. His love was pure, his affectionate smile had pleased her every day, his kindness was true, and his touch comforting. The wind blew her hair in circles. She could hear Donald's voice. *Don't worry. I'll watch over you.* It was as if Donald was telling her to begin again.

The sun slid behind a bank of dark clouds and the temperature dropped. Grace's eyes burned from the biting cold, so she retreated to the shelter of her house. Once inside, the warmth of the small home felt good. As she took her coat off, she accidently walked into the edge of the small desk. She must not have pushed it back far enough against the wall when she swept that morning. The writing table fell over, spilling its contents across the floor. Before she knew it, she was on her knees picking up the envelopes and papers. The letters she had saved from her father caught her eye. She put another log on the fire and sat down to reread the last words to his family.

46

May 1910
JUNEAU

WALTER EXPECTED IVAN any day now. His annual visit to collect and buy Walter's furs had become a celebratory event. They had developed more than a business partnership; they were good friends.

Ivan's visit would usually take Walter away from the house, but only for a short time, as the two ventured to Amalga Harbor. Bessie and Matthew never minded, they still looked forward to the burly man's arrival. It always meant laughter and more money.

Uncle William did not want either of the two white men in the village and several other men agreed. They sided with the uncle, wishing Walter and the Russian fur trader would leave. Occasionally, Walter would see these men whispering outside, near Uncle's part of the house. As Walter went about his chores, he always made a point of glowering at them, hopefully making them uneasy with just his presence.

It was late in the day when Ivan knocked on the door. "Hello in there."

Everyone stopped eating and then Matthew ran to let him in.

"Come here and give me a big hug, young one." Ivan scooped the boy into his arms and tussled his blonde hair. "You are growing so tall."

Walter rose to greet his friend.

Bessie stood to give him a welcoming hug.

"Bessie, you are more beautiful than before. Walter, you're a lucky man."

Bessie, embarrassed, hurried to the kitchen to set a place for their visitor.

Walter gestured to Ivan. "Come and sit."

It was a small table, so Ivan was relegated to a place near Uncle William and his family. With a serious tone and no smile, he greeted him, "Uncle William."

Uncle William responded with silence.

The seal oil burned long into the night as Ivan regaled all with his stories, at least for those who wanted to listen.

On the second day of Ivan's visit, Walter and his friend planned to follow the Breadline Trail for Amalga Harbor. Provisions were readied, including sleeping bags, rations, rope, blankets, and canvas bags for the extra furs that would be purchased from the area's trappers. The day of departure came on a fine spring day.

Bessie embraced her husband to say goodbye.

Matthew ran toward his father, fisting one hand. "Father, did you forget your lucky charm?"

Walter picked his son up and looked at the small boy's open hand. It was the white marbled stone that Matthew had given his father a year ago. "I'm so happy you reminded me." He placed it in his pocket and then gave Matthew a final hug. "Be good and take care of your mother. I love you."

"Yes, Father." He jumped out of his father's arms and ran to his mother's side. With feet spread apart and hands on his hips, he looked like a warrior.

As Walter turned to leave, he saw Uncle William standing off to the side. He walked over, grabbed the old man's arm and whispered to his nemesis. "If I discover that you hurt my wife or child while I'm gone, I will see to it that you never witness another sunrise."

Ivan heard his friend issue the threat. He joined him on the path. "Well said."

Walter agreed with a nod.

Within the second hour of following the shoreline, the two men came to the inlet. The tide was almost out. They sat on the rocks and waited until they could cross over to the trail to Amalga Harbor.

"You're a fortunate man, Walter Ellis." Ivan sat open-legged with hands on knees, as if he were king of the universe, surveying his empire.

Walter took a deep breath and closed his eyes. "You're right. I've been given a second chance for happiness."

"Do you ever miss your old life in the outside?"

"Sometimes I can't sleep, but then I reach over and feel Bessie next to me. She has healed me in more ways than ever. I'm grateful."

"Understood."

"Fate dealt me a bitter blow, but when I see Matthew, I know he was the reason I survived. I can't wait to find out what great things he will do."

The seagulls began to circle and crowd the tidal flats looking for fresh seafood. Ivan grabbed his supplies. "Ready?"

"Right behind you."

Once across the inlet, they walked past the markers for the new cannery, scheduled to be completed next year, then climbed the slope next to the black stone outcrops. Walter could see the opening where Matthew had hidden his special box, when the two had camped on his birthday. He smiled. At the edge of the woods, the men followed the wooded path, listening to the ocean on their left. Walter could feel his right hand swell from swinging it low as he walked. He nestled it into his pocket. After a few steps, his fingertips touched Matthew's good luck charm. He pulled it out to show Ivan. "What a kind son I have. Did you see what he gave me for good luck?"

Ivan glanced at it as they kept a lively pace. "We can always use good luck."

Walter cautioned as he walked ahead. "Keep alert. The bears are waking."

Ivan remembered the man's warning back in Juneau. "Right behind you."

They approached a denser part of the woods. Walter scanned between the gnarled tree trunks and standing pole pines. He felt for his lucky charm. It was gone. "Ivan, you go ahead, I must have dropped Matthew's gift. I'll catch up."

Ivan saluted and kept walking.

Walter thought the white marbled stone would be easy to find against the deep green moss that cushioned the forest floor. He kept his eyes down. He'd be quick. After 100 feet or so, it seemed to be a lost cause. He decided to turn back toward his friend.

From inside the dense woods, he heard a rustling. Walter stopped to listen but saw nothing. He took hold of his rifle with both hands, ready to fire. Within seconds, from behind him, the largest bear he had ever seen stood tall with paws outstretched and huge teeth exposed. Walter slowly backed away with his rifle cocked. The bear rose to almost eight feet. Walter knew it would do no good to turn and run so he got off one shot into the behemoth's chest. It didn't faze the beast. He reloaded. With the lift of his arm, to send another bullet into the brute's head, the monster was upon him with one leap.

Ivan stopped when he heard the first shot. He turned and ran toward his friend. A writhing mound of black fur blocked his way ahead. Walter's feet extended flat on the ground under the bear. Ivan froze in his tracks, cocked his rifle, then aimed for the massive creature's head. The bullet met its mark but only made the monster angrier. It turned in pain with a deafening roar. The bloody giant stood tall once more with its sharp fore claws fully extended and ready to attack its next victim. Ivan drew his axe and with the skill of a marksman, he sent the blade in a death spiral, meeting its mark and splitting the bear's skull in half. The colossal mammoth fell over the edge of the cliff and crashed to the swirling waters and sharp rocks below.

47

Present Day, Tuesday
CAPE COD

BY 8 A.M. TUESDAY, Neil Hallett was on the road in case the women returned sooner than expected. He wanted the first look, even if he had to break the attic door down.

The dusky morning cast a somber spell over old Provincetown. It was off-season and Neil laughed to himself that it was perfect for someone who may want to commit a crime.

As he approached the house, he saw a car and a van backed into the driveway. Hallett recognized the woman as the liquidator from the estate, but he didn't know the guy loading up boxes into the van. He decided to drive past the house, circle back then park a short distance away to watch. Once parked, he saw the two people talking. Caldwell was nowhere in sight. Disappointed he couldn't gain entrance, he stayed put and continued his vigil. Within the hour, the car and van left.

Using the key from within the fake rock, Hallett finally stepped inside. He bypassed the near-empty parlor and headed straight upstairs to the locked attic door. To his surprise it was open. Must have been jammed, he thought. He gave a quick look through file cabinets, boxes, trunks, and then rifled through the stacked paintings but found nothing he thought was important. As he was about to leave, he pulled out his flashlight from his backpack to scan the darker corners of the attic one more time. He noticed a long metal tube in the back. It leaned against the wall behind a ladder, mixed in with pieces of lumber and iron rods.

Hallett retrieved the tube and carried it over to the window for better light. With a strong grip, he was able to loosen the rusted screw-type lid. Inside was something that resembled a scroll. His heart beat faster. He thought *treasure map*. With a careful touch, he unrolled the paper to reveal a set of house plans. His heart sunk, until he read the address of the house and the written names of Matthew Ellis, Abigail Ellis, and Maria Ellis. Abigail's name piqued his interest. Abigail E. was the signature on his favorite painting. He wondered if they were the same person.

His cell phone rang. It was Rick Sanderson. "Everything okay?"

Agitated, Hallett nestled his phone between his neck and shoulder. His answer was quick and terse. "Yeah." He kept studying the plans, hoping to find a clue about his prized painting and the infamous ruby ring.

"Just checking. I'll be home in a few weeks."

Ignoring his boss's words, Neil Hallett rolled the plans up and inserted them back into the cylinder for later. "Gotta go. See ya."

Downstairs, he checked to make sure nothing was out of place then he quietly closed the door with the tube under his arm. He left after he replaced the key in the rock.

Hallett remembered the name of the antique store that he found when he'd turned his beloved painting upside down. He made a right onto Bradford Street, instead of driving to the highway, then he circled back around to Commercial Street. Not much traffic in early spring, so he was able to slow down. Out of the corner of his eye, he spotted the words, Provincetown Estates, on a sign with a small white paper next to it. He pulled over to the right and parked. The street was so deserted that he didn't need to look for oncoming cars. He rushed over to the glass door. The paper sign read, *Open by Appointment*, but there was no number listed to call. Frustrated, he left to drive home, but not without a spark of excitement. No one will ever miss what he found in the attic. He couldn't wait to examine the original plans of the Provincetown house.

Halfway home, Neil Hallett heard a funny sound coming from the car's engine before it just stopped on the highway. He coasted to the side of the road in Wellfleet. "Shit!"

He wasn't good with cars and had purchased AAA road service because of his lack of talent with moving vehicles. He called for help. The tow truck arrived within the hour and drove him home, it then delivered the disabled car to an auto repair shop in Eastham. Hallett wasn't going anywhere for the next two days. It was a good thing he had plenty of beer and take-out delivery was available.

48

1910
JUNEAU

IT PAINED IVAN to look at his friend. The sight of Walter's scalp torn away and his stomach ripped open made the powerful man crumble to the ground like a fearful child.

"Walter."

The half-dead man opened his eye. "Ivan."

Ivan slowly regained his composure. "My friend, you will survive." He quickly took off his coat and pushed it against Walter's bloody abdomen to stop the bleeding. He didn't know what to do about the gaping skull. He frantically looked around for something else to cover the wound.

Walter reached for his partner's arm. "Ivan, come close."

He leaned nearer to Walter's face.

"Promise me you'll watch over Bessie and Matthew."

"Yes. Yes. I will." Tears fell down the big man's cheeks.

"Tell them I love them." Walter closed his eye and what was left of him lay quiet.

Ivan leaned back on his feet and yelled into the deep woods. "Noooo…"

It was dusk before Ivan was able to finish building the pole stretcher that would carry Walter's body back to the village. He tied a blanket around Walter and secured it tight so his friend would be protected.

As he picked up the two poles to begin his sad journey, he spotted Matthew's good luck charm off to the side of the wood line. As he bent to pick it up, his eyes swelled. He swiped his nose dry, pocketed the stone, and whispered to no one but himself, "I'll take you home, my friend."

With the light of a full moon, Ivan's soulful passage was made possible. He thought that was lucky. He remembered when his parents died, when he was in his early teens, and so young. It was the first time someone close to him had left through death. As he dragged the remains of Walter behind him, Ivan tried to think of the words that people had comforted him with, as he once again grieved. What would he say to Bessie and especially to young Matthew?

Several miles away, Bessie tried to keep her mind on her household duties and not on how much she missed her husband. She also kept her eye on Matthew and made sure he was in view all the time. She didn't want him to wander off by himself, thinking Uncle William would take advantage of any opportunity to blame him for things he didn't do.

Supper was simple with fresh salmon, *wapato* – "Indian potato", greens, and dried berries. As the house settled in for the night, Bessie heard a commotion outside. She opened the door to see Ivan sitting on one of the tree stumps next to a pole stretcher, surrounded by several people. She could not understand their whispers. As she approached the gathering, their talk stopped and the men broke ranks. Bessie continued walking nearer while Ivan stared at the ground.

"Where's Walter?" She glanced at the stretcher, then back to Ivan. "Where's Walter?" She asked again, her voice louder.

Within seconds, she knew Walter was gone. Her wails echoed into the pines as she ran to her husband's body.

No one moved to comfort her. All stood in silent prayer for the widowed woman. Ivan could hear the village women repeating, "*Uhxha du`jeet oowathlixh.*" He knew what the words meant, "the paddle was broken in her hand." A paddle is important in Tlingit society; it cannot break in a storm. Now Bessie's spirit was broken.

Walter's adopted Eagle clan could not help with his burial, according to Tlingit tradition. Bessie's Raven clan held that honor but Uncle William, now the restored housemaster, was purposely slow to respond to his duties.

Before preparations would begin, the first item on Uncle's agenda was to reclaim the clan's Chilkat ceremonial robe. He had felt cheated when Bessie's father awarded the honor of caring for the robe to Walter. This gesture on Thomas of Tee Harbor's deathbed had increased the Uncle's hatred for all *Die 'it Khaa*, or "white people."

That night, he quietly entered Bessie's side of the house and stole the cherished robe for himself. Later, encouraged by other Raven clan members, he agreed to begin the funeral preparations, but the ceremony was going to be simple and quick.

Bessie was inconsolable and Matthew would not leave his bed. Ivan grieved in silence, watching from afar with mixed feelings. The old ways meant nothing to him. His thoughts remained with Bessie and Matthew, not Tlingit traditions.

The cremation began at sunrise. A center fire pit within the house was readied. Bessie averted her eyes as the wrapped corpse was brought inside. She lay in her bed, crying, as the smell of death drifted out the top of the roof. By evening, her husband's ashes and remaining bones were gathered into a box and lifted, according to tradition, out of the opening in the roofline. The following day, Walter's remains would be buried.

Morning came with a foggy dawn. Uncle William took to his role of Chief with a vengeance, ordering Bessie to remove her husband's personal possessions from the house by the end of the next day.

Bessie sat quiet, unable to move. She heard his command, but the depth of his cruel words fell on closed ears, overshadowed by grief. By afternoon, the burial ceremony was over, and she returned to her mourning, making no effort to collect Walter's belongings.

Ivan entered the house and took his seat next to the widow. "I want to help you." He held her hand. With his touch, she collapsed onto his lap in tears. Ivan rubbed her back and stroked her black hair.

"Walter wanted me to tell you that he loved you and Matthew." He waited a few seconds. "Those were his last words to me."

Her cries grew louder.

Ivan stayed with her until she was calm. Finally, he helped her lay down and covered her with a blanket. "I will tend to Matthew."

Bessie didn't want to let go of his hand. Her eyes pleaded for more comfort.

"Stay. Rest your soul. I'll soon return to be with you."

Ivan found Matthew in the back of the house, carving with his knife, near the salmon drying racks. His hand went fast and furious into the wood.

"What are you making?" Ivan stood tall over the visibly angry boy.

Matthew stayed silent.

"Would you like to honor your father?"

With Ivan's words, the boy looked up.

"Come with me." Ivan led him inside the house. "We need to gather your father's favorite things and find a safe place to keep them. You must do this for your father... and your mother." He waited for a response. "Will you help me?"

The boy pocketed his knife and nodded.

They found Walter's duffle bag in the storage room. Inside the bag were his tablet of paper, pencils, more blue beads, his wallet, and the picture that he had saved of his previous family.

Matthew studied the portrait. "Who are these people?"

Ivan hesitated, but only for a few seconds. "They were very important to your father before he came to Juneau."

"Okay." The boy slid the photograph inside the tablet.

Then the two went to gather Walter's tools from the rear of the house. After they filled the duffle bag, Matthew was determined to carry it himself.

As he struggled to carry the bag into the house, Uncle William appeared at the doorway. "What do you have, boy?"

"My father's things." He stood as tall as he could muster with the weight of the bag on his shoulder.

Ivan took a stance next to the boy. "Leave him alone."

"Leave, you Russian half-breed. We've had enough of a creole living amongst us." Two of Uncle William's men appeared behind the old man.

"I'll leave when I'm ready. Step aside." The Russian towered over all three men as he led Matthew through the doorway.

Ivan welcomed an end to the confrontation, for now. No need to anger the uncle any more than necessary. He knew he had to leave for Juneau in a few days and he wanted to make sure Bessie and Matthew were able to regain some normalcy in their daily routine before he left.

When Ivan did leave, he was uneasy for the whole journey and eager to return, fearing the worst for Bessie and Matthew.

Racist anger and jealousy reared its ugly head as soon as Ivan left. While Bessie and Matthew went to visit where Walter had been laid, Uncle William's cohorts ransacked Bessie's side of the house. Upon the shattered family's return, they found the second duffle bag was empty. Walter's clothes and tools, and anything of value, had all been divided among the Raven clan. His personal papers were untouched. A few women had even confiscated Bessie's special hide tanning equipment.

Matthew watched as his mother ran through the house looking for any evidence of Walter and screaming, "Why?" There was nothing left. It was almost as if her Walter had never existed. The young boy noticed a pile of items by the fire pit and quickly walked over to see what they were. There, ready to be burned, lay his father's wallet, writing paper, pencils, and the pouch filled with beads. He checked inside of the tablet for the photo. It was still hidden where he'd tucked it. Matthew scooped the last of his father's presence up into his arms, grabbed his pack then ran outside. His anger focusing him, he didn't stop running until he reached the inlet, where a few cannery men were standing on the stone shoreline. They paid no attention to the little boy.

The tide was out, so Matthew ran across to the other side of the water, his heart burning with a mission to do what he had to do. He glanced around, to make sure the men were out of sight and that it was safe for him to complete his task. After he scrambled to the black outcrops, he stepped upon the highest flat stone then reached into the black opening to retrieve the metal box he had hidden there.

Keeping only the tablet with the photo and pencils, Matthew placed his father's wallet and bag of beads into the box, next to the other blue beads he had already stashed there, the year before. When the box was safely out of sight again, he sat facing the shoreline and promised himself he'd return one day to fetch the few treasures and memories left of his father. As the tide rolled in, he flew across the tidal pools with the confidence of an older boy, and a passion to make his father and mother proud in whatever he chose to do in the future.

Later, Matthew found his mother in her bed, not from mourning, but from punishment leveled by her uncle. She had a blackened eye and her lip was bleeding.

"Mother. What happened?" He ran to get a wet cloth.

"We have to leave our home." Bessie took the cloth and dabbed at her face. "Do not be afraid. Ivan will return in a few days. Until then, we must do whatever Uncle tells us to do."

"But, Mother..."

She held his small shoulders and looked into his blue eyes. "Do you understand?"

He nodded.

49

Present Day, Wednesday - Nancy
PROVINCETOWN

ON THE WAY TO THE old house, Ally said she was sorry about returning without me the day before our scheduled visit. It didn't bother me, not to be included. I thought of all that still lay dormant up in the attic room.

The parlor was almost empty. I sensed it would be a shortened day and once upstairs, I quickly determined there really wasn't much left to explore. In one corner, I spotted two unopened boxes. Soon, I discovered both held more books. I managed a quick glance in each, and to my good fortune, at the bottom of one box, underneath some children's books, was a leather journal. I sat on the top step of the attic, near the window for better light, and opened the old chronicle. The first page of the half-filled book was dated 1750, Barnstable, Cape Cod.

My loving Matthew surprised me today with you. He thought I would like to record my thoughts. And I do. Young Matthew and Abigail have grown into such blessings for us. Of course, our son has his moments that bring us to our wit's end. I look forward to tell you my deepest feelings. At this moment, I'm tired and can't think of what to write. Until tomorrow...

Now we're getting somewhere, I thought, and read more. As the words drifted past my eyes, I admired this woman of the past. She was giving the reader first-hand insight into what it was like to live in the late 18th century on Cape Cod.

Her first name didn't appear until a third of the way in: Maria Ellis. No surprise, since we were in the Ellis house. As the years flew by across the pages, with occasional gaps between months, Maria's handwriting noticeably deteriorated. There were fewer words and she sounded older with each turn of the page. One of her last entries was different and caught my attention. The year was September 1781. She wrote, *The pigeon's blood lies warm and deep, hidden by the woman who now sleeps.* In the middle of the page, under the phrase, was a crude circle, about two inches wide, containing the first letters of the directional coordinates: North, South, East, and West. I recognized the rough sketch as a compass rose.

I read the phrase out loud, hoping it would make me understand its meaning. Then I sat quiet, trying to decipher what the words meant, if anything. The following pages were blank. Disappointed, I assumed Maria must have died. I scanned through the pages again, hopeful of finding something related to the mysterious words and symbol.

Ally and I left Provincetown and pulled into our Brewster parking lot a little past noon. "Let me know if you need any more help." I stood by the open door of the car.

Ally echoed back, "And you let me know if you find anything new about that painting and the sketchbook."

I laughed. "Absolutely. Hey, and don't forget the journal I found today."

"Have fun."

After dinner, the sun was shining and there was still time for a walk on the beach.

I opened Paul's studio door and peeked my head in. "Want to go for a walk at Crosby Landing?"

Without hesitation, he got up and greeted me with a hug. "Let's go."

Temperatures were hovering right below the 50-degree mark, so we still needed our jackets. We started our walk via the dog path, which runs parallel with the shoreline, Mac leading the way. The further we got from the parking lot, the windier the air became.

Paul asked, "Want to turn back? Are you too cold?"

I zipped my jacket up higher and pulled my hood tighter. "Let's go to the end of this path and return the same way we came."

Paul donned his gloves. "Whew, the wind is coming right off the ocean. It was much calmer at home."

We kept walking. Out of the corner of my eye, I saw Paul trip, but he quickly righted himself. Over the wind I called out, "I'm impressed. You've got good balance." I grabbed his hand. "Let's get up to the top of the dune for a peek at the water." We stood side by side, whipped by the strong sea air. "You know, together we can face anything that blows our way."

Once in the safety of our car, we breathed a sigh of relief. Mac shook his chills off.

"That was brutal." Paul started the car and cranked up the heat.

"But exhilarating."

Halfway down the street, my cell found some bars for reception. I had a voice message. As we turned left onto Route 6A, I said, "You'll never believe who I got a call from." I didn't wait for Paul's answer. "Steven Boudreaux from Los Angeles."

"No kidding. How is he?" Paul turned into our driveway.

"I guess he's coming to the Cape for business. He wants to visit."

"It will be good to see him. I wonder if he's still with Valerie?"

"I don't know. I'll give him a call later."

Once we arrived home, I contacted Stephen and discovered that he would be on the Cape tomorrow. Stephen never wasted time when he wanted something. He said he wanted to talk with me about FBI business. The FBI, I thought. A few years ago, when I went on a motherly visit to see our son Jim in Hollywood, I never imagined myself being involved with that crime fighting force. Evidently, here I was again, even if it was just a question. Let's hope this time that it's not regarding serial murder and mayhem.

Stephen showed up at our door on schedule the next morning. Mac greeted him with several loud barks.

"Nancy. It's great to see you." We hugged. "I noticed you have a security system besides old Mac." He rubbed our beagle's back and scratched behind Mac's floppy ears.

We moved into the kitchen for coffee and cookies.

"Where's Paul?"

"Meeting with a client about his latest painting commission. He'll be back soon." I handed him a cup of coffee. "So, tell me. How's Valerie?"

Stephen was quiet but didn't miss a step. "That didn't work out. But it's okay."

"I'm sorry. I thought you were so good together."

"I thought so, too, but… you'll never guess what happened after we broke up?"

"Tell me."

"If you remember, I had a son in college when we met at the National Treasure Hunter's Society conference."

"Yes."

"He recently got married. I'm a grandfather!"

"Whoa. That's calls for another cookie."

"And… I've been seeing his mother, my ex-wife." He downed the extra treat in a few bites.

"That's wonderful. I'm so happy for you."

"It is, isn't it?" He pulled out his phone. "Now for the business end of my visit." Stephen showed me a man's picture. "Recognize this guy?"

"No. Should I?"

"Maybe. He's disguised himself pretty well."

I stared at the image. "Who is it?" Now I was getting annoyed. I usually have a great memory.

"Neil Hallett."

I grabbed the phone from his hands to look closer. "Oh, my God, you're right. It is him! Look at that bushy beard. He's bald now?" I felt a quick flip of my stomach but regained my composure. "What about him?"

"As you know, he's been out of prison for over ten years. He still lives in Eastham."

"I was aware of that, but why are you interested in him?"

"Money laundering via art galleries."

At that moment, Paul came into the kitchen. While he and Stephen were getting to know each other again, along with Stephen telling him the good news of his ex-wife's return, I couldn't stop thinking that I had seen Hallett lately, but where?

50

June 1910
JUNEAU

SMOKE FILLED THE AIR outside as Bessie exited the house. She whispered, "What's burning?"

Others looked to the top of the tree line, wondering the same thing.

Matthew stood by his mother's side. "What's wrong, Mother?"

Bessie held her son close. "It's coming from the direction of my brother's cabin." She grabbed her jacket, took hold of her son's hand then followed the trail of the embers. By the time she reached her brother's cabin, where Walter had lived when he'd first arrived, its roof was gone, and the sides were engulfed in flames. The totem stood untouched, for now. There was nothing Bessie could do but watch as the fire pushed its rage closer to the carved pole. Uncle William stood to the side with a gasoline can in his hand. There was no doubt in her mind who had done this vengeful deed.

An evil smile grew across his face, pleased that Bessie had come to see his power.

Bessie knew in her heart that her uncle's intention was to erase any trace of Walter and possibly of herself and her child. She turned away with Matthew in tow and hurried back to the house.

The next day, Bessie secretly gathered whatever was left of her family's life, including an old photo album of their history. Inside it were pictures of her father, mother, brother, her son, Matthew and, of course, Walter.

Matthew busied himself with his carvings and never noticed anything unusual with his mother's routine. The one thing that was added to the boy's daily habits were the words, "When does Ivan return?"

Bessie would answer, "Soon." The frightened widow kept her fears inside. She, too, looked for Ivan's arrival. Her heart grew heavy at the thought of leaving her birth home with the fur trader. She bolstered her decision by remembering Walter's words before he left for Amalga Harbor, "Would you be against us leaving for the outside?" Bessie touched her blackened eye, the result of her uncle's temper, and wished she could leave now.

Two miles away, Ivan thanked his transport man and jumped out of the canoe. He headed straight for the Big Dipper house through the woods. He thought it strange to see Walter's old cabin had burned to the ground, even its totem. The Tlingits were a tidy society, nothing wasted. As he ventured further in, his instincts told him to be cautious. Something was very wrong.

As he approached the house, Ivan saw new faces standing outside. Bessie and Matthew sat on the tree stumps with Walter's filled duffle bag next to them. He didn't like what he saw and grabbed his rifle from his shoulder. "Wáa sá iyatee." He slowly walked toward Uncle William.

The housemaster stared and said, "You are not welcome here, Dle`it Khaa."

A few men closed ranks behind Ivan as he held his rifle across his chest. "I will speak to Bessie." He waited for a response, scanning the faces of the men. "Don't make me angry." He caught Bessie's eye.

She nodded and stood up. Tension filled the air.

Within seconds, Ivan tossed his rifle to Bessie and pulled his Bowie knife from his leather sheath with the other hand.

Bessie aimed her weapon toward the men.

Slowly, the fur trader backed closer to Bessie and Matthew, wielding his blade, hoping to keep all at bay. The boy opened his carving knife, ready to defend his mother.

Ivan moved closer to the two people he wanted to protect. He stood in front of them and whispered over his shoulder, "Bessie, will you come with me?"

"Yes. I'm ready."

Uncle William knew that even four of his men against the one big man were powerless and would be easily defeated. The Russian was not a man to be messed with. The uncle signaled to stand down, and then waved the three exiles away. "Sh Kahaadi!"

Bessie and Ivan knew what he meant. He had called them crazy and mentally unbalanced. It was a terrible insult, but they cared little about the attack on their dignity. Ivan carried their bag on his back as the trio ran for Bessie's canoe near the water's edge.

Once they had ventured out through the water about a mile toward Juneau, Bessie noticed Matthew was crying. "Don't be afraid, my son. We are safe now."

"I'm not afraid." He wiped his eyes.

"What is it?" She pulled him close as Ivan took over the paddling.

"I'll never see my treasures again." Matthew explained how he had hidden his father's wallet and special beads.

"I love you, Matthew." Bessie hugged him. "If you have hidden them as well as you say, then they will be safe, and one day you will return for them."

Matthew appeared to understand. He took hold of his mother's paddle and joined Ivan in their lifesaving voyage and their quest to find a new life.

51

April 1911
PROVINCETOWN

JENNY STARTED HER labor around midnight, but Mrs. Nickerson thought the midwife was not needed yet. At 8:00 a.m. she was finally summoned to the house. Jenny's brother fetched Grace around 9:00 a.m. By late afternoon, Charles Mendes was born, April 25, 1911. There was a beautiful sunset.

By the second month, mother and baby had grown more comfortable with each other and needed less attention.

Down the street, Grace grew bored at home by herself, so she began to take daily walks into town, in search of some purpose. She became intrigued with the many strange and interesting people who now visited the latest tourist attractions across Provincetown. The warm June air, the pier, its fishing vessels, and the sound of the train whistle to destinations unknown, taunted Grace with thoughts of adventure.

An older gentleman passed her on Commercial Street. "Is that you, Grace Ellis?"

Grace stopped and recognized Mr. Silva's father. "Hello, Mr. Silva. How's your granddaughter?"

"Granddaughter?" He scratched his chin. "Oh, you mean little Alice. She's fine. Doing just fine."

Grace had heard that her old boss's father was getting forgetful and the family was worried about him suffering from *a softening of the brain.*

"Have you heard from your father?" The old man took out his handkerchief to blow his nose.

His question took Grace by surprise. No one had mentioned her father to her in years. Understanding the man's affliction, she humored him. "No, sir. I'm afraid not."

"Well, when he returns, tell him old Mr. Silva said welcome home."

Perplexed with emotions of sadness for her loss of father and husband, and worries about her future, Grace walked home along the shoreline in solitude instead of along the crowded sidewalks. When her hand finally touched the white enamel doorknob of the back door, it seemed to calm her with a yearning for closure.

She pulled out her father's letters from the old desk and read them once more. This time, Grace felt his words summoning her to find him. Through the night, she thought of reasons why she should stay home. Was she strong and brave enough to find her father by herself? Was she fearful of finding the truth about his disappearance? Then she switched to the positive. Travel would not be an issue as far as wintery weather and she had enough money for the trip. She had connections in both New York and Seattle, convenient stops to communicate her whereabouts to loved ones, or if she felt unsafe.

Morning came with a determination to journey ahead. Grace found a small leather book to be used as a travel journal. She wrote her father's name at the top, with a question mark after it. Next, she penned a letter to her mother relating her travel plans and her goals of finding her father. A similar note was sent to Mrs. Barnes in Seattle.

Grace spent every day over the next week finalizing her travel itinerary, based on her father's letters. She did a quick sweep of the house downstairs before Jenny and her little family would move in as caretakers for the Ellis homestead while Grace was away. Up in the attic, she boxed and packed away sentimental pictures, important documents, and special pieces of furniture that belonged to the Ellis family's history. She locked the attic door and hid the key in the usual spot above the doorway. Jenny would have use of the whole downstairs.

On the coming Monday, Grace would leave for Boston on the fast ferry, as locals called it, or the S.S. *Dorothy Bradford*, owned by Cape Cod Steamship. Two suitcases stood empty and ready to be packed with a minimum of necessities and clothing. Her brown woolen suit with an above ankle A-line skirt, white blouse, and loose-fitting jacket would be her travel outfit. Paired with sturdy, short-heeled oxford shoes, and a simple felt hat decorated with a small collection of tiny feathers, these clothes would ensure her safety by bringing little to no attention to her as a solitary traveler.

A three-quarter length, double breasted, woolen coat trimmed in fur, for cooler weather, was folded at the bottom of the case. A pair of patent leather, square heeled shoes, adorned with a square shiny buckle, was nestled within the folds of the coat. They would serve to accent her afternoon tea dress just in case the occasion presented itself during her travels. Alongside two knit sweaters, two white blouses, and one extra skirt, lay Grace's special Edwardian split pantaloon skirt. She had paid no mind to the disparaging looks and comments from those around her when she'd picked up the special order from Nickerson's. She might be going into rough territory and wanted to be prepared. No hobble skirts for her. Leave those restricting clothes to the socialites.

The other case held Grace's nightgown, slippers, woolen socks, under-garment pantaloons, toiletries, lace gloves for summer, and a fur lined woolen pair for cold weather. Her last dinner was of simple fare; nothing too heavy. As she waited for the teapot to boil for a final cup of tea, she reminisced about the last year. The changes in her life were many, and at times, insurmountable. But Donald's presence was stored in her heart, next to family memories, and she felt confident.

Grace glanced around the kitchen and remembered the few days before her father had left for Alaska. She had marveled at all the supplies he knew to pack, even when not knowing what was ahead of him. One event made her smile. She could hear her mother remind him several times, "Please don't forget your long underwear; in fact, take both sets."

Her father would answer with a smile, "There's not much room in my duffels."

She would yell up the stairs, "Well, make room!"

"Long underwear," Grace whispered. She returned to the attic and found the box labeled Donald. At the very bottom was his long underwear. She held it up against her waist, a little big but they'd work. She was thankful they could be squeezed in around her packed clothes. Now she was ready.

Colorful flags waved in the sunny air as Jenny, Jonathan, and little Charles said goodbye to Grace. Buoyed by her youth and a renewed sense of life, Grace blew a kiss to the little family as the steamer left the dock.

Jenny held Jonathan's hand on the return to their new home, rent-free in trade for keeping everything shipshape for Grace.

The steamship arrived in Boston as scheduled. Grace's next stop was South Station, to catch the train to New York, then on to Sarah and Andrew's house.

As Grace stepped off the train in New York and into Grand Central Palace, the temporary terminal in use while the new Grand Central Terminal was being built, the station bustled with confusion. Signs had been mislabeled and trains rerouted, to accommodate the demolition of the old station.

Grace waived a red cap porter for help with her two large suitcases.

"Where to, Miss?"

She checked her journal. "#2 at 79th and 5th Ave."

The porter tilted his cap, "Follow me."

Grace stared through the car's window at the streets filled with horses, wagons, pedestrians, cars, and trolleys, which all seemed to move with no rhyme or reason. It didn't take long before they arrived at her destination. The driver got out, lifted the suitcases onto the sidewalk, then helped Grace from the car.

She stood in front of a huge limestone chateau. "Are you sure this is the correct address?" Stone carved heads flanked the second-floor windows.

"Yes, ma'am, #2 at 79ᵗʰ and 5ᵗʰ Ave." He then asked, "Would you like me to carry your bags to the door?"

Still a little dumbfounded at the grandeur of Andrew's home, Grace replied, "I think so. Thank you kindly."

She tilted her head back to take a better look. The parapets were decorated with gargoyles and the chimney sported a winged monster. She followed the driver up steps that had iron dolphins on either side of the railings, then through a stone archway to double-glassed doors covered with beautiful scrollwork. The door opened before she could raise her hand to ring the bell.

A tall man dressed in an Edwardian black-tailed uniform stiffly asked, "May I help you?" He looked at Grace dressed in her plain travelling suit, then at her suitcases, back to her with the air of a well-paid servant waiting for an answer.

"I'm Grace Costa. Here to see Andrew and Sarah Fletcher."

"Please come in." The man stepped aside and reached for the suitcases.

The driver waited near the car.

The beauty of the foyer stunned Grace. Out of the corner of her eye, she saw her mother burst out of two closed doors and rush past the manservant to hug her daughter. "Oh, Grace. It's so good to see you. Franklin, take care of her bags and the nice gentleman who brought her here."

"Yes, ma'am."

Andrew came flying down the grand stairway ornamented with carved seahorses all the way up to the top floor. His arms opened wide. "Grace. We've missed you. How've you been?"

The trio walked through the massive oak doors and into the front drawing room. Grace couldn't stop admiring all the paintings hung in every corner. So distracted, she walked as if in a daze, marveling at all that lay before her.

Concerned, her mother held her daughter's arm. "Are you feeling all right?"

Grace blinked her eyes. "Of course, Mother. You never mentioned any of this to me. I assumed Andrew was wealthy, but not like this." She walked away to inspect the detailed seahorse carvings on the stairway.

Andrew held Sarah's hand. "Let her explore." They followed Grace wherever she walked, like loving parents witnessing a child's wonderment. As she passed the many ornately designed rooms, then climbed the breathtaking stairway to each level, Grace would look to Andrew for permission to enter or continue, and Andrew would nod with a smile.

"Where are your paintings?" Grace asked as the trio descended to the main floor.

"In my study and Sarah's sitting room." He stopped between the second and third floors. "My Uncle Isaac favors his collection of art and believe me, they are exquisite."

Grace recognized the works of David, Gainsborough, Rembrandt, Reynolds, and Rubens among others she did not know, all displayed throughout the stately mansion.

For a moment, Grace wished she knew where the painting of her grandmother was, and who may have bought it. If the family still owned it, she would have hung it in a special place. She noticed her mother looked so happy, why mention the tragic loss of the portrait. She changed the subject. "And mother, where is my dear brother, Charles W.?"

"Off to summer camp and loving every minute of it."

Grace looked to Andrew. "Where is your Uncle Isaac?"

"I'm afraid he's taken a turn for the worst, since he asked us to move in with him. He and Aunt Mary are at the doctor's now. We try to stay positive."

"I see. They won't mind if I visit?"

"Given the size of this townhouse and their eight servants, they may not even notice whether you're home or not."

Grace felt a little more at ease.

"My uncle's ill health sometimes requires him and my aunt to take their meals in their private rooms. If it weren't for my duties here and his illness, Sarah and I could have stayed longer with you in Provincetown."

"I understand. I was fine and Jenny was wonderful to me."

Sarah turned to her daughter. "The first thing we're going to do tomorrow, is go shopping."

"I don't need anything." Grace smoothed her modest skirt and perked her blouse.

"There are a few social events that we must attend and you're coming with us." She summoned Alice, their latest employee. "Alice will help you settle in. Whatever you need or may want... just ask."

Later, in their private quarters, Andrew couldn't help but notice how happy Sarah was. "It's so nice to have Grace visiting us."

After over a year of worrying about her daughter, Sarah finally felt at ease. Finding Grace coping with Donald's death was comforting. Knowing that her daughter had purpose in her life was gratifying.

52

1910
JUNEAU

BESSIE AND MATTHEW huddled inside the entranceway of Madsen's Hotel. Ivan approached the front desk and pulled out several gold coins.

The clerk looked over Ivan's broad shoulder at the two Indians behind him. Bessie held Matthew closer.

Ivan stared at the man. "Have a problem?"

The man stared at the huge hulk standing before him then handed Ivan the key. "Up the stairs and to the right."

The rooms had changed since Bessie's last visit with Walter. The walls, paper thin and faded, showed evidence of water damage and the aftermath of violent behavior. She smelled the sheets and blankets and decided even though they had an odd scent, it was far better than sleeping outside.

It was almost dark before everyone was settled. Bessie sat stone-faced on the edge of the bed. Matthew watched people moving around below, through the window.

"You'll be safe here. Keep the door locked. I'll return tomorrow." Ivan held Bessie's shoulders and repeated, "You're safe now."

She nodded.

As soon as the sky grew into night, exhausted from their long and stressful journey, the two runaways climbed under the covers. Matthew quickly fell asleep. Bessie placed his carving knife under her pillow and then lay wide-eyed, lost in her thoughts. What was to become of them? She missed her father, mother, and especially Walter. She rolled on her side so Matthew wouldn't see her tears. She'd had no other choice but to leave her home, especially after learning that Uncle William had planned to sell them as slaves to a neighboring clan. How could he? They were family. Bessie wiped her eyes with the edge of the blanket. Ivan was so kind and protective. Thank you, Walter, for sending him to us. But now what?

The sun woke Bessie. It was a new day. Decisions must be made. She stared at the dingy ceiling. Would she have the courage to find the right path for her and her son? She had no money; their treasures lay deep in her heart and in Matthew's. Maybe Sister Elizabeth at St. Ann's Hospital could help.

Bessie heard a knock on the door and then the sound of a key in the lock. She hoped it was Ivan, but to be safe, as soon as her feet touched the cold wooden floor, she popped Matthew's knife open, ready to defend her family, if needed.

The door creaked as Ivan pushed it in. He saw Bessie in an attack position and immediately called out, "Bessie, it's me."

She relaxed and rested her hand on Matthew's uncovered foot as he lay quietly sleeping. Her heart pounded with the aftermath of adrenalin as she stared at Ivan.

He upended a pouch filled with breads, jams, and cheese onto the top of the dresser. "Did you sleep well?" A bottle of cold tea rested next to the food.

Bessie gently shook Matthew awake. The boy smelled the fresh baked bread before he opened his eyes and reached over to taste the treats. She quickly got dressed behind the screen then joined the two people in her life who now meant everything to her.

Bessie wiped her hands after a satisfying breakfast. "Ivan, I've been thinking. I want to go to St. Ann's and talk with Sister Elizabeth about returning to work."

"I will go with you." Ivan stood to gather his things. "Are you ready now?"

"Yes." She turned to Matthew. "Fetch your jacket."

As they walked through the streets of Juneau, nothing seemed to have changed since the last time Bessie had been there with Walter. They walked past where the new governor's mansion was soon to be built. Signs of racism were still evident. Bessie felt uncomfortable as she held Matthew's hand a little tighter.

Ivan waited with Matthew on the sidewalk in front of St. Ann's while Bessie went to find her friend, Sister Elizabeth. He was anxious to talk with Bessie about their future together and waited patiently, as thoughts of family filled his head and heart. Thoughts that he had harbored since they'd stepped into the canoe after their escape from Uncle William's evil.

Secretly, he always wished for a family of his own but was too stubborn in his selfish ways to seek a woman. Ivan remembered his promise to Walter. He watched Matthew carving a small stick with his knife. He favored the boy, and Bessie was very beautiful. Could they grow to love each other if they stayed together?

Bessie appeared from behind him.

"You look distressed?" Ivan stood to face her.

"There is no work here for me."

"I'm sorry."

She pulled out an envelope. "Sister Elizabeth gave me this letter stating my credentials and recommendations for anyone in need of nursing skills." She returned the envelope to her pouch.

"But where will you go?" Ivan wanted to tell her his intentions of marriage but hesitated.

The three travelers were silent on their way back to Madsen's. Matthew yawned a few times and then lagged behind as they climbed the stairs to the hotel's second floor.

"Feeling tired?" Ivan picked the boy up into his arms for the last steps. Once through the door, he laid him across the bed. The boy quickly fell asleep.

Bessie sat in the lone chair by the window with the letter in her hands.

Ivan's heart raced with a nervousness that he had never experienced before. He took a chance and whispered, "Bessie, will you come with me?"

She looked up. Before her was a bear of a man who always spoke gentle words to her and Matthew. She wanted to open her heart to her protector, but her feelings for Walter and Ivan twisted together in her head.

Ivan noticed her uncertainty but continued explaining himself. "My fur trading will be coming to an end soon. The seal population is gone and there are too many government restrictions. I have gold and supplies. Would you and Matthew join me on a journey to the outside?"

"Ivan, you are a kind man. Walter always spoke of you with such respect. You are good with Matthew and you make us laugh." Bessie looked down at the letter then took a deep breath. "I am Tlingit and always will be. My family stories are kept within me, honoring my ancestors and the beautiful land that has nourished us." She looked up to Ivan. "I fear the time has come for me to say goodbye to my homeland."

Bessie rose and stood next to Ivan. She took his hand, then kissed it. "I'm ready to go with you."

Ivan Baranov's heart leapt with joy. He returned a gentle kiss to her hand.

By noon, the trio of wanderers had left the hotel with a plan to stop and see Sister Elizabeth for one more favor before they left Juneau.

Ivan towered over Bessie outside of the hospital. "I will return by evening with my things. Please ask your friend if she could help us."

"I will. Hurry back."

Bessie and Matthew disappeared between the doors of St. Ann's Hospital.

A few influential people owed Ivan favors. He intended to take advantage of them, and quickly. His first visit was with the lawyer, Mr. Behrends. Ivan wanted him to contact the bank to withdraw his money and gold. Mr. Behrends could arrange travel money faster than Ivan could himself.

"I need National Bank notes and the rest of my gold in a strong leather satchel. Where do I sign?"

Mr. Behrends looked pensive. "Mr. Romanov, I'm not sure I can do this."

Ivan stood with a hand resting on his Bowie knife. His massive body imposed a threat for cooperation. "I'll meet you at St. Ann's in four hours. We leave on the PS *Portland* tonight." He turned and left. His message was understood by Mr. Behrends.

Next stop was the mayor's house.

After Ivan finished tying up all his loose ends, he arrived at the hospital. Bessie, Matthew, Sister Elizabeth, and Mayor Valentine were in the small chapel…waiting. Everyone knew a man and woman can travel with less curious eyes if they were married. It had to be done. Time was of the essence.

When the civil ceremony uniting Ivan and Bessie concluded, and the certificate was certified by the mayor, the newly married couple and their son enjoyed a fine dinner, compliments of St. Ann's.

Bessie watched Ivan talking with Matthew and thought she could someday see Ivan as more than a friend and savior. She knew she would never forget Walter and promised herself to leave her heart open for a second chance.

As preparations were finalized for their departure, Ivan explained his plans to Bessie. "When we arrive in Seattle, I have a connection with a furrier near First Avenue. He's looking for an investor and I'm him."

She agreed it was a good plan but still looked worried. "Where will we live? In the city?"

"My friend has a small house for us to rent while I look for property. I will build you and Matthew a grand mansion."

"How can that be, Ivan?"

Before Ivan could answer, two rough-looking men dressed in black suits delivered the travel money. Bessie stood back, next to Matthew, and watched the men struggle to carry in a leather satchel and one suitcase. The satchel was filled with gold and the suitcase full of bank notes, both an easy carry for Ivan as he took hold of his possessions. As soon as the men left, he knelt down and opened them to show Bessie the rewards of his hard work over his years in Alaska. Ivan smiled up at his new wife. "You will never have to be fearful again." He closed both bags, equaling over a quarter of a million dollars.

53

1911
NEW YORK AND SEATTLE

THE LATEST FASHIONS from Paris hung in Grace's closet. Her favorites were the Poiret tea dress and the Paquin cream satin summer coat. These extravagant gifts from her mother were worn with other new outfits to several social occasions Sarah had arranged for her daughter. She closed the cabinet's door on a whirlwind of fantasy and then latched her suitcases shut, filled with practical clothes she would need on the next leg of her journey. Grace glanced around the room before she left for the train station. Her new book, purchased at Brentano's, would have to wait to be finished until she returned to New York.

Andrew and Sarah stood waiting for their daughter by the front entrance. Andrew grabbed her luggage. "Do you have your itinerary?"

Grace smiled. "Yes, Andrew." She hugged the two most favorite and beloved people in her life.

"Once you get to Chicago, I know you'll really enjoy the train ride along the route called *The Milwaukee Road*. The Chicago Milwaukee & Puget Sound Railway boasts all new steel rail service all the way to Seattle." Andrew beamed because Grace had accepted his gift of first-class tickets.

"You shouldn't have spent so much money." She gave him one more hug. "Thank you, Andrew." Grace was looking forward to the luxury of her first-class accommodations and was grateful for his kindness.

The butler opened the massive door. "Your car has arrived, Miss Grace."

Sarah stood back, quietly whimpering. She didn't want her daughter to see her upset. She had grown anxious over the possibility of losing another loved one but moved closer for a last embrace. "God speed, my dear. I pray you find answers that finally bring peace for all of us. I see strength and a determination in you, like your father."

Inside the car, on her way to the Grand Central Palace, Grace read the information on her ticket and anticipated the latest comforts from Pullman and an experience of a lifetime on the extravagant *Olympian*.

Once on board the CM&SP train, Grace settled herself in her wood-paneled stateroom, anxious for the 2200-mile journey to begin. The porter told her they would pass through five mountain ranges and fifty-two tunnels on their way to Seattle's new Union Station. On the third and final day of travel, Grace enjoyed a special treat for herself of salmon with hollandaise sauce and plum pudding for dessert. While she waited to be served, she studied her father's letters. His last letter came from the Barnes' home in Seattle and that would be her first connection to her father.

The city of Seattle was known for rainy and foggy days and it didn't disappoint. Grace's view out the rain-splattered window was hindered as she settled in the rear of the taxi that would take her to the Barnes family, over in Queen Anne Town, near Denny Street. The car pulled up out front of a large house with three floors and decorated with two small turrets on its roofline.

Grace asked the driver to wait. She wasn't sure what to expect from these strangers and wondered if they had received her letter telling of her coming visit.

The door opened and Rebecca Barnes smiled, "Can I help you?"

"Yes. My name is Grace Costa, Walter Ellis's daughter."

"Oh, please come in. We've been expecting you. I'm Rebecca Barnes." She looked over Grace's shoulder. "If you like, you're welcome to stay in our house while you're visiting Seattle."

Relieved, Grace thanked her hostess and returned down the three stone steps to the street to pay the driver and retrieve her suitcases.

"Mother is resting, but she'll be up soon. Would you like a cup of tea?"

"That would be nice." The house smelled like fresh cookies.

"Would you care for a butter scone? My mother is famous for her sweets."

"Yes, please."

Rebecca sat across from Grace in the parlor. While they enjoyed their afternoon tea, waiting for Mrs. Barnes, Rebecca was curious. "Tell me about your train ride from Chicago. I've heard it's luxurious."

With Grace's last descriptive words of her travels, the Barnes matriarch appeared in the doorway. "Well, this must be little Gracie." She hobbled over to her stuffed chair with the aid of a cane and sat down. "We've been expecting you."

"Then you received my letter?"

"Yes, my dear." She removed her glasses. "I'll tell you what I remember about your father and my Rebecca here will try to fill in with other details."

Grace reached into her purse for her travel journal and retrieved a pencil for her notes. "I'm ready."

Mrs. Barnes settled into the tufted fireside chair while her daughter fetched tea for her mother. "If I recall correctly, it was my Rebecca who first met your father at Seattle General, while she was working as a nurse."

Grace listened intently.

Rebecca joined the conversation. "He was so nice. Seemed to really care about his family. He showed me the family portrait."

Grace remembered the day they had posed for that picture in Mr. Nickerson's Provincetown studio. Her father had wanted to take it with him, so they had two copies made.

The elder woman added. "I wasn't too pleased that my daughter invited a stranger into our house with no recommendations, but after I got to know Walter, I mean your father, I liked him quite a lot." She sipped her tea. "He helped me in the kitchen with my bakery orders.

Each day he seemed to grow healthier and stronger. Soon, he was fit and able. Luckily, my Leu found him work on the *Elder* to Alaska."

Grace underlined the name, *Elder*, in her journal. "Was there anything else that might help me find out what happened to him after he left your home?"

"I'm afraid not, but Leu will be stopping by for dinner. We can ask him then."

Leu and his new bride arrived a few minutes before dinner. Everyone immediately sat down at the table.

Mrs. Barnes looked over to her new daughter-in-law, "So nice that you could join us this evening."

Before Grace tasted her first bite, she asked Leu, "Do you recall anything about my father other than he left on May 31, 1899 on the *Elder*?"

"I'm not sure how much more I can add to what mother and Rebecca have told you, but I'm happy to say that I have some other good news." He sipped his wine.

Grace dropped her fork. "What is it?"

"I've arranged for you to see the logbook of the *Elder* from when they sailed from Seattle to Alaska."

She sat back in her chair. "Does that mean they might have my father's name listed somewhere and maybe what happened to him?"

"Well, I'm not sure. That's for you to find out."

"Thank you, Leu." Now Grace was hungry, and the food never tasted better to her.

"I'll pick you up tomorrow morning."

The Pacific Coast Steamship Company was located up the street from the docks. Leu walked Grace into the main offices. "Mr. Jacobs, this is the young woman I spoke to you about. She's looking for her father. He sailed on the *Elder* with Harriman in 1899."

"Yes. I'll be right with you." Mr. Jacobs closed a file on his desk. "Come with me."

Grace kept her gloves on as she scanned the dates from the *Elder's* older logs. May 31, 1899 finally appeared. Under the listing of crewmembers were over thirty names. At the very bottom of the list were the stokers. Her father's name, Walter Ellis, had an asterisk before his name. What does that mean, she wondered? She looked in the margins and found nothing. At the very bottom of the page, she found what she was looking for. In scripted letters, with a tiny blotch of ink at the beginning of the sentence were the words:

Stoker accident – burned, disembarked in Juneau,
June 5, 1899.

54

Present Day, Thursday - Nancy
BREWSTER, CAPE COD

IT WAS SO GOOD to see Stephen but my mind kept circling back to where I'd seen Neil Hallett. I focused back on our guest. "Where are you staying?"

"I was planning to settle in down the road at the Orleans motel."

"You're welcome to stay with us. We certainly have extra bedrooms with all the kids gone except for Danny."

"Are you sure? I don't want to put you out or anything."

"No bother. It will give us time to catch up. Are you hungry?"

"A little. I took the red eye and haven't eaten anything healthy yet."

"Go unpack and I'll call you when brunch is ready."

After we ate, we settled in for a glass of wine, at least Paul and Stephen did. I had my usual piece of dark chocolate, no wine for me.

Stephen's cell rang. "Excuse me. I need to take this." He left the room.

"Must be FBI business." Paul looked pensive. "Nancy, I'm really happy you never took Stephen's offer to join him on cases concerning lost art antiquities."

"Yeah. I'm pretty happy with what I'm doing now. Just being a grandma."

Stephen returned with a sober look on his face.

"Something wrong?"

"Not really. Just a snag in a case I've been working on."

I was curious, as usual. "Can you tell me anything?"

"Well, it involves your guy, Neil Hallett."

"My guy? I don't want anything to do with him. Nope. Never."

Paul sat up and seemed concerned. "What about Hallett?"

Stephen didn't answer Paul. Instead he said, "I can tell you this. I've been assigned to a Specialized Art Unit called the Art Crimes Team."

"I've never heard of it."

"It's everything about money laundering. Dirty money is easy to hide if you know what you're doing."

"I've always known Hallett bought and sold antiques but focused mostly on his supposed ancestor, Goody Hallett, and her connection to the pirate Sam Bellamy from 1717."

"That's right, but this time, we think he's involved as a middleman with something bigger but doesn't know it. We're hoping he can assist us."

"If I can be of any help, let me know."

Paul shot me a serious look.

Stephen sipped his wine. "If I recall, your treasure finds were pretty notorious."

"I guess so. I'm still fascinated that Bellamy was a real pirate and his ship, the *Whydah*, earned the title of, 'the only pirate ship authenticated in the world'."

Stephen smiled with confidence. "And you just happen to have some of the spoils from the wreck. Don't you?"

"I suppose you could say that. I'm pretty familiar with his legend." I fingered the 18th century necklace around my neck that I had uncovered back in my adventuring days, then glanced over to him. "Want to come with me later this afternoon to visit Casey at her gallery? I need to pick up an old painting and a sketchbook I found in an old house in Provincetown."

"I'd love to." Stephen stood to go and unpack.

Paul left for his studio as I loaded the dishwasher. I called after Stephen, "On the way, I can explain to you the 'what and how' of finding those items."

"Give me a minute to change and I'll be ready."

"Since it's not full season yet, Casey opens later, around 1:00 p.m., so take your time."

The sun glistened across the water in Pleasant Bay on our way to Chatham. I explained to Stephen why I was in the Provincetown house and how I had uncovered the outlines of two paintings above the mantle. I mentioned the sketchbook and the strange words in the journal. "What do you think the words mean?" I recited them again to him. "The pigeon's blood lies warm and deep, hidden by the woman who sleeps."

Stephen kept his eyes on the road. "I've heard of a rare ruby called the pigeon's blood, but I'd need more time to think about the other words and what they might mean."

Up on Main Street, we saw Casey coming from the rear parking lot with key in hand. She waved at us as she opened the front door.

We both gave her a hug. She was so pretty, dressed with a beachy, upscale sophistication. Very stylish, I thought.

"Hi, Mom. Great to see you, Stephen." She turned on the gallery lights, music, and her computer.

Stephen admired Paul's artwork and then turned his attention to Casey. "You look great. Haven't seen you since Brian's wedding. So, you're a gallerist now?"

"Yes, I am." She turned the sign to open and offered us some coffee.

"Would you show Stephen the old painting?"

"I'll get it."

I wasn't sure what sparked me to remember where I'd seen Neil Hallett, but it popped into my head like a light bulb flipping on. I turned to Stephen. "I know where I saw Hallett. He was the guy from the home watch company that met Ally and me in Provincetown. He showed us where the key was hidden and took off as soon as I joined Ally on the porch." I felt a twinge of concern.

Stephen chimed in with, "He probably recognized you. That's why he left so suddenly."

Was it just a coincidence or was there another motive for us meeting? There was no way Hallett knew I was going to be there. I pushed the whole idea behind the strange words from the journal.

Casey laid the Impressionistic painting next to the sketchbook.

Stephen examined it and then leafed through its pages until he saw the words 'pigeon's blood' written in the margin by the drawing of the ring. "That's interesting. And you said there were no paintings in the house with a ring like this in them?"

"Couldn't find any."

"Maybe the ring was in the artwork that hung under this Impressionist piece."

"You might be right."

Casey closed the sketchbook. "These drawings and watercolors are beautiful."

I leaned on the front table. "You know, Casey, Stephen says he's still with the FBI and now works in the Art Crimes Unit."

"Correction. The Art Crimes Team." He laughed but, as usual, wanted to be right.

Casey added, "We took a course in college about that. I was shocked at how easy it was to hide money in the art world."

She helped us take the painting and sketchbook out to the car and to say her goodbyes.

On the ride home, I wanted to know more about how dirty money becomes clean money using fine art. "Can you explain how the money thing works?"

"Someone gets a bunch of cash from drugs or other illegal activities. They need to hide it because it's off the books, so they buy several art pieces from a notable art gallery with cash then leave them on consignment at the same gallery. Now they've invested the money. In a few months or even a year, they'll return to the gallery and ask to liquidate the artwork, fast. The art sells, maybe a little higher than what they'd paid, and presto, they now have clean money in their bank."

"Interesting. With the right opinion on the appraised value of older antiquities, that would work."

"Usually, they enlist a middleman to do the buying and selling, so there's no way of tracing the money back to the original source. They never use their real names and the clean money is deposited into a fake company. Any other questions?" A call was coming in. Stephen ignored it.

I leaned back. "You know, Casey went through a random audit a year ago. The IRS was testing a new tax rule for businesses. It was brutal. The investigator was rude and accused her of hiding money because art galleries were notorious for dealing in cash."

"How did she do?"

"Well, it cost her a few thousand for accountant fees, and several sleepless nights, but they found no irregularities. She's in a tourist area where most people use cards, not cash, and she proved it."

"That's good news. Remember I mentioned the role of a middleman in these schemes?"

"Yes. What about it?"

"That's where Neil Hallett may come into play."

55

1911
SEATTLE - JUNEAU

GRACE STOOD IN FRONT of the high oak cabinet; her eyes glued to her father's name written in the logbook of the *Elder*. Burned? Disfigured? Crippled? She closed the book. She didn't want to believe that her father had been hurt. Did he suffer? Was he still alive?

Mr. Jacobs came near. "Is everything all right, Miss?"

Her hand rested on top of the leather book. Her thoughts were with her father.

"Miss? Have you found what you were looking for?" He sounded impatient. "I have another appointment within the hour."

"I'm sorry. Yes. Yes, I've found him." She turned to leave and hurried out the office doors, headed to nowhere in particular. Images of her father burned and suffering filled her head. She bumped into a gentleman entering the Steamship's office. "Forgive me."

Grace ran down the street, trying to distance herself from the horrific news. Out of breath, she leaned against the outside of a tall stone building. After a few minutes, she felt her composure returning. She wanted to go back to ask Mr. Jacobs more questions, but remembered he had another appointment. She dabbed her eyes with a handkerchief and hailed a car to return to the Barnes house. Finding her way to Juneau was more important right now.

That evening, after dinner, Grace related what she had discovered about her father. Leu stopped by as she was finishing her story. It took all of her courage to retell it again without tears, but Leu needed to hear. "I have to go to Juneau. Leu, can you find passage for me?"

"Of course. Tomorrow, it will be my first task of the day."

"You're so kind."

"You should start packing right now."

Grace stood to get her purse and then handed him money for her fare. "If you need more, I have it."

By mid-morning the next day, Leu appeared with her tickets. "The first passage out is tonight at 9:00 p.m. It will be on the Pacific Coast Steamship's Totem Pole Route aboard the *Spokane*."

"The Totem Pole Route?" Grace wasn't pleased. "I'm not here as a tourist."

"I'm well aware of that, but it's the safest and the earliest passage, especially if you're travelling alone. I hear Juneau is still a little uncivilized."

"I'll be ready."

"Good. I would advise you to go and do some extra shopping this afternoon."

"For what?"

"You'll need a sealskin raincoat and warmer boots."

"I'll get right on it."

"One more thing you'll need." Leu carefully pulled from his vest pocket a small royal blue 1908 Colt. "I bought this for my wife, but I want you to carry it while you're travelling."

"Oh, I can't take this. Although I do know a few things about firearms. My late husband gave me lessons. I still can't accept this."

"Return it, hopefully unused, when you're back in Seattle in a few weeks. Remember, it's a round trip ticket."

Reluctantly, Grace agreed to carry the gun with her and was hopeful that it would be out of her hands by the end of June.

Leu stood to leave. "I'll be back at 7:30 tonight to take you to the steamer."

After a quick shopping trip, Grace copied Harry Cavanaugh's return address from Juneau into her travel notebook. She wrapped the 4.5-

inch Colt in a handkerchief and pushed it next to the journal in her purse. Her father's letters were hidden among her clothes in the suitcase.

The *Spokane* steamer left Seattle on time the night of June 14, 1911. Leu had secured a stateroom for Grace on the Hurricane Deck with a private bath and two brass bedsteads for $250 plus meals.

Grace retired soon after boarding. While the passengers slept, the ship crossed Puget Sound's calm waters and headed for Victoria, B.C. The next morning, breakfast tasted good. According to the ship's schedule, passengers would sightsee today. Grace stayed on board and reread the itinerary in her stateroom.

She decided to begin a daily routine of strolling across the Hurricane, Upper, and Saloon decks, then retrace her steps back to the observation area. She sometimes followed this route three times a day. Usually during the first two strolls, her head battled anxious thoughts about what could have happened to her father and what her future held, living by herself. She continually yearned for closure and hope. By the third stroll of the day, she was oftentimes able to finally concentrate on the scenery around her.

The ship's course took them northwest, through channels, gulfs, bays, and straits, then finally into the Inside Passage. The scenery was beautiful, but Grace still preferred to stay in her cabin. It was not that she minded travelling by herself, but everywhere she looked, couples held hands, snuggled in each other's arms, and looked so in love. Their affections were only grim reminders of what she had lost.

One morning, Grace decided to go up on deck for some sea air. She stood alone on the observation deck as she listened to the loudspeaker announce that they were passing Graham's Reach with its thousand waterfalls. Later, Grace saw mile-high mountains flanking each side of the ship. As the steamer passed through Chatham Sound and along the shores of Tsimpsean Peninsula, the *Spokane* crossed the boundary line into southeastern Alaska. Over the next days, scheduled stops were planned in Metlakatla, Ketchikan, Sitka, Funtor Bay, Skagway, and the famous White Pass, ending with an opportunity to climb the Muir Glacier.

Grace was surprised to see how many people wanted to participate in the glacier climb, leaving the ship almost empty. By early afternoon, fellow travelers slowly drifted back on board the steamer. Grace sat on one of the deck chairs next to a well-dressed woman in her sixties.

"Hello." The woman straightened a blanket across her legs.

Grace returned a smile.

"I've noticed that you're travelling alone. So am I." The woman moved her head to look at another beautiful image of the landscape that lay before them.

For some reason, Grace felt comfortable with this woman. "I'm searching for my father."

"That's very admirable of you. Might I ask you as to the whereabouts of your husband?"

"He's dead."

"Oh, I'm so sorry. Actually, I'm a widow also."

Grace began to engage in small talk. "Not interested in climbing a glacier?"

"Not for me. But I do enjoy travelling." She extended her hand. "I'm Maggie MacIntyre, from Boston."

"Nice to meet you. Grace Costa from Cape Cod."

Maggie settled back in her chair and closed her eyes. "Such a coincidence. We're both from New England."

Grace put her feet up on the lift of the chair and closed her eyes, inhaling the fresh air.

On the next day, the scheduled stop was at the Treadwell Gold Mines. Grace preferred to stay on board again. She looked for her new friend on deck and found her in the same chair near the observation deck. "Good morning, Maggie," she said, sitting next to her.

"Good morning to you, Grace. I trust you slept well?"

"Actually, yes." She noticed that Maggie's legs were covered again. The temperature had risen to the low sixties and the sun was hot.

"So, tell me about your father. This task of finding him seems insurmountable for such a young woman as yourself."

Grace liked Maggie, so she explained her story and how she was on a journey to bring closure to her family, and that she was going to leave the ship in Juneau, and not return with the others to Seattle.

"I will repeat. Admirable."

A young woman pushing an empty wheelchair came closer and stopped in front of them. "Shall we have lunch?"

"Yes, Kathleen." Maggie struggled to stand. Only with the aid of Kathleen was she able to transfer from the deck chair to her wheelchair. Once seated, she introduced Grace. "This is Grace Costa. A very brave woman from New England."

"Nice to meet you, Grace."

As they turned to leave, she heard Maggie ask her nurse, "Did you enjoy the Treadwell Mine?"

Grace never had a chance to say goodbye to Maggie. Tomorrow the *Spokane* would land in Juneau, and those who wanted to visit the city could do so, as long as they were back in time before the ship left harbor. Grace had purchased a round trip ticket and leaving early was frowned upon. She would wait until everyone had left and the gangplank was empty, so no one would notice her carrying her suitcases off the ship.

56

THE LONG DAYLIGHT hours still bothered Harry Cavanaugh, even though he had lived in Alaska for almost twelve years. He was proud that he could afford heavy drapes for each bedroom to block out the long days of summer light. Business was good and he enjoyed his role as partner in the R.C.E. Pacific Mining Company. Max Reynolds was a silent partner and spent most of his time back home in Idaho.

His new residence on Chicken Ridge was prestigious in local eyes, even down to an office on the first floor, built to his personal specifications. The windows that spanned one side of his headquarters highlighted the majestic mountains that surrounded his custom-built house. Harry preferred to be inside with paperwork, rather than outside in the mines, where he worked when he'd first arrived in Alaska. He was fully aware of the toll that a solitary life, hard labor, and sparse living conditions had on a miner. The entrepreneur, at thirty years old, never regretted his past choices, but now yearned for a family.

Today, he grew tired of the sound of the carpenter's hammers reverberating throughout the house. On his way out for some fresh air, he turned and straightened a favorite photo of his. Three men, all smiles with arms wrapped around each other, posed in front of a steamship's smokestack. The words, *The Beginning of R.C.E Mining Co. – S.S. Newport – March 1899*, were written below the image.

Mount Juneau towered over the city, which seemed as busy as other cities to Grace, just not as many high buildings. Signs advertising food, souvenirs, adventure cruises, and clothing shops all beckoned the newest visitor to come and explore for a price.

Grace carried her two suitcases down Front Street, then checked into the Occidental Hotel. The three-story wooden structure was a welcome sight in a strange area. The lobby was comfortable and her room adequate. Her first night, she made sure her door was locked and pushed a chair against the doorknob and tucked her blue Colt under her pillow. In the morning, she would try to find Harry Cavanaugh.

The sun rose early at 3:52 a.m. and by 9:00 a.m. Grace found the desk clerk distributing mail to the row of wooden boxes behind the front desk.

Grace tapped the bell. "Excuse me?"

He turned. "Yes. May I help you?"

She took out Harry's letter and pointed to the printed words on the envelope: R.C.E Mining Company, Juneau, Alaska. "Do you know of this company?'

The clerk scratched his head. "I'm new here, but I believe I've heard of it." He opened a large ledger book. "Let me see." He flipped back several pages and then ran his finger down the list. "Yes, here it is. A Mr. Reynolds stayed here late last year. He registered as R.C.E. from Idaho."

Grace took out her travel book and pencil.

"If I remember correctly, he hired our car to take him to Mr. Cavanaugh's house. We thought it was strange when he could have walked. It's only a few minutes away."

"Would you write down directions for me?"

"Of course. It may take a while. I have other duties."

"Thank you, I'll be back within the hour." She scooped her book and pencil into her hands and ran up the stairs to her room.

True to her words, it wasn't long before Grace stood in front of the hotel desk, dressed in her brown travel suit. She pocketed the scrap of paper the clerk handed to her containing the requested directions. "Thank you again."

The sun warmed her back as she walked by the post office, Jorgensen's Hardware, and St. Ann's Hospital on her way to Chicken Ridge. Grace took note of the words written in the margin on the paper; *large glass windows and turret on left side of house.*

Up a slight incline, she saw a good-sized house with a turret on its left side. She followed the path that led to its front entrance. A sizeable wooden door greeted her and to the right, painted on the bottom window, was R.C.E. Mining Company - Est. 1899.

She turned the small iron handle to ring the bell, then waited. Hammers in the background echoed in an erratic rhythm. Finally, the door opened and a distinguished gentleman stood before her. "May I help you?" He was well dressed, clean-shaven and pleasant looking.

"I have come to see Harry Cavanaugh. Is he at home?"

"Why, yes, he is. In fact, you're talking to him." He smiled, then moved aside to welcome her in.

That was easy, she thought, and entered into a beautifully paneled foyer.

Harry smiled a little broader. "Shall we step into my office? It's a little noisy out here."

Grace followed him. The large expanse of windows caught her attention first and then she introduced herself. "My name is Grace Ellis Costa."

"Grace Costa!" He reached over his desk to shake her hand. "It's so good to finally meet you. Please, sit down."

As she turned to sit, Grace noticed the many pictures on the wall. "May I?"

"Of course, the pleasure is all mine." He watched her walk the edges of his office admiring his mix of oils, copper plate engravings, photos of various mines, equipment, and a few portraits. "Let me show you one that I'm especially fond of." He led her toward the doorway.

It didn't take long before she recognized her father standing with a younger Harry and another gentleman. Her fingertip touched her father's face. She tried to hold her tears back.

Harry offered his handkerchief.

"Forgive me. Seeing my father in an image different than the few portraits at home brought me closer to my sadness."

"I understand." He paused before speaking again. "What can I do for you, Grace?"

"I want to know what happened to my father and why he never returned home to us."

"As I said in my letter to you and your family, I would also like to know. Please sit down."

Grace pulled out the last letters from her father and spread them out on his desk.

Harry leaned in. "The only fact I'm sure of was that he never met us in Seattle."

Grace pointed to each letter as she explained her travels. "After leaving Provincetown, I tried to retrace my father's journey. I went to Boston, New York, and Seattle, that's where I found the log of the *Elder* steamship. It listed my father as a stoker. Sadly, I also discovered there was an accident on board that caused him to leave the *Elder* in Juneau." She shook her head. "He seemed so determined to continue on to Alaska. Why didn't he come home?"

Harry examined Walter's letter from Seattle.

Grace leaned over the desk. "That's all I know. I was hoping you could fill in anything else about him."

He sat back into his chair. "When your father didn't show up that morning, we were worried, but Max and I had to continue on to Dyea. We kept hoping to meet Walter somewhere along our journeys. Finally, we settled in Juneau a few years ago. I'm not sure if I can be of any more assistance."

Grace saw he had a kind face and looked straight into his eyes. She hoped he could help her. "Mr. Cavanaugh."

"Please call me Harry."

"Harry. It seems that I know more about my father's path than you do. I now realize the last time you were in contact with him was on the steamer S.S. *Newport*, in 1899. But I also know in my heart there must be something you can help me with."

He swiveled his chair to the windows in thought. "I assume that if there was an accident on the ship, and they couldn't treat him on board, they must have taken him to a hospital."

"That's what I thought."

"The only hospital at that time was St. Ann's."

"Of course, I passed it today on my walk to your residence."

"Would you like me to accompany you to St. Ann's?"

"That would be very kind of you."

"Will tomorrow be soon enough?"

Grace stood. "Yes. I'm staying at the Occidental." She turned to leave.

In seconds, Harry moved to block her path. "Grace. I assume you eat? May I escort you to dinner in town?"

Without hesitation, she answered, "Certainly." That was so nice of him, she thought, his company would be pleasant after travelling alone for so long.

Three hours later, Harry walked into the hotel's lobby at 5:00 p.m.; Grace was waiting for him.

Dressed in her extra skirt and a fresh blouse, she carried a blue woolen shawl for the evening air.

Harry opened the door. "We could go to the Grand Restaurant across the street, but my personal favorite is the Owl Café, a few doors down. Chef Lindig serves everything *First Class* according to the newspaper, and they're right."

Grace laughed. "Show me the way."

After a delicious meal, the two sat and talked some more. Harry explained how his business achieved such success. "In the beginning, we formed our partnership on the steamship, the three of us named our company the R.C.E. Pacific. The letters stood for Reynolds, Cavanaugh, and Ellis. Less than six months later, Max and I struck gold. Then we sold our claim. With the high profits, we were able to purchase other miner's claims, then sell them. Money rolled in and doubled with each new investment."

Grace was quiet, thinking of the wealth her father never had a chance to enjoy. "And my father never showed up the next morning when you left Seattle?"

"That's correct. I wrote a letter in case he did appear later in the day and dropped it at the steamship's office, but that was the last time either of us saw your father."

"What time will you come by to pick me up tomorrow?" Grace dabbed her lips.

"I hope to leave early and get to you at 10:00 a.m."

"Will I be able to see the hospital records?"

"I hope so. The hospital is run by the Sisters of St. Ann. It's an excellent facility with a school for the children and a nursing program. I know of a Sister Elizabeth who can pull a few strings, if we encounter any problems. The hospital is our best hope for finding anything about your father after he left the steamship."

"God willing." Grace's eyes grew weary. It had been a long day and she was tired. "I think it's best that I return to my hotel. I hope I can sleep."

"I'll look forward to our adventure tomorrow." Harry rose to pull Grace's chair out.

What a gentleman, she thought. It had been almost two years since Donald's death and Harry's attention was welcome.

57

Present Day, Wednesday – Friday
CAPE COD

AFTER GETTING DROPPED off by the tow truck, Neil Hallett made some coffee and unrolled the house plans across a table in the kitchen. The drawings were simple, showing each floor, living spaces, and their dimensions. At the bottom of the last page, under the architect's name, was another business listing. A company called Compass Rose from Provincetown had built the fireplace hearths in the house.

For part of the next day on Wednesday, stuck at home waiting for his car to be repaired, he busied himself online Googling the name of the builder, but found nothing out of the ordinary. He did think it was odd, though, that the mason, E. Nesbit, was listed, so he searched for that name next. On the second page of listings was a small article from the *Codder* newspaper, dated five years ago, about *Mysterious Cape Cod Houses*. Within the highlighted text was Compass Rose, Provincetown.

The article stated:

> *In the late 1700s, Compass Rose Company of Provincetown,*
> *owned by E. Nesbit, was known for leaving a secret hole or*
> *opening for their clients in their fireplace to hide valuables.*

Hallett read and reread the words to make sure he understood. He had one more day to wait for his car to be fixed before he could return to the house. Not sure what he was looking for, he only knew that now it involved the fireplace.

Friday arrived and the car was ready. Hallett Ubered over to the repair shop, then drove home to collect his things, including the house plans, before he left for Provincetown.

His cell rang. It was Dominic DeSorta. Hallett wondered if he'd found something more his speed to buy. "What's up?"

"I've got some more work for you, if you're interested. I need you to deliver a briefcase to a gallery in Boston. Can you help me out?"

Sounded easy to Hallett. "Sure. When and where?"

"Right now."

"Now?" He glanced back at the house plans and then over to the clock. It was already 1:30 p.m.

"Yeah. Now."

"How much?"

"Three hundred."

"Okay. Where am I going?" His car was fixed so there should be no problem.

"Near Newbury Street. And wear a sport coat.

"You're kidding? Right?"

"Nope. When you get back on Cape, call me and I'll meet you at the Watering Hole in Hyannis with your money. If you do good, I've got more jobs."

58

Friday - Nancy
BREWSTER, CAPE COD

THE IDEA THAT NEIL Hallett might be involved in crime again bothered me. One would think after years in prison, a person would not want to go back there. Hallett must think he's invincible – or he's just dumb.

Stephen came into my office after lunch "Busy?"

"A little." I spun my desk chair around to face him.

"Remember I mentioned Hallett may be involved with some money laundering?"

"Go on."

"I was going to pay him a visit. Not sure if he's even at home. Want to see where he lives?"

My curiosity started to rise. "Maybe I would. But I'll stay in the car."

"Okay. In fact, I was going to ask you to stay in the car."

"When are you leaving for his house?"

"Around 2:30 p.m."

EASTHAM

Neil Hallett's place was on one of those desolate beach roads where seasonal houses are spaced far away from each other. We drove down the sandy road until we saw the quarter board across his garage that read: Goody Hallett.

"I guess we're here."

Stephen turned off the ignition. "Don't see any cars. Looks like no one's home."

The driveway was all sand with big ruts where cars drove down, using the same tracks. "I'll still wait here."

I watched Stephen knock on the front door then walk around the back. I waited until he appeared again and signaled for me to come out. I could see no one was home, so I felt a bit more confident and exited.

The sun warmed my head, but as soon as I joined Stephen in the rear of the house, the shade cooled me. I felt a shiver move down my back but ignored it, still wanting to look inside. In the daylight, the windows only reflected my face and the landscape behind me. I leaned in closer and shielded my eyes from the glare. There was nothing spectacular; the small beach house was cluttered and messy with only the barest of furnishings. I walked to another side and peered in to see a large desk with a computer. No big deal. I slid over to the next window and was surprised to see a painting above the fireplace on the opposite side of the room. As the light shifted, I moved back and forth between windows, trying to get a better view of the art piece.

Stephen came alongside of me. "Nothing in the garage of interest to me. Did you find anything exciting?"

I stepped back. "Take a look. Can you make out that painting?"

He positioned himself like I did near the glass. "It looks old. The woman has black hair... dressed in red... with a black shawl." He moved so I could get closer.

I really focused this time. Now that Stephen had planted the idea of a woman in my head, I could almost see her. My eyes moved down to her folded hands and that's when I saw a big red ruby ring.

I stepped back and looked to Stephen. "She's got a huge ring on her finger."

"Let me take another look." He moved in front of me.

I waited patiently for my turn. "Boy, would I like to get inside."

Stephen walked over to the back door. I heard him jiggle the lock.

"You can't do that. Can you?" By the time I got next to him, he had the door opened.

"There's no security or cameras. Come on."

I followed with a little trepidation and a lot of curiosity.

Once inside, I noticed a hook by the back door that held a sweatshirt. I whispered, "Stephen," and showed him a sleeve with the security company's name on it. So, it was Hallett on the porch in Provincetown. He lifted a thumb as if to say that he knew what I was talking about. I felt like a little kid up in my parent's bedroom looking for whatever interesting I could find. I glanced over to Stephen. "Why are we whispering if no one's here?"

He started to laugh.

Shelves and boxes that held 18th century memorabilia were scattered about the kitchen. Stephen wandered into the front room to Hallett's computer.

I joined him and instantly froze in my tracks when the painting came into full sight. I wasn't positive, but I could see elements in the painting taken right from the sketchbook. I check-marked each detail from the sketchbook in my head as I moved closer. The figure in the painting was dressed in 18th century clothes. She had dark flowing hair and posed next to a small table. I stood inches from the canvas. The ring on her hands was definitely a pigeon's blood ruby. Coincidence? Maybe. Then I noticed a blue and white teacup and saucer on a table next to the woman. That image stunned me again. It was not among the sketches but had the same pattern of the old teapot on my shelf at home; the one that matched the china from the treasure I'd dug up. This woman could be Maria Hallett! An Abigail E signed the portrait. How is she connected to Abigail E? Is the Maria Ellis from the journal in the attic... the same as Maria Hallett? The painting is hanging in a Hallett's house.

Stephen came over to me. "Everything okay?"

"It's the same images as in the sketchbook." I quickly took a picture of it then guessed at its measurements.

He headed over to the back door. "We better get out of here."

I kept staring at the painting. "Stephen, I think this woman is...."

"Nancy!"

244   BARBARA EPPICH STRUNA

"I'm coming. I'm coming." As I left the front room office, I noticed a closed door to my left. Do I dare open it? Always curious about what's behind a closed door, I pulled my sleeve down over my hand and turned the doorknob. It was Hallett's bedroom. My jaw dropped once more. From across the room, I came face to face with a grainy image of me pinned to a corkboard. My voice cracked. "Stephen."

"What's the matter?"

"Look."

He gave a low whistle and stepped closer for a better look.

I couldn't move. All I could see was a big 'X' across my face.

"He's got pictures of your house, Paul getting the mail, and you in the garden. Must have been taken from a distance and then blown up, pretty blurry but recognizable."

"It's creepy." Now I wanted to get out of the house as fast as I could. I put the coincidences of the painting on the back burner.

Stephen closed the bedroom door, wiped the doorknob and followed me out. He relocked Hallett's back door and repeated his cleaning of the outside door.

On our way home, I looked over to Stephen. "Don't tell Paul what we found. He worries too much."

"You sure?"

"Yes, we do have a great security system installed." I started to reason myself out of my uncomfortable zone. I knew I had ruffled a few feathers over the years of finding lost treasures, but I couldn't live my life in hiding. "You know," I said, "we're right on Main Street, kind of an open book to whoever passes by."

Stephen agreed with a nod.

"I'll be careful."

We were in Brewster within ten minutes. I wasn't hungry for dinner; my stomach felt queasy. Danny was off to a friend's house, so I asked Paul to order a pizza. The three of us sat at the kitchen table, comparing the drawings in the sketchbook against the image on my phone and the teapot to the cup and saucer in the portrait. There was no doubt; the sketches and china pattern were good matches. We all sat there in deep thought.

I broke the silence. "What do we do now?"

Stephen spoke up. "Well, you're not going to do anything."

I knew Paul was already concerned that we went to Hallett's house. He eased up at Stephen's words of caution to me.

Both noticed that I was upset. I'm not a fan of being told what to do or say and he knew it, as well as Paul did. I have a good right arm and know all about self-defense, if I need it. I got up to clean the dishes and put away the leftover pizza. The kitchen was quiet. You could cut the tension with a knife. "Well, tomorrow I'm going to Provincetown to return the Impressionist painting, sketchbook, and journal. Do I need anyone's approval?"

Paul gave me a hug. "Just drive safely."

Stephen added, "Can I go with you? I'd love to see the old house."

"Of course."

59

Present Day
PROVINCETOWN

Friday Evening

It was dark when Neil Hallett finally pulled onto his road. Traffic in Boston had been brutal and he was tired. In between cars cutting in front of him and honking horns, he thought about the house plans. He ripped off the sport coat and threw it in the closet. An ice-cold beer waited for him as he counted his money for completing the delivery, all in small bills. He unrolled the plans once more across the table. He would return to Provincetown tomorrow.

Saturday 9:45 a.m. Provincetown

In Hallett's eyes, the old Provincetown house looked cleaner than before. A lot more of the boxes were gone. He entered the kitchen and put the key on the table, then ran his hand across the bricks of the chimney. He then positioned a chair in front of the hearth, sat down, and stared straight ahead. Squinting, he looked for an odd brick or a different color mortar. He used a broom to swipe the dirt and soot from the stone's surface as the morning sun filled the kitchen with light. He sat down again. Dust particles floated all over the room. Hallett maintained his stare as he ate a deli sandwich he had picked up on his drive out. As he was finishing the last bite, the sun's rays began to recede across the bricks and cast a long shadow to the left of the hearth, revealing a small circle stamped into a brick. He stood and wet the brick with a finger covered in saliva. A feint compass rose emblem appeared. His blood pressure soared. He had to sit down. He thought, now what?

Tools? Why didn't he bring his tools? He crumpled up the bag that had held his sandwich, threw it in the corner, then left for the hardware store on Commercial Street as rain clouds moved in over his head.

60

Present Day, Saturday Morning - Nancy
BREWSTER

PAUL WAS UP EARLY and had made coffee for all of us. It smelled delicious as we bantered back and forth about the weather. "Stephen, would you mind carrying the painting to the car?"

"No problem." He picked it up by the frame. I put the journal into my purse and filled my water bottle for the ride. Paul grabbed the sketchbook and walked us out to the car.

As Stephen and I entered Orleans, I assured him that it was okay to return a day earlier to Provincetown. "We should be all right. I made a call to Ally and told her we were going to return the art."

Stephen stared at his phone.

I looked over at him. "Something important?"

"No. When I first arrived, I stopped by the police station to let Tony know I was in town on business. They always like to be aware of who's in their territory. I was hoping he had some information for me." He put his phone down. "I guess not yet."

"Can you tell me about it?"

"All I can tell you is we're looking for a local guy, like Hallett, who can connect us to the top, the one who's funneling the dirty money."

We stopped for coffee in Truro and got back in the car just as a few drops of rain hit the windshield.

Stephen looked over to me. "I was thinking about that sentence from the journal."

"What about it?" I was eager to hear his thoughts on its meaning.

"One of the reasons I wanted to come with you today was because I think the answer to the riddle is in that house."

"I do, too. I mean, everything circles back to Provincetown. So, what's warm and deep?"

At 10:10 a.m., we pulled onto the driveway by the old house. Still lost in my thoughts, I said aloud, "And who sleeps? Does that mean they're dead?"

I handed Stephen the extra blanket we always carry in the car for emergencies to keep the rain off the painting. I ran ahead to retrieve the key. It was gone. I tried the closed door. It opened. Strange, I thought. Ally and I have been so careful about locking up.

Stephen came behind me and leaned the painting against the inside wall.

I mentioned to Stephen, "That was weird; the door was unlocked." After I took the sketchbook from him, I placed it on the kitchen table, the only flat surface available in the house. "Do you smell baloney?"

He quickly glanced around the rooms downstairs, ending in the kitchen. "Smells like a deli." He picked up a crumpled brown bag on top of a half-filled black garbage bag in the corner. "Here's the smell."

"Wonder who was in here?" I was uneasy, knowing someone besides me or Ally had been in the empty house. "I'm going to give Ally a call." I saw Stephen looking up the stairs and gave him a thumb's up that it was okay for him to see what was in the attic. "Hi, Ally. I'm here at the old house with Stephen and we think someone else has been in here besides us."

She answered my question. "We had the water turned off last week, maybe it was the plumber."

"And the door was unlocked. Should we be worried?" I happened to spot the house key on the table. "Never mind, I found the key. The plumber must have forgot to lock the door. I'll replace it in the rock."

"Okay. Thanks."

"We won't stay long. Are you meeting the art appraiser here next week?"

"Yes. Want to join me?"

"Thanks, I would like that. Call me later."

I went upstairs and found Stephen looking at the stored paintings.

"Nice, aren't they?"

"What treasures. You said there were no known relatives to the estate alive?"

"That's right, and if they can't find any, all the proceeds will be donated to a halfway house in Hyannis for Mothers and Children and to a home for homeless."

"I hope the profits are big. Those are good causes."

"I guess we should be going."

61

HALLETT DROVE DOWN the street to return to the old house with a brand-new chisel, screwdriver, and hammer. As he got closer, he noticed a car in the yard. "Shit. Who's that?" He parked across the street, down two houses, and waited.

The steady rain blurred the windshield as he tapped his fingers on the steering wheel. He checked his phone, pulled the packaging off his purchases and threw the tools into his backpack. Finally, he saw a man, and a woman who resembled Nancy Caldwell, get into the parked car. He hit the steering wheel. "Christ! I hope it's not her. That woman makes my blood boil."

After the car drove away and was out of sight, Hallett grabbed his backpack and cautiously walked down the street toward the old house, turning his head back and forth to see if the car might return.

He tried the doorknob. It was locked. Instinctively, he checked the fake rock and found the key inside it. After opening the door, he replaced the key in the rock, as usual, and went straight to the kitchen. Hallett took off his wet jacket, dumped the tools onto the table, rolled his sleeves up, and set his sights on what was hidden behind the stamped brick. Moments later, he heard something that sounded like a car door. He grabbed the hammer and hid against an inside wall of the parlor.

A woman's voice called out, "I'll only be a minute." The key clicked in the lock.

As Hallett watched the woman enter the kitchen, he gripped the handle of the hammer tighter. He only saw the back of her as she paused by the table and picked up the chisel, then cocked her head. It was Caldwell. In an instant, he lunged toward her. She turned. His hammer missed its mark and crashed against the table.

She backed up against the hearth. "Hallett!"

He raised his weapon high in an attack position. "Well, we finally meet again."

One hand fell to her side, the other went in front of her face. "Please don't."

"Look, Caldwell, I've thought about killing you every day. You ruined my life." He inched a little closer to her.

Unbeknownst to Hallett, Caldwell's hand brushed against the handle of an iron poker. She seized it and held it in the air to hit him. Hallett dodged her swing, which gave her enough time to run past him and out the door.

62

Present Day, Saturday - Nancy
PROVINCETOWN

MY HEART WAS BEATING so fast that I thought it would burst. I ran down the slippery, rain-soaked porch steps toward the car, not caring if I fell or not. Stephen scrambled to get out and met me halfway on the grass. "What's wrong?"

"Hallett's in there." I could feel Stephen's hands tighten on my shoulders as adrenaline shook my body. "He tried to kill me."

Stephen looked up toward the house and then to me. "Stay here." He reached behind his jacket and pulled out his gun.

"Wait. You can't go in their alone," I pleaded. "We've got to call 911."

"Get in the car. Did you find your phone?" He ushered me closer to the car.

"No. I couldn't find it." I followed Stephen's orders and got inside the car.

He tossed me his phone. "Lock the doors and hold off on the 911 call."

Through the foggy window, I watched him position himself to the side of the open door and then disappear into the house. Five long minutes went by. No sign of Stephen. I found some inner strength and pulled a large flashlight from under the seat. It felt heavy enough for a possible weapon. I opened the car door, pulled my hood up and walked to the side of the house to peer into a window. My attacker sat at the kitchen table with his hands cuffed behind his back. Stephen stood in front of him with his gun pointed directly at Hallett's head. My shoulders dropped in relief.

I went around front and walked inside.

Hallett glared at me.

Stephen acknowledged my presence and then threw a question at Hallett. "Why are you here?"

Hallett kept his mouth shut.

"What's with the tools? You looking for something?"

More silence.

"You know, I've got no place to go and neither does my friend." He glanced at me. "I suppose we could call the police. But that wouldn't sit well with your police record. Would it?"

With that bit of information, Hallett seemed as if he might talk. "You don't have anything on me. It's her word against mine." He sneered at me.

"Maybe so, but I believe her, and I know a lot of crimes I could nail you with…unless you want to co-operate?"

"What do you mean?"

I wondered what Stephen was doing. I really thought we should have already called the police. The guy almost killed me. I was about to speak up when he explained his reasons.

"We know you've been doing some jobs for Dominic DeSalvo."

That got Hallett's attention.

"We also know that DeSalvo is working for a company called Pacific Antiques."

"So what? I didn't do anything wrong."

"Nancy, can I have my phone."

I handed it to him, still curious about his intentions.

With one hand and one eye on Hallett, he pulled up a picture and showed it to him. "Is this you?"

"Yeah. So what?"

Stephen extended his arm so that I could view the image on his screen. The picture showed Hallett carrying a black briefcase in front of an office building. The next image was of Hallett inside and halfway up the stairs. On another, the letters on the glass door were blown up and read Pacific Antiques. Then he showed him more pictures.

"That doesn't prove anything."

"I've got a list of charges I will personally level against you if you don't do the FBI a favor."

"I'm listening."

I stood in the kitchen trying to make sense of what Stephen was telling the guy. After I realized that I was in no more danger from Hallett, my thoughts drifted to why he was in the house in the first place, especially in the kitchen with a hammer and chisel.

Hallett grudgingly agreed to Stephen's plan. "Can I leave now?"

Stephen leaned into his face. "I know where you live and so do the police. Don't try anything funny. We'll find you."

He began to squirm in the chair.

"We know DeSalvo is going to call you tomorrow to deliver another package. You'll be wearing a wire. Here are some questions we want you to ask him." Stephen threw a piece of paper across the table. "I'll see you tomorrow at your house."

The cuffs came off. Hallett picked up his instructions and dashed out the front door, leaving his tools and backpack behind.

"Can you trust him not to run?"

"If the FBI has him in their sights, he can't hide."

I leaned against the table to look at the bricks. "Why did he bring a chisel?" I answered my own question. "Breaking bricks."

63

Present Day, Saturday Evening/ Sunday Morning - Nancy
BREWSTER - PROVINCETOWN

BEDTIME CAME EARLY for me. Stephen retired to the solace of his room to work via his phone and computer, preparing for whatever was going down in Boston tomorrow with Neil Hallett. Paul watched the news.

I'm never one for keeping secrets between Paul and me, but I couldn't bring myself to tell him about the unsettling events that happened over the last few days. I did tell him that Hallett was in the Provincetown house when I returned to find my missing phone and that Stephen had convinced Hallett to co-operate in catching the money launderer. I went to sleep listening to the rain on the skylight, hoping for a good sleep, knowing it would be easier to explain things in the morning.

Sunday
Stephen was up and gone on Sunday by 7:30. I joined Paul for coffee. As I was about to speak, my cell rang.

"Good morning, Ally."

"Hi, Nancy. Can you do me a favor?"

"Sure." I sipped my coffee.

"The art appraiser asked if he could meet us today instead of Monday, but I'm really swamped. Will you go?"

I hesitated for a few seconds. I was just there yesterday and was not very fond of the old house since my near-death experience at the hands of Hallett. I acquiesced. "I don't mind. Maybe I can get Paul to come with me for the ride." I looked over at him reading the *Times*. He nodded without question. "What time, and what's the guy's name?"

"It's not until 4:00. Is that okay?"

"Sure. We'll catch some dinner at Napi's."

The rain had stopped for a few hours, but more was forecast for later that afternoon. I spent the day going through papers at my desk. I looked at the old, faded letter that I had brought home from Juneau and studied the W. E. on the leather wallet. It could very well stand for Walter Ellis, one of the names from the old house. The address started with a 'P' in front of C.C. MASS. It's too co-incidental, I thought. But isn't life filled with chance meetings and choices of going one way over the planned path?

By 2:45 I was ready and waiting for Paul to take Mac out before we left. We were on the road by 2:55 so we could be in Provincetown by 4:00 p.m. to meet with Mr. Glass.

As we approached Orleans center, Paul asked, "Did you have a good adventure with Stephen yesterday? It must have been pretty cool to see him in action again with Hallett."

I hesitated. "I guess so. I knew I was safe, but Hallett still gives me the creeps." I put my hand on Paul's leg. He mimicked my gesture with his hand. "I neglected to tell you one thing about yesterday."

"Uh huh."

"It was raining pretty hard in Provincetown when we left the old house. I was trying to brush some of the wetness off my coat and hair when I realized I didn't have my phone. We turned around and headed back. I just wanted to run in quick to look for it. I didn't know Hallett was inside. Stephen stayed in the car."

"And?" Paul gripped the steering wheel.

"Hallett tried to hit me with a hammer. I dodged his swing and ran out to get Stephen." I paused for an angry reaction.

Paul was silent.

"I'm sorry to keep that from you. I knew you'd be angry. I don't blame you. But..."

He interrupted me, "Nancy, I am upset, but I'm also aware of your penchant for getting involved with elements of danger. I'm trying to accept you always going that extra step to figure a mystery out. I can't lock you up. So, I'm resigned to loving you every minute just the way you are, no matter what. I will not try to change you."

I almost cried. "I love you so much and I promise I will be more vigilant wherever I go."

We drove several more miles in quiet thought, our hands entwined.

By the time we reached Truro, Paul asked, "Do you have your phone?"

I felt it nestled in my jacket pocket. "Yes. From now on, I'm going to zipper the pocket shut so it doesn't fall out between the seats, like it did yesterday. And I'll make sure the sound is on, except when in meetings."

We arrived in Provincetown at 3:45, a little early. I found the fake rock and opened the wooden door.

"This house is beautiful," Paul whispered. "It must have been filled with treasures. How old did you say it was?"

"Around 1780. Maybe we should bring the paintings down into the parlor."

He slowly walked through the downstairs empty rooms. "Okay. I'll help you."

We climbed the stairs. "Let me show you where I found the skeleton key to the attic."

Paul followed me into the bedroom where I pointed to the small opening above the doorjamb.

"You're pretty smart."

By the time we had carried half of the art downstairs, about a dozen pieces, Mr. Glass was knocking on the front door.

I greeted the appraiser. "Come on in." I shook his hand. "Hi, I'm Nancy Caldwell. Ally asked me to meet you in her place. This is my husband, Paul Caldwell.

Mr. Glass shook Paul's hand. "Nice to meet you." He leaned his umbrella against the foyer wall.

I spread my arms out. "Here they are. Paul and I will bring the rest down to you."

As we walked back up the stairs, Mr. Glass adjusted his horn-rimmed spectacles and went right to work. I watched him twist his handlebar mustache as he inspected the paintings. I stopped midway up the stairs, tapped Paul on his arm, and pointed to the look alike Salvador Dali. He also noticed the similarity and turned around to smile at me. No words were needed; we understood each other and who the art dealer resembled.

After all the artwork was brought down, we waited in the kitchen. Paul looked over the tools and picked up the hammer. "Was this Hallett's?"

I whispered, so we wouldn't disturb our visitor. "Yes, they all belong to him. I guess after Stephen un-cuffed him, he ran out and forgot them."

"What was he doing with them, besides hitting you?" Paul held the hammer close to his face and mumbled, "I'd like to smack him with this."

I deserved that comment.

Paul replaced the *weapon* on the table and moved closer to the hearth. "So, you think Hallett saw something on these stones?"

"I've been thinking that exact thought." I ran my hand over the bricks.

After only a short time, Mr. Glass stuck his head around the corner. "I'm done. Based on a conservative estimate, I believe the paintings are worth around $100,000. We know they are old and very lovely, but they're unknown artists. I need to do more research and get back to you with my final appraisal."

"Fine. Thank you again, Mr. Glass. I'll relay your opinion to Ally." We shook hands then he was gone.

As I closed the door, the rain came down in torrents. "Paul, I really want to get my hands on those tools and investigate the bricks more, but..." I checked my phone. "...according to the weather channel, this isn't going to stop anytime soon, in fact, it's supposed to get worse."

Paul looked out the front window. "Agreed. I know we planned to get dinner. Maybe we should just go home."

I locked the door but decided to bring the key with me. I didn't trust anyone anymore.

64

1911
JUNEAU

HARRY AND GRACE waited in the hallway for a meeting with Sister Elizabeth. The sounds and smells of a sterile environment made Grace uneasy. She knew it was a place for healing and hope, but she'd prefer to be anyplace else.

Inside her office, the sister's black habit was slightly off-putting to Grace, but she and Harry followed through with their intention of finding answers.

The sister's face looked distant as she greeted them. "How can I help you?"

"I'm looking for my father, Walter Ellis."

Sister Elizabeth's face softened. She looked down at her desk. "I remember Walter." Her eyes focused on Grace. "He came to us back in 1899. He had third degree burns over his right side and a badly damaged right eye. We were not able to save his use of that eye."

Grace put her hand over her mouth in shock.

"My dear, are you feeling well enough for me to continue?"

Harry reached for Grace's hand. It was a bold gesture on his part, but Grace accepted it. She needed something to ground her. "Please go on."

"Walter stayed with us for over five months. He had no money to support himself, and two duffle bags filled with, I assume, his clothes."

"What happened to him?"

"He had nowhere to live. Fortunately, a young Indian nurse was compassionate. She offered a small cabin near her family's home for him to live in. The day he was discharged, we gave him money for supplies. A small stipend that would help him survive, at least through the coming winter in the remote territory that he was entering. He was guided to Auke Bay, twenty miles from here."

"Is he still living there?" Grace's heart beat faster with hope. She sat on the edge of her chair. "Is he alive?"

Sister Elizabeth wasn't sure she should say anymore. The woman before her looked so pale. She spoke with care. "I'm afraid not."

Grace leaned back in her seat; her face expressionless. She shed no tears. In her heart she knew he was gone. The sister's words brought closure, but she needed more.

Harry sat stone-faced.

Sister Elizabeth looked concerned for the young woman. "May I offer you a cup of tea?"

"Yes, please." Grace summoned more courage. "Can you tell me more?"

"I saw Walter about five years after his discharge. He visited the hospital for a memorial for one of our sisters who had died. Bessie, his wife, was Sister Marie's friend."

"Wife?" Grace couldn't believe her father had married someone else. How could he do that to her mother? Her face reddened in anger.

"He married the Indian nurse. They had a child together."

"A child?"

"A little boy, Matthew. He was around two years at the time of their visit."

Harry listened quietly.

Grace tried to speak but her thoughts twisted in her head. Her father was a good and decent man; he must have had good reasons for his behavior. She loved him. She stared at the steam from the hot tea drifting into the air. Her face now appeared unreadable.

Sister Elizabeth looked to Harry. "Should I go on?"

After several seconds, Grace seemed to awaken from her numbing trance of hearing devastating news that toyed with her emotions. She looked straight at the sister. With determination, she said, "I've come a long way to find my father. I want to know every detail."

Harry was impressed. He had never met a woman with such courage, guts enough to seek the truth, no matter how much it hurt.

Sister Elizabeth explained how Walter had died in 1910, and about Ivan. She talked of Ivan and Bessie's last day in Juneau, before they left for the outside.

"Does that mean I have another brother?" She cocked her head in more thought.

"Yes, it seems so."

Grace looked distant again, trying to decide how to deal with the sister's words.

"Wait." The sister shuffled through a few drawers in her desk until she found something. "I remember receiving a holiday card from Bessie. Would you like to know where they are now?"

Grace hesitated.

Harry looked interested.

Grace finally pulled her travel journal out. "May I see the return address?" As she wrote down First Avenue, Seattle, she commented on the letter writer, "Very nice handwriting." She pushed the letter back across the desk. "A few more questions, please?"

"Of course."

"What was Bessie's last name before she married my father? And how may I reach her family?"

"Her name was Bessie Wright." Sister Elizabeth looked to Harry. "Mr. Cavanaugh, I'm sure you can help Grace with your connections to locate Bessie's family, if she wants to look further?"

Grace turned to Harry. "Harry. Can you help me?"

"Yes."

As they left the hospital, she asked, "So… where is Auke Bay?"

That same afternoon, Harry returned to the Occidental Hotel, after making arrangements for travel, and summoned Grace down to the lobby. "We leave tomorrow morning by canoe, at 7:00 a.m., for Auke Bay and Tee Harbor."

Grace had a lot to process that night. She lay in bed thinking of what was going to happen the following day. She prayed to be strong enough to face whatever was thrown at her. She rolled over to look at the clothes she would wear. Laid out on the chair were her split pantaloon skirt, blouse, woolen jacket, and seal raincoat. Her all-weather boots were lined up on the floor and her socks stored in each boot. The blue 1908 Colt was under her pillow, ready to be packed into her shoulder purse for the journey.

Grace had sailed with her father, but never in a canoe. Their guide was kind and professional. She felt safe as she sat between him and Harry. The snow-capped mountains that surrounded them as the canoe glided across the waters were exquisite. Several hours went by before the canoe swerved to the rocky beach and was pulled to shore.

Grace listened as Harry conversed in Tlingit with the guide, who agreed to lead them to the Big Dipper house. Harry followed with Grace behind him, offering his hand whenever she needed it. She was pleased that she had chosen the right footwear for the climb up the incline. They passed a burned-out area near the remains of an old totem pole but kept walking.

A trail of smoke in the sky pinpointed the location of the long house. They walked closer.

An elderly woman came to the door and watched the trio approach. The guide asked her in Tlingit if anyone remembered a Walter Ellis. The old woman looked at him and then glanced over to Grace and Harry. Grace stood closer to Harry with her hand on her purse.

The woman took a few steps toward the two white people. "What do you want with Walter Ellis?"

Grace was surprised she could speak English. "He was my father."

"Come."

No one spoke as they followed her into a side woods by the house and up a slope of grasses. They stopped at a small wooden house. Grace thought it was not big enough for a family, with only one room. Seconds later, she realized that it represented a house for the dead.

The woman pointed to a slab of wood in an upright position on the side of the house. The name Walter Ellis was carved across it with the words, *Dead 1910.*

Grace fell to her knees. Tears flooded her face. She had finally found her father.

The Tlingit woman stepped behind the crying woman and placed a hand on her shoulders.

As Grace cried, Harry looked into the tiny window. Two urns, with mementoes in front of each, were on the floor toward the back wall. One had carved letters: Thomas of Tee Harbor and the other William something, the last name was smudged.

The woman quietly turned around to walk back to the long house. She waved them to follow. Harry helped Grace up and held her against his body as they walked behind the woman.

Florence Johnson offered her visitors tea. They all sat at the table. Grace held her head in sorrow.

The Tlingit woman put her hand on Grace's shoulder for a second time. "I liked Walter. My husband did not. I'm sorry for my William's actions."

Even in her grief, Grace was curious. "What do you mean?"

"William did not like your father, nor any white man."

"I understand."

"Since William has been gone, the Raven family has been at peace." She moved over to a small chest and withdrew a photo.

Grace immediately recognized her father as he posed with a Tlingit woman and a Tlingit boy of maybe three years old. He had light hair.

The woman touched the face of Bessie. "I miss my niece. She was very kind."

Walter's daughter stared at her father in the picture; he looked older and a little sad. It was strange to see the black patch over his eye. His right side was somewhat slumped with his shoulder forward.

Florence looked again at the photo and whispered, "Walter was kind to me. I miss all of them. I do not miss William's meanness."

Their guide stood in the doorway, signaling it was time to leave or they would have to stay the night.

Harry stood next to Grace. "We must go."

Florence held Grace's hand and slipped the photo of Walter and his Tlingit family onto the grieving woman's palm. "You take this." Grace hugged her. "Thank you."

As the canoe slipped into the distance, Grace never took her eyes off the picture. Feeling some closure, she knew her journey was still not over.

65

IT WAS A FEW MINUTES before 9:30 p.m., and dusk was finally settling upon Juneau after eighteen hours of daylight. Harry lingered in the lobby with Grace, wanting to stay longer with her.

She yawned a few times. "Thank you, Harry, for being there for me through all of my wanderings."

"It's been an honor." He took her hand. "May I call on you for lunch? I'm assuming you'll sleep in later than usual. I know I will be a little lazy tomorrow morning."

"That would be nice. Thank you again." She climbed the stairs to her room.

Harry watched until she disappeared from view. With mixed feelings about his intentions toward this brave woman, he left in search of a nightcap.

He chose the Imperial Billiards and Bar. It was a place miners and locals would frequent, and occasionally the higher-ups in Juneau. After ordering his drink, Harry turned to look for any familiar faces.

He noticed a well-dressed gentleman leave a table after finishing a card game. "Mayor Valentine. How are you?"

The mayor acknowledged Harry and sidled up to the bar next to him. "How's your construction going on over in Chicken Ridge?"

"Almost finished." Harry turned to stare at his drink. "Have you ever had any dealings with an Ivan Baranov?"

"Why do you ask?"

"It's for a friend of mine. A lady friend."

"Oh, I see. Well, he left for the outside sometime last year. He was a very successful trapper. I think he was off to Seattle. Planned on joining up with someone to open up a fancy fur shop."

"Is he a good man? You know, honest, upstanding?"

"I would have to truthfully answer a resounding yes."

"That's good to hear." That was all Harry needed to know. "I appreciate your words." He paid for his drink, said goodbye, and then left. Harry had an idea that might bring a solid end to Grace's search for her father, and maybe a satisfying one at that.

At noon the next day, Harry entered the lobby of the hotel. Grace was sitting in a chair waiting for him.

She stood to greet him. "Sleep well?"

"Yes, I did, in fact." He held Grace's elbow as they walked to the Owl Café.

As they ate lunch, Harry explained his plan for Grace to finish her quest.

She liked what she heard.

He added, "And I'll go with you."

"Are you sure? It's a long journey to Seattle, and costly."

"I'm well aware of my finances and time commitments. Not to worry."

"Then it's a deal." Grace held her hand out to Harry.

He returned a handshake with a slight squeeze and a lingering glance. Grace blushed and smiled at the same time. That afternoon, two separate cabins were booked on the S.S. *Jefferson* steamship to Seattle. They would leave on June 24 and not travel along the slow Totem Pole Route.

On June 24, the steamship cut its way through the Pacific Ocean. Harry and Grace talked, walked, and talked more as they strolled each deck three times a day. He told her about when he had first met Walter and everything he could remember about him.

Grace told Harry about her life in Provincetown. They laughed that she grew up near the water and he grew up on a farm. On the second day of travel, Grace broke down as she retold the circumstances surrounding Donald's death. Harry held her and just listened.

During breakfast, lunch and dinner, they talked about what made them happy and their dreams and hopes.

Within a week of sail, they arrived in Seattle.

Harry hailed a car. "First Avenue, please."

Minutes later, they turned onto a street that was lined with businesses. "Driver, would you please slow down? We're looking for a particular storefront. I think it's a furrier."

"Oh, you mean Jones & Baranov?"

Grace and Harry looked at each other and said in unison, "Yes!"

The driver stopped the car in front of the shop. Elegant fur stoles were draped in the large windows next to a beautiful full-length coat trimmed in beaver. "That must be it." Harry leaned into the front of the car. "Would you mind waiting with our luggage?"

The driver tipped his hat.

Inside the showroom, a few ladies were milling about the luxurious furs. A petite woman came from behind them. "May I help you?"

Grace turned to face her. "Yes, I'm looking for an Ivan Baranov."

Ivan heard his name from the back room. He hesitated, wondering who would be asking for him; it was unusual for someone to request him personally. He saw the young couple and thought they seemed to be all right, maybe a newly married couple. He decided to greet them.

Grace was taken aback by Ivan's sheer stature. He towered over Harry. His hair was shoulder length but well groomed. He sported a mustache and goatee and he appeared handsome in a rugged manner.

His voice boomed. "I'm Ivan Baranov. Who's inquiring?"

Harry took a step back in awe of the man before him.

Grace regained her composure and replied, "I'm Grace Costa. My father was Walter Ellis."

Harry was impressed with Grace's fearlessness.

Ivan stared at the young woman before him. Images of his friend Walter materialized in his head. He paused, and then, with utmost respect, extended his hand to Grace. Next, he greeted Harry. "Mr. Costa."

She quickly added, "Oh, he's not my husband. I'm a widow."

"I'm Harry Cavanaugh from Juneau, Alaska."

And with that Ivan relaxed. "It's a pleasure to meet both of you. Won't you please step into my office?"

They followed him through the backroom and into another private room. Ivan's desk was filled with papers. "Please excuse the chaos. I wasn't expecting visitors."

Harry and Grace sat in front of the oak desk. To the side was a family portrait. A beautiful dark-haired woman was seated in an ornately carved chair. Ivan stood behind her and a fair-haired boy held the woman's hand.

She knew at first glance it was Bessie and Matthew. She had studied the photo that Florence had given her every day since they'd left Juneau. She pointed to the portrait. "I recognize Bessie and Matthew." Grace explained how they had traveled to Auke Bay and met Florence. She showed Ivan the old photo. "I wanted to find my brother and meet Bessie."

Ivan was quiet. "Did you happen to come across a man near Auke Bay and the Big Dipper longhouse called William?"

"Yes, we did."

Ivan grimaced. "I hope he did you no harm."

"His wife, Florence, apologized for her husband's prior behavior and informed us that the Raven clan was at peace since his death."

"I'm pleased to hear that news."

"Would I be able to meet with Bessie and Matthew?"

The big man leaned back in his chair. "They're visiting me today but they are not here."

"When will they return?"

"They always go to Pioneer Place. Why don't you go and meet them there?"

Grace looked over to Harry who was listening intently. "Would you mind if we went? The car is waiting. I'm sure he would drive us there."

"Of course. We should go. Thank you, Ivan. You've been very generous with your information." Harry pulled Grace's chair away from the desk as she stood up. Harry turned around to Ivan. "How will we know where to find them?"

Ivan laughed and bellowed, "You'll have no trouble finding the two loves of my life."

66

1911
SEATTLE

THE DRIVER, KNOWING exactly where Pioneer Place was located, drove down First Avenue to Yesler Way. In the middle of an intersection of several roads, a small patch of green grass lay ahead of them. On one end was the largest totem either of the passengers had ever seen. The magnificent carved pole rose to over 45 feet in height. A wrought iron fence enclosed the little park. At the other end was an iron pergola with a glassed roof and bathrooms below that provided shelter and relief for cable car passengers. It was as grand as the totem.

Grace recognized Bessie and Matthew from the picture on Ivan's desk and the family photo from Florence. The two stood alone near the totem, apart from the others congregating under the pergola.

Grace signaled the driver, "Stop here." Harry was right behind her as she exited the car.

As she stepped onto the street, she called out, "Bessie?"

The woman turned. She held her son's hand but said nothing.

"Bessie Baranova?"

"What do you want?"

The boy stared at Grace and Harry. "Mother, who's that?"

Grace walked closer. "Please don't fear me. I only want to talk with you."

Cautious, Bessie answered, "About what?"

"I'm Grace Costa. My father was Walter Ellis."

Bessie's face turned pale. She squeezed Matthew's hand and started to retreat toward the pergola.

Grace pleaded, "Please don't turn away from me. I just want to know what happened to my father...and meet my brother." She smiled at Matthew.

Bessie looked deep into Grace's eyes and could see Walter reflecting back at her. She couldn't move. She gently bit her bottom lip in hesitation, having known this day would eventually come and force her to meet with Walter's past.

Matthew pulled on his mother's hand and whispered, "Is that the girl in that old family picture?"

"Yes, Matthew."

Bessie took a deep breath and stood tall. It was time.

Grace attempted to ease her unannounced presence with a simple distraction of making a connection. She stepped closer to the iron fencing and gazed at the totem. "It's beautiful, isn't it?"

Bessie slowly moved next to the young woman. Matthew stood on the other side of her.

All three focused on the intricate carvings and colors.

Bessie pointed to a figure halfway up the totem. "It honors a woman of the Tlingit Clan of the Raven Moiety, Chief-of-all-women."

"How proud you must be." Grace held onto the iron bars and tilted her head back to view the top figures and symbols.

Matthew interrupted. "The white people stole it from us."

"Hush, Matthew." Bessie scolded him. "Please excuse my son, sometimes he speaks without thinking."

Grace leaned down to the boy. "I would love to hear why you think they stole it. Maybe your mother could explain also."

Bessie pointed higher up the pole. "In the summer of 1899, business folks from Seattle went on a vacation to Alaska. They found a deserted village at Fort Tongass and wanted a souvenir to remember how the gold rush helped settle Seattle. They cut down this Tlingit totem and took it home."

"That doesn't sound as if they stole it."

"We were at our summer camp and intended to return. If they knew about our culture, they would have known that the village was not deserted."

"That's terrible. I'm so sorry." She touched Bessie's shoulder.

Matthew piped up, "See, they stole it."

"Why is it called Chief-of-All-Women?"

"The totem belonged to the Kinninook family, a Tlingit clan of the Raven Moiety. It was carved in 1790 to honor a Tlingit woman who drowned in the Nass River while traveling to visit her sick sister."

Grace shook her head. "Bessie, I would love to talk more." She caught Harry's eye.

He returned a smile. "Maybe we should return to Ivan's shop?"

Bessie hesitated again.

Harry suggested, "Would you care to ride in our car?"

Matthew held onto the fence and leaned back to get his mother's attention. "Can we go with them? Please, Mother?"

Bessie agreed.

Over tea in Ivan's office, Grace discovered why her father had fallen in love with the young Indian nurse. She was kind, funny, and absolutely beautiful, in a mysterious way.

Bessie explained how sick Walter was when she'd first met him and how, as he got better, he felt certain his return to Provincetown would be a terrible decision. She dabbed her eyes. "I want you to know he believed there would not be enough work for a cripple back home. He felt he could not be a good provider for his family." She touched Grace's hands. "He loved all of you but could not see any path home that would be good."

Throughout the afternoon, time and tears passed between two women who grieved over the same man, a father to one and a loving husband to the other.

Eventually, Ivan interrupted, "We need to close the shop and go home."

Bessie was apologetic to her new friend. "I wish you could stay with us, but the home we live in now, before our other house is finished, is very small."

"Not to worry." Grace added, "Harry has made arrangements for us at the Olympic Hotel. In fact, it overlooks Pioneer Place."

"Then please come for dinner tomorrow evening?"

"We would be delighted."

Grace left Ivan's office and joined the two men as they talked business in the main sales room. Matthew whittled at a small desk in the corner. She walked over to the boy and pointed to an image of a raven resting on a piece of driftwood. "This one is very nice."

Matthew beamed. "You can have it."

She picked it up. "Thank you, Matthew." She kissed him on his blonde hair.

Matthew glanced up at Grace. "Are you really my sister?"

"Yes, I am."

"I'm glad." He returned to his carving, then looked up again. "You're real pretty."

"Thank you, Matthew. I look forward to talking more with you tomorrow over dinner."

Harry went outside and hailed another car to take them back to their hotel.

Alone in her hotel room, Grace studied Matthew's carving. What a treasure, she thought, the boy was so talented, and he seemed very smart. She smiled and remembered Charles W. at the same age as Matthew. The stolen Tlingit totem stared back at her through the window of her hotel room. She wondered what she could give Matthew in exchange for his gift.

She shed her clothes, slipped into her nightgown and then climbed into bed. Restless at first, images of her father with his patched eye and slumped body circled her thoughts, along with her mother, Sarah, and the day he'd left them. The Provincetown house appeared in her mind along with the lost portrait of her grandmother. She straightened her covers, rolled over and her eyes flipped open with an idea. The teacup and saucer could be her gift! She was sure Bessie would like it and Matthew may someday, when he grows up, cherish this family heirloom from his father's family. As soon as she arrived back in Provincetown, she would send it to the boy.

Grace finally felt at ease. Her journey was almost at its end. After Seattle, she would travel back to New York before going home. She felt grateful for finding answers and wanted her mother to be strong enough to understand the reasons for all the changes in the family's life. She hoped Sarah's happiness with Andrew would soften her words.

And what about herself? Her own future? Was there a chance Harry would be in it? Her spirits lifted with the thought of Mr. Harry Cavanaugh by her side as she fell asleep.

In the morning, Grace ordered room service. While she waited, she composed a letter to Matthew. He would have it in his hand by dinnertime.

Dear Brother Matthew,

Your father, Walter Ellis, was a good and just man. I know he loved you as much as he did us. Before he left for Alaska, he told me a family story.

"Once upon a time, a beautiful lady fell in love with a pirate. She was your great-great-great-great-great-great-grandmother, Maria Hallett Ellis..."

67

Present Day, Late Sunday Afternoon
CAPE COD

THE RAIN STOPPED in Boston by early afternoon. Neil Hallett was almost to the bridge and considered himself lucky, even though it was still raining on the Cape. He thought he did a pretty good job today and did everything he was supposed to do. As soon as the FBI had heard what they wanted, they'd moved in. Hallett felt good not to be the one in cuffs. Once outside, by the police van, he was told to leave. The Fed who had convinced him to become a stooge had said he'd see him again in a few days.

Too tired to return all the way to Provincetown, he lit up a cigar and drove straight to his second favorite place on the Cape, The Beachcomber at Cahoon Hollow Beach, in Wellfleet. He knew it wasn't open for the season yet, but he didn't care. He popped open the glove compartment revealing two nip bottles; just enough to celebrate his near escape from the law and the chance of possibly uncovering the find of a lifetime, tomorrow, at the old house.

No other cars were parked in front of the Beachcomber, as he'd expected. Who would visit the beach in a rainstorm? Hallett parked near the split rail fencing that edged the twenty-foot cliff. Another cigar was lit then a mini bottle opened. He cracked the front windows and puffed with pleasure at the thought of chiseling away at the mortar around the brick in the Provincetown house. His hand reached for the seat release so he could lean back. Another puff. He thought he heard a low rumbling. He sat up, then within seconds, the rumbling grew louder as the parking lot split apart beneath his car.

Hallett fumbled to release his seat belt, but it wouldn't budge. He held onto the wheel, wide-eyed, as the car quickly sank then slowly slid down the dune that collapsed around and on top of his car. Hallett tried to reach for his phone on the passenger seat but felt a stinging pain in his upper body. As the sand hissed with a deafening finality, it buried the car and sprayed itself across its interior. He couldn't breathe. Tears rolled down his cheeks as he grabbed his chest and realized that he was not going to get out of this one. The pain near his heart increased and then his eyes closed.

The cigar fell from his lips and rolled into the sand. The rushing mounds of granular rock and minerals, along with pebbles, stones, and dried dune grasses eventually slowed their assault to a trickle, until there was silence.

68

Present Day, Sunday Evening - Nancy
PROVINCETOWN

THE RAIN BEAT AGAINST the outside of the car as we drove home to Brewster. We had to slow down as the fast-paced wipers flew back and forth across the windshield.

When we finally reached Eastham, the rain stopped a little and released the tension in the car. "Want to go back tomorrow and do some chiseling?"

Paul turned on the defroster. "Sure. I'll go with you. You probably should ask Ally if it's okay."

"You're right. I'll call her when we get home."

"I'll bring my tools; in case we need a repair."

We both laughed.

Once in my pajamas, I settled on the couch with Paul. "Ally said no worries. It's okay to go back in the house."

Around 10:30 p.m., I headed to bed and got a text from Stephen. *Stuck in Boston. Call you tomorrow.*

Curled up under the covers, I couldn't sleep. The mystery sentence repeated in my head. I began to have a conversation with myself. *The pigeon's blood,* that's the ruby ring, and *lies warm and deep,* that means… it's buried someplace warm… inside the fireplace? Neil Hallett had somehow figured out the ring was hidden there because he had a chisel with him. But which brick?

69

Monday Morning
CAHOON HOLLOW BEACH, WELLFLEET

AT SIX O'CLOCK IN THE morning, the next day, a lone figure walked his dog along the coast near Cahoon Hollow Beach. Remnants of the prior rain-filled days were scattered across the shoreline. His dog stopped every few feet to sniff the carcasses of dead birds, along with new smells that had been washed up or uncovered from the storm.

The walker was impatient. "All right, one more sniff."

The dog pulled his owner to the bottom of the cliff beneath the Beachcomber.

The man glanced up. "Oh my God." He stepped back to get a better view of the collapsed dune.

The dog continued digging.

"What do you got there, boy?" He watched his dog slowly uncover the bumper of a car with a Massachusetts license plate. He punched in 911.

70

Monday - Nancy
BREWSTER

MONDAY STARTED WITH sunshine, a welcome sight after several days of rain. Paul and I decided to return to the old house after lunch. By mid-morning, I was at my desk when Casey called.

"Mom. I've got some information."

"What?"

"I decided to deep dive into the internet to look for the Abigail Baranova from the letter that was sent to you, which got lost under your desk, until you spilled your coffee and found it."

"Go on." I grabbed a pen, ready to write down anything new. The very letter was sitting to the left on my desk. I picked it up.

"When I Googled Abigail Baranova, I learned that she's a photographer in Rhode Island. On Wikipedia, her father is listed as Matthew Ellis Baranov, a well-known sculptor in New England. Then I checked the different last names and discovered that Russian surnames change with gender. Baranov is male and Baranova is female."

"That's interesting. Wait! Did you say Ellis?"

"That's right, it's his middle name. He's famous all over the world for his nature sculptures, particularly featuring the Pacific Coast. What was in her letter again?"

I pulled it out of the envelope and read the beginning over the phone.

Dear Ms. Caldwell,

I'm writing to you because my father, Matthew Baranov, recently passed away. Whatever extra information we knew of my ancestors went with him. We have only stories but no facts. We do have a teacup and saucer, (see enclosed picture,) and a fantasy story about its history involving a supposed relative and the New England pirate Sam Bellamy from 1717. My father would tell us this tale when I was small, along with stories from his childhood in Juneau. He was a Tlingit. My father's legal name was Matthew Ellis Baranov. I've started a family tree at Ancestry.com but could only go back to 1910.

I held my breath. "Casey, I read the letter a few times before but never connected the middle name or probably never noticed it. I've been in the Ellis house in Provincetown all this time. I wonder if Baranov is connected to the same Ellis family?"

"Maybe."

"Of course, that's a popular name here in New England and on Cape." I could hear some talking in the background through the phone.

"Gotta' go. Call you later, Mom."

"Thanks. Love you."

My brain started whirling. I looked up Matthew Ellis Baranov online. Casey was right, he was a sculptor born in December 1902 in Juneau, Alaska. Then I signed onto Ancestry.com and dug deeper through the censuses. I was so engrossed with what I was finding that I didn't hear Paul behind me, asking about lunch.

"Nancy, want to eat lunch now?" he repeated.

"In a minute. You won't believe what I've found in the 1920 Seattle census."

"What?"

"That Matthew from the letter you pulled out from under my desk was listed in the census with an Ivan Baranov as his father, and a Bessie Ellis, his mother. He was 18 years old in 1920."

Paul leaned closer to the computer screen. "Anything else about Bessie Ellis? Could she be connected to the Ellis family from the old house?"

"I don't know. There's not much about Bessie, as expected for a woman during the early years of record keeping."

"And Walter Ellis?"

"To my surprise, there were two Walter Ellis's that fit into my search. One was listed in the 1890 Barnstable Cape Cod Census with a Sarah as wife, and Grace as daughter. Then in the 1910 Barnstable Cape Cod census, Sarah and Grace were listed with another child, Charles W., but no Walter."

Paul started to leave. I heard his stomach rumble with hunger.

"Wait, it gets more interesting. The second Walter Ellis was listed in the 1910 Alaska census with Bessie as wife, and Matthew Ellis as their son, age eight."

"You think they're the same Bessie and Matthew from Seattle in 1920, but with a new husband?"

"I think so, the dates and ages would be correct."

"So, Walter had two families."

"I believe so." I began to write the details on a clean sheet of paper. "It seems that Walter left his family on Cape Cod for some reason that we'll never know sometime between 1890 and 1910, moved to Alaska, and married again. If Bessie and Matthew are listed in the 1920 Seattle census with Ivan Baranov as father, then Walter must have died."

As we walked into the kitchen for lunch, my cell rang. It was Stephen.

"Nancy?"

"Hi, Stephen. Coming back to the Cape today?"

"Not yet. I'm still in Boston, tying up loose ends."

"Too bad. Paul and I are heading back to Provincetown. We'd wait for you if you were on your way. I also found some interesting facts about the people who lived in that old house."

"Nancy, are you sitting down?"

"Yes?"

"I got a message that our 'middleman', Neil Hallett, is dead."

"What?"

"A dog walker found his car out at Cahoon Hollow Beach buried under a collapsed dune. He was in it."

"Oh my God. I know I hated the guy, but what an awful way to die."

"Pretty gruesome. An autopsy will give us more information."

"Keep me posted." I was stunned, but not too sad. After all, he was not my favorite person, and I knew he felt the same way about me. Karma was a bitch, especially if you're on its wrong side, which I suspected Hallett was.

As we were about to leave, a police car pulled into the driveway. I watched our friend and Ally's husband, Tony, get out and walk toward the deck.

Close friends, I still greeted him with a formal greeting I like to use out of respect for his position. "Detective Anthony Gomes, how've you been?"

Tony repeated his formal salutation for me. "Fine, Ms. Nancy Caldwell."

We stood in the foyer.

Paul joined us and extended his hand. "Hi, Tony, good to see you. What's up?"

Tony stood with one hand on his belt and the other on his gun. "Do you have a minute to talk?"

"Of course."

We went into the kitchen and sat at the table. "A dune collapsed last night out at Cahoon Hallow Beach. As you know, we've had a lot of rain and the ground can only hold so much before it gives way."

"You found Neil Hallett in his car, right?" I didn't mean to interrupt, but I felt comfortable enough to casually talk.

Paul looked over to me. "How do you know?"

"Stephen just called me from Boston, a few minutes ago."

Tony looked straight at me. "You mean Stephen Boudreaux?"

"Yes."

Tony continued, "The Wellfleet police dug the car out, found him and his ID, then ran the license plate. After searching his house with the Eastham police, they discovered some disturbing evidence...it concerns you." He held his stare on me.

I remained quiet.

Tony added, "When we got the call in Brewster, and I heard your name, I offered to come and talk with you. I know it doesn't matter now, because he's dead, but were you aware that he had photos of you and Paul on a wall in his house?"

"I knew about the pictures."

Paul looked disturbed. "What do you mean? You knew about it?"

Tony took out a small notebook.

I started to explain. "The other day, Stephen and I went to Hallett's house. He wanted to question him. No one was home. I stayed in the car while he looked around. Before I knew it, Stephen had the door open and we were inside. That's when I saw those pictures."

Tony looked serious. "That's breaking and entering."

"I know, but I was with Stephen and he's FBI."

Tony's eyes narrowed. "I'll keep that news to myself. Has Hallett ever threatened you?"

"No, not since before he was sent to prison."

Paul was now visibly angry. "And you didn't tell me?"

"I tried to explain but for some reason, always held back. I guess I was worried about your reaction."

"Oh, for Christ's sake." Paul stood to get a glass of water.

I felt guilty and knew I had made a mistake. "I'm sorry, Paul."

Tony closed his notebook and stood to leave. "Well, it's over now. The threat is gone." His tone softened. "If I can be of any more help to you, please call me."

I followed him back into the foyer. "Tony, wait. If the police find any information in reference to this old house in Provincetown," I wrote the address on a paper, "please let me know."

"What does the Provincetown house have to do with Hallett?"

"It's the house Ally and I were cleaning out. I think it might be connected with him." I opened the door. "Just a hunch."

"I'll see what I can do."

"Oh…I almost forgot. I have one more thing, kind of an odd request."

Tony smiled and politely listened.

"When I first met Hallett, and then throughout his trial, I knew he had no living relatives, so, if and when they liquidate his belongings, there's a painting in his house that I would be interested in buying."

"You're an unusual lady, Nancy Caldwell. I'll keep you posted."

"Thanks."

Paul was in the kitchen staring out the windows.

I reached to hold his hand. "Please don't be mad at me. As you can see, nothing happened."

He accepted my gesture. "I'm trying. I love you so much, Nancy."

"I love you too." For all of Paul's inner strength and courage to be a successful artist, against all odds, he was oftentimes caught off guard by some of my choices. He always respected my passion for finding answers as much as he has always followed his own creativity.

We stood and hugged each other. I could feel both of us calming down.

His face relaxed. "Do you want to go out to the old house?"

"You still want to go with me?"

"Yes, but I've got a few things to finish first in the studio. Okay?"

"I really love you."

While I was waiting for Paul, Tony called again. He informed me the police found a set of construction plans for the Provincetown house that I was interested in, based on the address I had given him. If I wanted to, I could pick the plans up at Hallett's house. The police would be there most of the afternoon. I valued my friendship with Tony and knew he had something to do with the authorities following up on my request for information. I assumed he vouched for me based on my involvement with the FBI back in the day.

I hurried out to the studio. "Tony called. The Eastham police found a set of house plans for the old house. We can pick them up on our way out."

"That was fast."

"You know what they say, 'I got a guy.'"

71

Present Day, Monday Afternoon - Nancy
CAPE COD

PAUL FOLLOWED ME into Neil Hallett's house. I introduced him and myself to the officer. "Detective Gomes said I could borrow the house plans you found."

"Yes. I'll get them."

While we waited, I pointed out to Paul the painting hanging above the desk. "I bet that's Maria Ellis, and... it could be Maria Hallett. Look at that ring." Paul admired it from the kitchen. I glanced over to the bedroom where I first saw the threatening photos.

As I was about to show Paul the bedroom, the officer returned and handed the plans to me. "Just drop them off at the Eastham station when you're finished."

"Thank you again."

Eager to get on the road to Provincetown, we hurried to the car.

I sat in the back seat so that I could unroll the large plans across my lap. "These are fascinating." I noticed that the name of the company who built the fireplace was listed along with its owner, Nesbit. "Paul, have you ever heard of an architect listing other people besides themselves on their plans?"

"Back in college, when I earned extra money part time by rendering what a house would look like before it was built, I don't recall seeing anyone else's name besides the architect."

"Why would they list this one?" I Googled on my phone for information about the company's name. Up popped Provincetown, Cape Cod, secret, and Compass Rose. "Well, it looks like the mason was famous in his own right."

By the time we reached Truro, my stomach was doing flip flops, anxious to get back into the old house.

Up on the porch, I almost forgot that I had taken the key. I fumbled for a few seconds but found it in a side pocket of my purse. We both headed straight for the kitchen. Paul carried the house plans. Hallett's tools still lay on the table. I watched Paul run his hand across the bricks, staring at the rough red surface. The clouds outside made everything a little darker. I flipped the light switch on and opened the plans across the table. "You see anything odd in the drawings?"

"Not really, pretty straight forward." Paul turned back to the brick surface. "There's no real break in this brick pattern, except when necessary for corners and such."

I pulled out my flashlight/pen for another look. Just as I was about to give up, I saw it. My heart jumped. "I see something." I pointed to a full brick on the left front face. "Look, there's a mark on this one. It's very faint but I can see it."

Paul took his handkerchief out, poured some water on it then rubbed the mark. He laughed and grabbed the chisel and hammer. "Shall we?"

I nodded. "Worst case is that we will have to return to cement the brick back in the hearth."

The only sound in the house was the clink of the chisel against the mortar. Paul worked slowly. With each tap, dark bits of cement dropped to the hearth. As he cleaned the last row out from around the brick, I swallowed hard to wet my dry throat. Paul placed his tools on the table and began to wiggle the brick back and forth to loosen it. There was a quick clunk and the brick came loose but not completely out.

"Nancy, will you do us the honor of removing the brick?"

I brushed my hands to clean them, then wiped them on my jeans, as if my hands had to be sterile to touch dirt. After handing the red brick to Paul, I grabbed my little flashlight and shined it into the black hole. I saw a dark, lumpy object wedged in the back. I stepped back and looked to Paul.

"Your turn."

He rolled his sweater cuff up and reached in until his hand disappeared. "I've got something."

I watched as he slowly pulled the object out. In his hand lay a faded, cracked leather pouch. "Now it's your turn." He put it on the table.

I tried to open the pouch strings but they didn't budge. The leather ties had melded together with the pouch as one piece. I dug in my purse for a tiny Swiss knife. "Do I dare?" I asked, opening the knife part. "I can feel something inside. What do you think?" I stood ready with the knife above the pouch.

"Go for it."

In the interest of lost treasures, I decided the leather wasn't as important as what was inside. With precision, I carefully penetrated the hardened leather. It was like fossilized skin. I closed the knife and used the scissor part to slowly cut about four inches across the top.

I saw a woven material inside that fell away when I brushed at it. "It feels hard underneath and much smaller than the leather pouch." I straightened up. "I think it's a ring."

Paul whispered, "The pigeon's blood lies warm and deep, hidden by the woman who sleeps."

I blew at the wispy fiber cover and there it was…the Pigeon's Blood.

The thrill of discovery lingered as we drove home to Brewster. I cradled the ruby ring in my hands all the way into Eastham. As we drove through the intersection where Ben & Jerry's sold ice cream, I calmed a little. The buzz returned as I walked up the wooden decking to our home, anticipating calls to Ally and Stephen. I wanted to shout it to the rooftops to anyone who would listen. I got keyed up again when I finally had a chance to talk with them.

Stephen thought it was par for the course for me, said he'd be on Cape in a few days but had to leave right away – FBI business. Ally was shocked we'd found a ring and said she'd be meeting with the lawyer who had originally asked her to liquidate the house on Wednesday with this new information.

Eventually, I sat down with a cup of chamomile tea.

Paul rubbed my back. "Nancy, I hope you'll sleep tonight."

"Me too." Then I called the kids and repeated what happened all over again. They wanted to know what I was going to do with it, but at that moment, I didn't know myself.

The ring landed in our safe. It was the first time I'd ever locked it. The strong box was only used for fire safety and the key was stored in my wallet.

I reread Abigail Baranova's letter about her father and the teacup set. I considered calling her, but then decided I should talk with Ally about who actually would be able to claim the ring. It wasn't mine; I had found it in someone else's house. The estate had no living relatives, but according to Casey's research and mine, Matthew Ellis Baranov might very well be the son of Walter Ellis. He would be the missing link, along with his daughter Abigail, and next in line for inheritance. There were a lot of legalities involved. Yes, Ally was the one to talk with first.

I arrived at Ally's office by 9:00 a.m. the following day with the ring wrapped in an old handkerchief of my mother's. It looked beautiful against the white linen cloth trimmed with red roses and green ivy. It took Ally's breath away.

"What a story that ring could tell us. If only it could talk." She picked it up in her hand.

"I was thinking the same thing on my way over here."

"Tell me what you found online about this Matthew Ellis Baranov."

I opened my laptop on her desk. "I can show you the information from Ancestry.com."

She took a few minutes to read. "Based on these records, it looks like you're right. Matthew could be a direct descendant from Walter Ellis and his estate. But we still need more proof." She looked further. "So, it's possible he had two families, one in Provincetown and one in Juneau, Alaska."

"What do we do now?"

"I'm meeting with the lawyers in Boston tomorrow. I'll forward the information you and Casey found over to them today and they'll probably hire an investigator, so everything is documented. I'll let you know."

"Would you mind if I took the ring over to the jewelry store in Orleans? They might be able to put a value on it."

"Great idea."

"I'll take it over now."

Within the hour, I was stunned with the knowledge that the ring could be worth millions. And that didn't include its value based on its age and back-story. I called Ally from the parking lot.

She was as surprised as I was. "Lock the ring up and we'll talk tomorrow."

72

Present Day, One Month Later
NEWPORT, RHODE ISLAND

THE MORNING OCEAN was calm as Abigail Baranova closed the door on her historic house. She walked a few blocks down Pelham Street to Bowen's Wharf, then passed the Black Pearl Restaurant and remembered the delicious birthday lunches with her father.

Abigail, approaching her mid-sixties, always carried a camera, and today was no different. She strolled to the wharf for some close-ups of boats, ocean views, and anything else of interest to add to her portfolio. After her husband died, three years ago, she had moved in with her father to care for him. She missed her father.

Upon her return to the house, she noticed mail sticking out of the black slit on the door. She shook her head. What was she going to do? There was just too much debt from her father's medical bills, supplies, and general upkeep on the old house. Devoting her time to his care gave her less attention for her own craft, causing photography sales and commissions to plummet. The house had to be sold. Was there even enough equity left for her to live on?

Abigail's cell binged with a text emoji from her daughter: a big red heart. It made her smile. The only good thing that came out of her unhappy marriage was her beautiful daughter, Sally, and granddaughter, Madison.

Wistfully thinking about the lawyer, Ally Grant, who called three weeks ago, about a possible connection to a Walter Ellis that might bring some money her way, she started to pay a few bills.

Her cell rang.

"Abigail Baranova? This is Nancy Caldwell. I'm the woman you sent a letter to, asking if I knew anything about a blue teacup and your father Matthew Ellis Baranov?"

"Of course, I remember you, Ms. Caldwell. I was hoping to hear from you personally."

"Would it be all right if my husband and I and Ally Grant come by tomorrow to talk? It's a nice ride and we'd love to visit with you."

"I'll be home. You might want to park on the wharf and walk over to the house."

"That's good advice. Thanks."

"See you in the afternoon."

Abigail leaned back in her chair. A three-foot totem pole painted in traditional Tlingit colors of red, black, and turquoise stood in a corner of the eclectically decorated living room. According to her father, the carved design depicted the story of his family. Atop the small totem, a black raven with a patch over its eye stared back at her. The patch always intrigued her and now as she aged, her curiosity grew stronger. Growing up, her father would laugh about it and then distract her with something else, so her questions were usually left unanswered. He seemed too busy with his career and rarely talked of his past before his family settled in Seattle. Maybe something was too painful for him to remember about Juneau, even though his intricate Alaskan carvings showed a deep reverence for his Tlingit heritage. His art seemed to speak for him instead of his words.

She glanced at a portrait of her Tlingit grandmother and Russian grandfather. They both had passed away before she was born. Right next to their frame was a photo of her own mother, who had died from pneumonia when Abigail was only ten years old. She still missed her.

Abigail reached for and cradled a blue teacup in her hands. She recalled the bedtime story her father told about a woman who loved a famous pirate; the china was part of that tale. He always said the woman was family. She regretted not asking more of her father and hopefully anticipated only good news from Nancy Caldwell.

73

Present Day - Nancy
RHODE ISLAND

THE SUN GLARED into the car as we drove to Rhode Island. "The Black Pearl opens at 11:00 a.m., we'll have plenty of time for lunch and then walk over to Abigail's house."

"Well, I'm getting hungrier as we drive." Paul adjusted his sunglasses.

I checked my briefcase for the computer, the ring, and some notes that Ally gave me to share with the last descendant of Walter Ellis. Ally kept busy on her phone.

By 1:00 p.m., I knocked on the old wooden door.

"Abigail Baranova?"

"Yes."

"I'm Nancy Caldwell. This is my husband, Paul, and of course you know Ally."

"Please come in." Abigail's gray-blonde hair fell to one side of her face.

"Thank you."

Paul and Ally followed behind me. Everywhere I looked, there were paintings, photographs, and exquisite carvings of Alaskan natives, seals, ravens, bears, eagles, and almost every animal imaginable from the Pacific Coast. "Are these all from your father?"

"Yes, they are. I also have a few of my own hanging."

"Your photographs are so lovely and poignant." I stopped at a sepia toned image of an older man and a young girl. "Is this your father, Matthew Baranov?"

"Yes, and my daughter, Sally."

The small girl in the photo sat watching her grandfather carve a raven in his studio. "You really caught that loving bond that connects us through all generations."

Abigail tenderly touched its gold frame. "I cherish this one the most of all the others."

Paul spotted a photograph he favored. "The tree shadows across this house are spectacular. It's an image I love to paint."

"Thank you. When I first found your wife in my online search, it was also noted that you were an artist, which led me to your studio page and your daughter's gallery site."

"It seems that both of our families are very creative." Paul continued looking around the room.

Abigail's face turned to worry. "I only wish I could afford a place to exhibit my father's work and mine, together, in a gallery here on Bowen's Wharf. He has quite a following after teaching sculpture for so many years at RISD."

"You mean the Rhode Island School of Design?"

"Yes. It's a wonderful school. My Sally went there for graphic design."

Ally held up her briefcase. "Shall we get started? I have some very good news for you. I think it will help you in reaching your goals."

Abigail led the way to the dining room table.

Ally calmly explained what her investigators had uncovered about Abigail's father and his connection to Walter Ellis.

The shock of hearing about her lost ancestors and inheriting so many treasures stunned Abigail. "I'm overwhelmed." She kept shaking her head in disbelief.

Ally paused after each item and its possible value.

"I can't believe this." Abigail stood up and retrieved an old writing tablet from the bookshelf. She withdrew from its yellowed pages a small photograph. "I wonder if this portrait has something to do with Walter Ellis?" She showed it to me.

I examined it. "This could be Walter, your other grandfather, and his first family from Provincetown. We now believe he had two families." I turned it over to see its stamp. "The back is signed with Nickerson Studios, Provincetown."

"When I found it, after father died, in some of his older books, I kept it, wishing it would mean something in regard to our family."

"I think this picture is of Walter Ellis. Nickerson was a photographer in Provincetown at the turn of the century."

While we waited for all the information to sink in, my eyes browsed what was around me and caught sight of the blue teacup and saucer resting on a windowsill. "May I look at the blue china?"

"Of course." Abigail turned her attention back to the legal portfolio.

I walked over to pick up the teacup. I held the blue flowered cup to the light and enjoyed its transparent essence. It was like looking into the past. "This pattern is just like the old teapot that I found a few years ago, in an antique shop." I looked over to Paul and then Abigail. "It's also the same as the broken china from the buried treasure chest I found in Brewster."

74

Present Day... Two Months Later - Nancy
CAPE COD

JULY CAME SUDDENLY; it seemed like spring never showed itself on the Cape. I sat at my desk, looking over the final numbers that Ally had sent to me about how much money Abigail had reaped from the estate of Walter Ellis.

The Provincetown house had sold for over $500,000, the Impressionist paintings found in the attic were auctioned off for a total of $150,000, and the lovely ruby ring, or the Pigeon's Blood, brought a sizable sum from Sotheby's Auction House in New York for millions. The philanthropist who purchased the ring turned it around and donated it to the Museum of Fine Arts, in Boston, for all to admire, along with its provenance. It was also nice to know that Abigail had made a generous donation to several social support houses in Hyannis.

I checked my email and noticed a message from the Eastham police that said I could pick up the painting from Hallett's house this morning. I hurried to find Paul. I was so excited that my hands shook as I gathered my purse and keys. Paul offered to drive to the station. I accepted.

After showing my ID, a check was exchanged for the painting. Paul carried it out the door and to the car. It didn't fit into the trunk, so he placed the precious cargo between the seats. I noticed something taped to the back of the wooden frame. "Hold up, Paul. What's that?" I reached to carefully pull a plastic baggy away from the frame. Inside the little bag was a brown scrap of paper. I took it out and read aloud, "Provincetown Estates and...." This confirms the painting must have come from a shop in Provincetown."

Paul inspected the small paper. "Could be. This old label might mean that Hallett was getting close to the painting's origin."

"Are you game for driving to Provincetown right now?"

"Let's go." He started the car.

As we drove, I began to Google online for Provincetown Estates. "I'm not having any luck."

We headed down Shore Road then onto Commercial Street and discovered a lot of traffic, as expected for July. We slowed to a crawl down the town's only main street.

We passed businesses opening, people looking for coffee or an early lunch, bicycles cruising, and people just wandering. When we had to stop for a UPS truck that was double-parked, it gave me a chance to take a closer look at the signs on storefronts, hopefully finding Provincetown Estates. I noticed, to my left, an older man sweeping off his steps. The sign above his head read, Provincetown Jewelry – We Buy Estates.

"Paul, look! That store might be what we're looking for."

Traffic started to move, and we drove past it. "Find a place to park...quick. Maybe at the pier. I don't want to miss talking to that man."

We got lucky and found a parking space at the far end of the lot. I jumped out of the car and power walked down the street. Paul followed, right behind me.

When we got to the shop, the door was locked. "Crap!" A small handwritten note said, Open by appointment only, but I couldn't find a phone number or website anywhere on the signage. I sat on the top step. "He was just here, a few minutes ago. I'm not leaving."

Paul stood in front of me. "You sure?"

"I'm not going anywhere."

"Want me to get some coffee?"

"That would be great, and maybe one of those malassadas?"

"Okay. You stay put."

Cars paraded in front of me as I waited. A young man approached me. I must have looked stressed. "Are you okay?"

"I'm fine. Thank you. Waiting for the shop to open."

"I just saw Mr. Abbot down the street at the post office. I'll bet he'll be back soon."

What a relief. "Thanks for the heads up."

Paul returned with coffee and my fried dough. "How long are you going to wait?"

"At least until I finish my coffee."

"Okay, then I'm going to walk down a little further. I'll be back."

As I wiped my sugary fingers, an older gentleman approached. "May I help you, young lady?"

I quickly stood up. "Mr. Abbot?"

"Yes."

"Nancy Caldwell. I wanted to ask you a few questions about an old painting."

"Let me open up and I'll be right with you." He slowly ascended the three steps, unlocked his door, then gestured me to follow.

Dark, wood-trimmed display cases flanked each side of the room. The glassed enclosures were filled with every shape, color and style of antique jewelry, and collectibles. The walls were crammed with paintings, photographs, and prints. I felt confident that I might be in the right place.

After a few minutes of waiting, Mr. Abbot said, "Now, how may I help you, Ms. Caldwell?"

I explained my reasons for contacting him. "I have the painting in the car Mr. Abbot, would you like to see it?"

"You've intrigued me. What might be the year of the painting and the artist's name?"

"It's signed by an Abigail E., which could stand for Abigail Ellis. I think it might be from late 1700 to early 1900."

"You bring the painting to me and I'll start searching my older records for that name."

"Thank you so much." I started for the open door.

"If the door is locked, just knock and I'll hear you in the back."

Outside on the sidewalk, I texted Paul to return ASAP. He stood next to me after only a few minutes.

Once at the car, we wrapped the painting in an old blanket and carried it through the crowds to the shop. The door was locked again. I knocked louder. The proprietor appeared and with a click of the bolt, he invited us in with a wave.

I introduced Paul.

Mr. Abbot took out his glass monocle to examine the painting. "It's definitely from the late 1800s, if not earlier." He stared at the label from the plastic bag. "The label did indeed come from this shop. We have records that show when we changed logos over the years. This one was introduced in 1900."

I wanted to know more. "Do you have any records of people's consignments or when you purchased items from that far back?"

"Yes. My grandfather opened in 1890 and kept pretty good records. When my father took over the business, around 1940, he started his own journal book. The older records were stored in the back." He led us to the rear of the shop.

To our left, on bookshelves, were black ledgers stacked upright. Years were written on white labels and attached to their spines. Wooden boxes, green desk lamps, and world globes all stood guard across the top of the shelves, along with multiple file boxes that filled in and around the perimeters of the small room. There were even a few stuffed squirrels and a big horned owl. A lone chair sat in front of a cluttered desktop. It was like walking into a disorganized museum.

"Just ignore the mess. I know where everything is." Mr. Abbot inched his way through the boxes to reach the old journals. "You know what they say, messy desks are signs of creativity."

Paul and I smiled at each other, thinking of our own work areas at home.

We watched Mr. Abbot scan the pages from 1899 through 1900. "Can we help?"

"Actually yes. That's a great idea." He gestured for us to get the other books down and unfolded another chair so that we could both sit.

Paul chose 1901-1902 and I picked up 1903.

Mr. Abbot went up front to take care of a customer.

As I thumbed through the pages, there were only a few listings for January and February of 1903. Mr. Abbot's grandfather used a system of recording that showed the date of consignment or purchase, its description, and then the date it was sold. During the month of March 1903, business resumed with moderation. April entries increased, reflecting the seasonal influx of tourists, just like today.

I glanced out the window of the old back door and could see the beach and edge of water. With a quick sigh, I returned to looking for Abigail or Ellis.

My finger stopped at an entry dated April 20th, 1903.

Seller: Sarah Ellis.

Item: Oil painting- Dim. 24 x 20-inch canvas.

Artist: Abigail E.

Description. Painted in late 1700s. Subject: Maria Goody Hallett, lover of pirate Sam Bellamy. Black haired woman resting with black shawl and red ruby ring on posed hands, blue china cup and saucer on small table.

I felt my heart skip. Tears clouded my eyes. A feeling of satisfaction and exhaustion overflowed me.

All these years, I thought, I've been wondering, guessing, and trying to solve the mystery of Maria Hallett. And now I'm looking at her.

Paul stood next to me, read the same words, then rubbed my back. "No wonder her trail went cold. She must have married an Ellis, not Sam Bellamy after all."

"The Ellis children came from Provincetown. Walter Ellis led us to where we are today."

As we exited the shop, I turned to Mr. Abbot, "Thank you so much. You can't imagine what your kindness has meant to me. By allowing me to look through these old books, I found information that has eluded me for many years. It is truly a special gift to me."

On the ride home to Brewster, I lay back against the headrest and watched the trees fly by the windows. Maria Hallett bore children and Walter Ellis was her descendant. He made it to Alaska but never returned to his home in Provincetown. The letter found in Juneau had to be his and it seems he had found love twice. That lovely old house held so many secrets, just waiting to be uncovered. It connected people of the past with the present in a patchwork of glorious stories. And I was privy to most of them.

When we stopped at the light near Marconi Beach, my cell rang.

Brian was calling from Alaska. "I arranged time off for when you and Dad visit us in October."

"That's wonderful. We're looking forward to it." I sat up to talk more. "We're on our way home from Provincetown with a lot of news. Can I call you later?"

"Of course."

"Give our love to Patty and little Sophia."

I looked over to Paul with a big smile on my face. "I guess I'd better make sure to pack my famous chocolate chip cookies for their little neighbor, Lizzy. I owe her a thank you from when she gave me that old wallet and faded letter."

75

Present Day, October - Nancy
JUNEAU

OUTSIDE THE AIRPLANE'S window, I noticed the leaves had changed to their fall colors, just like back home in Boston. After landing and retrieving our luggage, Paul and I exited the Juneau airport then waved at our son as he pulled up to the curb.

Brian lifted our suitcases into the back of his SUV. He reached for my backpack.

"Hold on. I'll keep that with me. It's carrying precious cargo."

Brian looked at me, curious.

"Cookies for Lizzy."

On the ride to Brian's house, the scenery was as beautiful as I remembered. Even the snow-covered mountains, a signal for the coming deep freeze, didn't take away from the picturesque view.

By the time we'd settled in, dinner was almost ready. Paul and I went to bed early soon after, but not until we got our fill of kisses and hugs from Sophia. Before saying goodnight, I reminded Patty to call Lizzy's mom to ask when the little girl would be visiting the Point.

The next morning, I woke to discover Paul was already up. The house seemed unusually quiet. I grabbed my robe in search of coffee, then found a note next to the carafe.

Good Morning, Mom.

Dad and I left for Home Depot to buy what we need for my
DIY project. Patty is at a check-up for Sophia. Make yourself
comfortable. We'll be home in a few hours.

Love, Brian

P.S. Patty made a call last night. Lizzy will be down at the
Point around 10:00 a.m.

I checked the time. It was already 9:15. After a quick shower, I headed to the Point with my gift.

The forest floor was lush with green moss and the morning sun filtered through the tall pines. I stopped to take a deep breath of Juneau's clean air. As I continued on to my destination, a black raven's caw echoed into the trees.

Below me, I could see my little friend was sitting on the black stone outcrops at the end of the land. I called out. "Lizzy."

She looked up then waved.

Carefully, I stepped down the slippery, stone-covered slope.

Lizzy smiled at me. "Hello, Nana."

I settled next to the small girl on the edge of the stone. "Nice to see you again, Lizzy."

"What's in the plastic box?"

I pried open the lid. The scent of butter and chocolate smelled delicious in the fresh air. "Remember that I promised you some of my famous chocolate chip cookies when I returned to visit Juneau?" I held the container closer to her.

She nodded then reached for one. "Thank you."

"What do you think?" I grabbed one of the tasty treats for myself.

Lizzy produced a big smile.

I explained what I'd found out about the old letter and wallet as simply as possible. We then sat in silence and enjoyed a few more cookies.

Before us, half a dozen sea otters bobbed and frolicked in the glistening morning water. They were thrilling. As young as Lizzy was, she seemed to appreciate the beauty of the view before us as much as I did.

I thought of young Matthew Baranov and wondered if he had ever sat here, as a young boy, and admired the same images. I'll never know how the metal box got where it did, but what I did know, was that life comes full circle, and there's always a reason for everything.

Feeling blessed as I walked back to the house, my cell rang. It was Molly, calling from college.

"Hi Mom. How's my big brother in Alaska doing?"

"Everyone's fine here. What about you? Are your classes interesting?'

"Yes. I actually called to let you in on a few things that have happened in the last few weeks."

"Oh?" I kept walking down Brian's driveway.

"Are you sitting down?"

"No. But I will be in a second." I took a seat on a small bench overlooking the ocean and watched the tide lap against the rocky shoreline.

"I think I got a teaching job."

"Oh, honey, I'm so happy for you! Your dad will be pleased." I fondly remembered Molly's first day of kindergarten. After the school bus came to a stop in front of our home, she literally bounced off and then skipped up the driveway singing all the way. I smiled, knowing she's always so full of life. "Where?"

"In Millbury. It's a small community but it was just what I was hoping for. You know I love the country over city life."

"Will you live close to the school?"

"That's the best part. One of the teachers knew of an old 1880 house in Millbury that will become available in the spring for rent and maybe with options to buy."

"That's lucky."

"And...Peter might be able to find a job in a nearby town also. He wants to move in with me."

A graceful bald eagle glided across the water. "My heart is filled with joy for you both. I know you and Peter will be just fine. You've been dating since seniors in high school."

"We're still young but there's so much potential starting out together. We love each other."

"Don't worry, your father and I will be there for you through everything."

"Oh Mom, I can hardly wait for the adventure to begin."

The End

FAMILY TREE

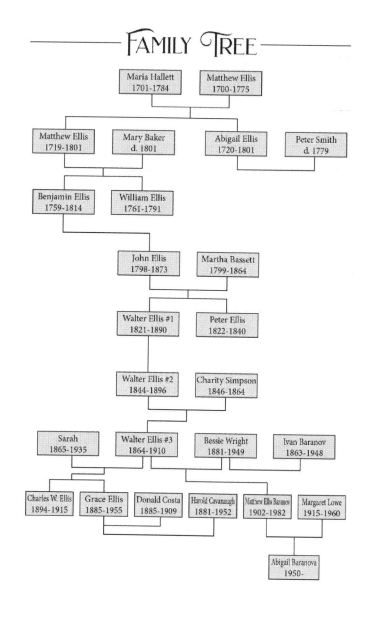

Maria Hallett
1701-1784

Matthew Ellis
1700-1775

Matthew Ellis
1719-1801

Mary Baker
d. 1801

Abigail Ellis
1720-1801

Peter Smith
d. 1779

Benjamin Ellis
1759-1814

William Ellis
1761-1791

John Ellis
1798-1873

Martha Bassett
1799-1864

Walter Ellis #1
1821-1890

Peter Ellis
1822-1840

Walter Ellis #2
1844-1896

Charity Simpson
1846-1864

Sarah
1865-1935

Walter Ellis #3
1864-1910

Bessie Wright
1881-1949

Ivan Baranov
1863-1948

Charles W. Ellis
1894-1915

Grace Ellis
1885-1955

Donald Costa
1885-1909

Harold Cavanaugh
1881-1952

Matthew Ellis Baranov
1902-1982

Margaret Lowe
1915-1960

Abigail Baranova
1950-

Author's Notes & Acknowledgments

EVER SINCE I WAS a young girl, I have loved to read. As I grew, my admiration for the written word flourished and keeping a journal became a part of my everyday life. I also wrote letters to friends and relatives and enjoyed receiving them in return. In fact, my husband and I dated through college and kept in touch through these penned romantic messages – I've kept them all.

It was natural for me in the process of writing this novel to include letters as an integral part of *The Old Cape Blood Ruby*.

A grateful thank you to my middle son, Tim, who, with his wife, Jenn, and their three little ones, have made their home in Alaska, the last frontier, living in Bethel, Anchorage, and Juneau.

The beginnings of my fourth novel took flight several years ago, on one of our semi-annual trips to Alaska. This time, we were on the island of Juneau.

One morning, we woke to a storm-tossed, exposed ocean floor. Outside the house's expansive windows that overlooked the mysterious Pacific Ocean was a large white object. Our son, Tim, went to see what it was. We watched him, as he walked farther and farther away from the house, until he stopped and took some pictures. Surprisingly, when he returned, it was the skeleton of what looked like a complete leg.

After finally uncovering proof that the skeleton belonged to a large animal, we all breathed a sigh of relief. But my imagination took off and my plotting began. I decided the narrative was going to include Cape Cod, specifically Provincetown, and Juneau during the Klondike Gold Rush at the turn of the century.

As the storyline grew, I wanted to discover every inch of the Alaskan wilderness, including historic downtown Juneau. With three little ones in tow, it was tense, but, in the end, we always had an adventure, especially walking down their road to explore the Point and occasionally pondering if we should attempt to walk the Breadline Trail.

I want to thank the following family, friends, and experts. The Stephen Gallant Jewelers in Orleans for their expert knowledge in gemstones and the Provincetown Town Hall for its availability of historical data.

Peter Stanton was my contact in Alaska for everything Tlingit or *People of the Tides*. He helped me with their language and customs.

My editor, Nicola Burnell, and proofreader, Cynthia Wckyoff, proved professional. My Friday Writers Group, who have been meeting weekly since 2008, always had the patience to really listen and catch the little discrepancies that make or break a great novel. My beta readers: Pat Meyer, Heather Struna, and Beth Brindo.

My oldest son, Scott, for his advice on the technicalities of building a chimney on top of a roof, and my future son-in-law, Tim Graham, for fine-tuning the beautiful cover.

As always, my husband Tim, plus my two younger children, Annie and Michael, who have always been there supporting me along the way in this crazy world of writing and publishing.

Thank you from the bottom of my heart!

Gunalchéesh!

ABOUT THE AUTHOR

INTERNATIONALLY BEST-SELLING author Barbara Eppich Struna is a storyteller at heart, who bases her tales on the history, myth, and legends of Cape Cod, along with her own personal experiences. She created a contemporary character, amateur sleuth, Nancy Caldwell, who is the vehicle that moves her novels between time periods in alternating chapters.

Her suspenseful historical novels, part of her *Old Cape Series*, have won numerous literary awards and accumulated thousands of reviews. Her books include *The Old Cape House*, *The Old Cape Teapot*, and *The Old Cape Hollywood Secret*. She also cowrote the memoir, *Family, Friends, and Faith*, with her late sister, Sister Barbara Eppich O.S.U.

Barbara is President of Cape Cod Writers Center; a member of International Thriller Writers; a Member of Sisters In Crime, National, New England, Los Angeles; and Member in Letters—National League of American Pen Women. She also writes a blog about the unique facts and myths of Cape Cod.

ALSO BY BARBARA EPPICH STRUNA

The Old Cape House (Historical Fiction) – Nancy Caldwell relocates to an old sea captain's house on Cape Cod with her husband and four children. When she discovers an abandoned root cellar in her backyard containing a baby's skull and gold coins, she digs up evidence that links her land to the legendary tale of Maria Hallett and her pirate lover, Sam Bellamy

The Old Cape Teapot (Historical Fiction) – Nancy Caldwell returns in this second novel in a series of adventures. The story is told using alternating chapters between centuries. After finding an old map on Antigua, she leads us on a journey across Cape Cod filled with danger and lost treasure.

The Old Cape Hollywood Secret (Historical Fiction) – In 1947, Maggie Foster and her cousin, Gertie, leave Cape Cod for Hollywoodland in search of glamour and fame. One girl returns home and the other disappears. Present-day Nancy Caldwell travels to Hollywood, where she discovers the paths of Maggie and Gertie. Along the way, a missing ring and a pearl-studded pouch are mixed in with Nancy's search. Using alternating chapters, across seventy years, the tragic stories of two young girls unfold and a murderous secret is uncovered.

Family, Friends, and Faith by Barbara Eppich Struna and Sister Barbara Eppich O.S.U. Co-authored by two sisters, this story is an inspirational memoir of how one woman made a difference in thousands of lives through an openness to God and a charitable heart. It may even connect you to your own faith journey.

Made in the USA
Middletown, DE
22 May 2021

40062363R00184